spy ski school

Also by Stuart Gibbs

The FunJungle series
Belly Up
Poached
Big Game

The Spy School series
Spy School
Spy Camp
Evil Spy School

The Moon Base Alpha series
Space Case
Spaced Out

The Last Musketeer

STUART GIBBS

spy ski school

A spy school NOVEL

Simon & Schuster Books for Young Readers
New York London Toronto Sydney New Delhi

SIMON & SCHUSTER BOOKS FOR YOUNG READERS
An imprint of Simon & Schuster Children's Publishing Division
1230 Avenue of the Americas, New York, New York 10020
For information about special discounts for bulk purchases, please contact Simon & Schuster Special Sales at 1-866-506-1949 or business@simonandschuster.com.
The Simon & Schuster Speakers Bureau can bring authors to your live event. For more information or to book an event, contact the Simon & Schuster Speakers Bureau at 1-866-248-3049 or visit our website at www.simonspeakers.com.
Book design and illustration by Lucy Ruth Cummins
Map illustration by Ryan Thompson
The text for this book was set in Adobe Garamond Pro.
Manufactured in the United States of America
0916 FFG
First Edition
10 9 8 7 6 5 4 3 2 1
Library of Congress Cataloging-in-Publication Data
Names: Gibbs, Stuart, 1969– author.
Title: Spy ski school : a Spy school novel / Stuart Gibbs.
Description: First edition. | New York : Simon & Schuster Books for Young Readers, [2016] | Summary: Twelve-year-old Ben's unexpected success outside the classroom causes the CIA to activate him for a mission to become friends with Jessica Shang, daughter of a suspected Chinese crime boss.
Identifiers: LCCN 2015037993|
ISBN 9781481445627 (hardcover) | ISBN 9781481445658 (eBook)
Subjects: | CYAC: Spies—Fiction. | Friendship—Fiction. | Skis and skiing—Fiction. | Schools—Fiction.
Classification: LCC PZ7.G339236 Ss 2016 | DDC [Fic]—dc23
LC record available at https://lccn.loc.gov/2015037993

For my best ski buddies over the past years: my parents, my sister, Darragh, Ciara, Andy Gibbs, Mike Matthews, Ken Parker, Mark Middleman, Adam Zarembok, David and Learka Bosnak, Jon Mattingly, Jeff Peachin, John Janke, Kent Davis, Garrett Reisman, "Ches" Thompson, and Ed Cohen—and my favorite new ski buddies, Dash and Violet

acknowledgments

In case it isn't obvious during the reading of this book, I like skiing. A lot. The first place I ever really saw anyone do it was in James Bond movies, which had so many incredible ski sequences that I couldn't wait to get out onto the slopes myself. Since I grew up in Texas, though, I didn't get much chance to ski until I was in my teens. And the first time I went was near Cleveland, Ohio, which isn't exactly famous for its skiing. Still, I'm grateful to the Klein family—Steve, Ann, Alan, and Rob—for taking me. And I owe huge thanks to Saul and Ilene Cohen, who later introduced me to skiing in the significantly better mountains of Vermont.

When I was in college, though, my parents moved to Colorado, and a whole new world opened up to me. I am indebted to the staff at Vail and Snowmass Mountains, particularly the ski instructors, for all their help in making this book—and for all the great ski days throughout the years. Also, thanks to my editor, Kristin Ostby (who is quite a good skier herself), for her enthusiastic encouragement on this story. Finally, an enormous thank-you to my wonderful, incredibly supportive wife, Suzanne, who doesn't ski, but who still let me spend so much time on the slopes to research this book. It was difficult work, but it simply had to be done.

contents

1: ACTIVATION   3

2: MEMORIZATION   26

3: ACCLIMATIZATION   38

4: RECONNAISSANCE   55

5: PUNISHMENT   72

6: CONNECTION   83

7: COMPLICATION   106

8: REASSESSMENT   120

9: DISTRACTION   133

10: ANALYSIS   151

11: ASSISTANCE   168

12: INFORMATION ACQUISITION 178

13: FLIRTATION 192

14: INFILTRATION 198

15: EAVESDROPPING 221

16: DISCOVERY 241

17: SNEAK ATTACK 254

18: SNOW SAFETY 264

19: INSPIRATION 276

20: SHOWDOWN 286

21: EVASIVE ACTION 300

22: NEGOTIATION 313

23: NUCLEAR DISARMAMENT 333

spy ski school

December 4

To: ████████████████████████

Given the evidence you have provided, the review committee has sanctioned Operation Snow Bunny for immediate deployment. Academy of Espionage students ████████ and ██████████████ have both been approved for this operation, with the option to activate additional operatives if needed.

However, the committee would also like to make clear that it has serious reservations about using such young agents on a mission of this caliber. It is only the absolute necessity of ████████████████████████—and the unfortunate failure of our previous operations to do so—that has led us to sanction this.

Should these young agents not be up to the task—should they fail due to their inexperience—the burden of this failure will be placed squarely on your shoulders. The CIA will disavow any knowledge that ██████████████ ██████████, or that ████████████████████████ ██████ in order to maintain the secrecy of ████████████████ ██████

Enclosed in the attached dossier, you will find plane tickets, ski passes, and forms for reimbursement of expenses.

Good luck on your mission, and God bless America,

████████████████████

CIA Director of Operations

P.S. There's a restaurant in ████ called Hänsel ünd Grëtel that has excellent fondue. Check it out while you're there.

Destroy this document immediately after reading.

ACTIVATION

Bushnell Hall

CIA Academy of Espionage

Washington, DC

December 6

1130 hours

The summons to the principal's office arrived in the middle of my Advanced Self-Preservation class.

Normally, I would have been pleased to have an excuse to get out of ASP, as it was my worst subject. I was only getting a C in it, even though, in real life, I had been quite good at self-preservation. Over the past eleven months, my enemies had kidnapped me, shot at me, locked me in a room with a ticking bomb, and even tried to blow me up with missiles—and yet I'd survived each time. However, my instructors at the CIA's Academy of Espionage never seemed very impressed by the fact that I was still alive. They just kept giving me bad grades.

"There's a big difference between running away and being able to defend yourself," my ASP instructor, Professor Simon, had explained, shortly before the call from the principal came. Professor Georgia Simon was in her fifties and looked like someone my mother would have played canasta with, but she was an incredible warrior, capable of beating three karate masters in a fight at once. "So far, all you have done in the field is run."

"It's worked pretty well for me so far," I countered.

"You've been lucky," Professor Simon said. And then she attacked me with a samurai sword.

It was only a fake sword, but it was still daunting. (The academy had stopped using real swords a few years earlier, after a student had been literally disarmed in class.) I did my best to defend myself, but it was only twenty seconds before I was sprawled on the floor with Professor Simon standing over me, sword raised, ready to shish kabob my spleen.

Which was all the more embarrassing, as it happened in front of the entire class. ASP took place in a large lecture hall. My fellow classmates were seated in tiers around me, watching me get my butt kicked by a woman four times my age.

"Pathetic," Professor Simon declared. "That's D-grade work at best. Would anyone here like to show Mr. Ripley how a real agent defends himself?"

No one volunteered. My fellow second-year students weren't idiots; none of them wanted to be embarrassed like I had been. Or hurt. Luckily for them, at that moment, the announcement from the principal came over the school's public address system, distracting Professor Simon.

There were plenty of other, far less outdated ways to deliver urgent messages to the classrooms at spy school, but the principal didn't know how to use any of them. In fact, he wasn't very good at using the PA system, either. There were a few seconds of fumbling noises, followed by the principal muttering, "I can never remember which switch works this stupid thing. This darn system's a bigger pain in my rear than my hemorrhoids." Then he asked, "Hello? Hello? Is this thing on? Can you hear me?"

Professor Simon sighed in a way that suggested she had even less respect for the principal than she had for me. "Yes. We can hear you."

"Very good," the principal replied. "Is Benjamin Ripley in your class right now? I need to see him in my office right away."

A chorus of "ooohs" rippled through the room: the universal middle-school response to realizing that someone else has just gotten in trouble.

Professor Simon gave the class a warning glare and the "ooohs" stopped immediately. "I'll send him right now," she replied. Then she looked down at me and said, "Go."

I leapt to my feet and hurried for the door, pausing only to snatch my backpack from my seat. Zoe Zibbell, one of my best friends, was in the next seat over. She looked at me inquisitively with her big green eyes, wanting to know if I knew why I'd been summoned. I shrugged in return.

Next to Zoe, Warren Reeves snickered at my misfortune. Warren didn't like me much; he had a crush on Zoe and saw me as competition, so he was always rooting for my downfall.

I made a show of hustling out the door for Professor Simon—and promptly slowed down the moment I was out of her sight. I was in no hurry to get to the principal's office.

I had been summoned to the principal four other times, and it had always been bad news: Previously, the principal had sent me to solitary confinement, placed me on probation, informed me that my summer vacation plans were cancelled in favor of mandatory wilderness training—and expelled me from school. (I'd been reinstated, however.) So I dawdled, wondering what trouble lay in store for me this time.

I exited Bushnell Hall and entered Hammond Quadrangle on my way to the Nathan Hale Administration Building. It was the week after Thanksgiving. Fall had been mild and beautiful in Washington, DC, but now winter had arrived with a vengeance. Frigid winds were stripping the trees bare of leaves, and a crust of icy snow carpeted the ground.

As I meandered across the quad, my phone buzzed with a text. It was from Erica Hale:

stop dawdling and get your butt up here. we're waiting.

I stared up at the gothic Hale Building, wondering if Erica was watching me—or if she simply knew me well enough to presume I was dawdling. Either was a likely possibility.

Erica was only a fourth-year student, but she was easily the best spy-in-training at school. However, she'd had a head start on the rest of us: She was a legacy. The very building I was heading toward was named after her family. Her ancestors had all been spies for the United States, going back to Nathan Hale himself—and her grandfather, Cyrus, had been teaching her the family business since she was born. When I'd been learning how to assemble Legos, she'd been learning how to assemble semiautomatic machine guns. Blindfolded.

I picked up my pace, hurrying toward the Hale Building. If Erica was waiting for me with the principal, that probably meant I wasn't in trouble. Plus, I was excited to see her.

I had a massive crush on Erica Hale. She was the most beautiful, intelligent, and dangerous girl I'd ever met in my life. I knew Erica didn't like me nearly as much as I liked her, but the fact that she liked me even a *little* was a big deal. Erica regarded most of her fellow students—and professors—with complete disinterest. As though they were rocks. And not even pretty rocks. Boring, gray rocks. Gravel. Even though her text to me had been curt and cold, it was still a text from her, which was more human contact than Erica usually parceled out. There were plenty of guys at school who would have killed to get a text from Erica Hale.

I burst into the Hale Building and took the stairs up to the fifth floor two at a time. The security agents stationed there quickly waved me through to the restricted area. "Come right on in, Mr. Ripley," one said. "We've been expecting you."

I stopped and spread my arms and legs for the standard frisking, but the second guard shook her head. "No need for that. They want to see you ASAP." She pointed me toward a door.

This was a different door than the usual one for the principal's office. A piece of paper was taped to it. It said PIRNCIPAL. Given the misspelling, I figured the principal had written it himself.

The principal was very likely the least intelligent person in the entire intelligence community. We had a lot of decent teachers at school, most of whom had been decent spies earlier in their careers. Meanwhile, the principal had been a horrible spy. He had failed on every single mission. No one wanted him teaching anyone anything, so he was made an administrator instead. He mostly handled paperwork that no one else wanted to deal with.

The principal wasn't using his normal office because I'd blown it up by firing a mortar round into it. (It was an accident.) The damage had been extensive, and since the government was in charge of the repairs, they were taking a very long time. The official completion date was set for three years in the future, but even that was probably optimistic; my dormitory had been waiting to have its septic system replaced since before the Berlin Wall fell. In the meantime, the principal had been moved down the hall.

Into a closet.

It was a rather large closet, but it was still a closet. Given the pungent smell of ammonia, I presumed that, until recently, cleaning supplies had been stored there. Instead of a nice big, imposing desk, the principal now had a card table. He sat behind it in a creaky folding chair, glowering at me from beneath the world's most horrendous hairpiece. It looked like a raccoon had died on his head. And then been run over by a truck. The closet would have been crowded enough with only the principal and me, but three other people were crammed in there as well, waiting for me. All of them were Hales.

Erica stood beside her father, Alexander, and her grandfather, Cyrus.

Alexander Hale had been an extremely respected spy for years, despite the fact that he was a complete fraud. The Agency had finally caught on and kicked him out, but he had subsequently proved himself on an unsanctioned mission and been reinstated. Now he was back to his usual debonair self, wearing a tailored three-piece suit with a perfectly folded handkerchief and a crisply knotted tie.

Meanwhile, Cyrus Hale was the real deal, as good a spy as there was in the CIA, even though he was in his seventies. He'd been retired but had recently reactivated himself. Cyrus didn't bother with fancy suits, which he considered impractical. Instead, he wore warm-ups, sneakers, and a fanny pack; he looked like he was about to go walk around the mall for exercise.

Erica wore her standard black outfit, her standard utility belt, and her standard bored expression. She barely glanced at me as I came in. "Nice of you to finally join us."

"Sorry I kept you waiting." I realized the closet didn't have a window. Which meant Erica *hadn't* seen me dawdling. She'd simply known I was doing it.

"No worries, Benjamin," Alexander said cheerfully. "I just got here myself."

"That's not exactly something to be proud of," Cyrus

told him disapprovingly. "Seeing as you were supposed to be here half an hour ago."

Alexander winced, the way he usually did when his father dressed him down, then tried to save face. "I was doing some important prep work for this mission."

"What mission?" I asked. In the cramped closet, there was barely room to move. "What's going on?"

"You're being activated!" Alexander announced excitedly.

Cyrus grimaced, as though Alexander had said something he wasn't supposed to.

"What?" The principal snapped to his feet, flabbergasted, obviously unaware of this news. "You're activating this little twerp? For a *real* mission?"

"It wouldn't make much sense for us to activate him for a fake mission, now, would it?" Cyrus asked.

"Well, he can't go!" the principal declared childishly. "He blew up my office!"

Cyrus exhaled slowly, trying to be patient. "As I have explained to you multiple times, that was not entirely Ripley's doing. It was a setup to make our enemies at SPYDER believe that he had actually been expelled so that they'd recruit him. . . ."

"He nearly killed me!" the principal protested, immune to Cyrus's logic. "It's bad enough that I had to take him back here as a student . . ."

"He *was* instrumental in thwarting SPYDER's plans," Alexander pointed out.

". . . but now you're going to send him out into the field again?" the principal railed on. "He hasn't even been at this academy a year yet! He's not qualified for the field!"

"He is," said Cyrus. "He's proved it."

"But—" the principal began.

"It doesn't really matter if *you* agree with me on this," Cyrus interrupted. "Because the chief of the CIA agrees with me. And he's the one who authorizes the missions, not you. The only reason we're even having this meeting here is that, as the principal of this institution, you officially have to be informed when students are being sent into the field."

If there had been anyplace to sit down in the office, I would have sat down. It was surprising enough to hear that I was being activated by the CIA. But I was completely floored to hear Cyrus defend me. Cyrus didn't give out praise easily. In fact, it was a good bet that he'd never given any to Alexander at all.

The principal sank back into his folding chair, glowering even harder at me.

I tried to avoid his gaze, shifting my attention to Erica instead. "You're being activated too?"

Erica arched an eyebrow at me but didn't say anything.

"I mean, you're *here*," I explained. "And your grandfather just said '*students*' were being activated. So it's not only me. . . ."

"Excellent deductive work, as usual!" Alexander pronounced, patting me on the back. "You're right. Erica will also be with you on assignment, as will my father and I!"

Erica's expression didn't change. I had no idea if she was pleased with any of this or not. She might as well have just been told she needed a root canal.

I was pleased, though. Even more than pleased; the idea of being on assignment with Erica was thrilling. In the first place, there was no one I trusted more. Second, it meant I now had an excuse to spend a lot of time with her.

In theory, I should have had plenty of other excuses to spend time with Erica, seeing as we both went to the same top-secret boarding school. But Erica could be as cold and distant as Antarctica. While the other kids at school bonded over pickup games of capture the flag or James Bond movie marathons, Erica kept to herself. Even though I was considered her closest friend on campus, that didn't mean much. A few months before, at the end of our last mission, when we were both doped up on painkillers after nearly being vaporized by a missile, Erica had said a few nice things to me and held my hand. But since then she had behaved as though that had never even happened. There had been weeks when she hadn't so much as glanced at me.

So I was excited for an excuse to hang out with her. Even one where my life might be in danger. As far as I was concerned, it was worth the risk.

"What's the mission?" I asked.

Cyrus produced a sealed manila envelope from the inner pocket of his warm-up jacket and handed it to me. It was labeled OPERATION SNOW BUNNY and stamped FOR YOUR EYES ONLY. My heart leapt. Getting an honest-to-God "For Your Eyes Only" manila envelope in spy school was like being named king of homecoming in regular school.

I broke open the seal and found several photographs inside. They were extremely grainy, as though they'd been taken from a long distance away with a telephoto lens. The first one was of a Chinese man with close-cropped hair wearing sunglasses.

"That is Leo Shang," Cyrus told me. "He's one of the richest men in China. Worth billions."

"What's he do?" I asked.

"We have no idea," Cyrus admitted. "The truth is, we know almost nothing about him: where he grew up, how much education he has, what he owns. He simply appeared on the scene five years ago, loaded with cash."

Erica shifted closer to me to get a better look at the photos. As usual, she smelled incredible, a combination of lilacs and gunpowder. She stared at the pictures in a way that suggested she'd never seen them before, which was unusual. Normally, Erica knew everything way before I did. I wondered why Cyrus hadn't shared these with her yet.

"Anyone with an untraceable background and that much money is suspicious," Cyrus continued. "So the CIA has tried to investigate him. However, the man has the tightest security I've ever come across. His organization is almost impossible to infiltrate. He keeps himself cloistered, interacting with only a few select people, each of whom is also extremely well protected. We've been trying to get an agent close to him for years with virtually no success."

"Why?" Erica asked. It was only the second time she'd spoken since I'd entered the room. "If he's a Chinese criminal, that's China's problem, isn't it?"

"We have reason to believe his crimes are not merely limited to China," Cyrus replied. "He seems to be plotting something in the United States. The last agent who investigated him reported he's working on a scheme known as Operation Golden Fist."

"What's that?" I asked.

"We don't know," Cyrus confessed. "Our agent was unable to learn any more before he was uncovered and the mission was terminated. However, in his final transmission to us, he did indicate suspicions that Golden Fist might be a Level Eleven threat."

Erica stiffened slightly in response to this, which was her exceptionally calm way of expressing great concern. "Level Eleven?"

"What's that?" I asked.

"Well," Erica replied, "a Level Ten threat would be extreme, causing the most chaos, danger, and destruction you can imagine. A Level Eleven threat is even worse."

I gulped, unsettled by the thought of this.

"Given this, it's of critical importance that we determine what Golden Fist is," Cyrus said. "That's where you kids come in."

"Us?" I gasped. "How are we supposed to get close to this guy when the entire CIA hasn't been able to do it?"

"Because everyone has a chink in their armor," Cyrus explained. "No man is an island. And Leo Shang's weakness is his daughter, Jessica."

I shifted to the next photo. It was of a Chinese girl about my age. It was even grainier than the first photo, so bad that I could barely make out anything about her except that she had hair. She appeared to be either baking a pie or holding a cat.

"You want us to get close to her," Erica said.

"Exactly!" Alexander cried. "Leo Shang might be suspicious of any *adult* who tries to get near him, but we doubt he'd ever suspect a teenager would be a CIA agent. And if you can get close to Jessica, you might be able to get close to her father."

"All right, I'll do it," Erica said. "It won't be easy, but I can handle it. With a few hours of extensive makeup, I can pass myself off as Chinese. If you give me the proper identification, I can then insert myself as a new student at Jessica's school. . . ."

A flicker of unease passed between Cyrus and Alexander, as though there was a subject both of them were afraid to broach. Finally, Cyrus seemed to realize he would have to do it. He cleared his throat and said, "Erica, *you're* not the one we're assigning to get close to Jessica."

Erica's eyes narrowed angrily. "*Ben* is the primary agent on this? You must be joking."

Cyrus signaled her to calm down. "Sweetheart, the objective here is to befriend Jessica. And the key to making friends with someone is actually being, well . . . friendly. You have a lot of wonderful qualities, but being nice to other people isn't one of them."

"Other people are usually idiots," Erica muttered.

"See what I mean?" Cyrus asked. "That attitude is exactly what I'm talking about. Now, when it comes to espionage, I know you have tremendous talents, while Ben here doesn't have many at all. . . ."

"Hey!" I said.

"But he *is* good at making friends," Cyrus went on.

"People like him. And that's nothing to sneeze at. Which is why he's going to be the primary agent on this operation, while you'll be his main handler."

"He was the primary agent *last* operation!" Erica snapped. "And I was his handler then! He's barely had any training, while I've been studying for this since I was a baby!"

"I've learned some things," I protested.

Erica fixed her angry gaze on me. "I can speak fluent Chinese. In Mandarin and Wu dialects. Can you speak fluent Chinese?"

"Er, no . . . ," I confessed meekly. "But I *can* order dinner in a Chinese restaurant."

"Great," Erica growled. "When you meet Jessica Shang, you can ask her for some egg rolls. I'm sure that'll go over well."

"That's enough," Cyrus told her.

Erica fell silent. She was obviously still angry, though. Which was unsettling. Erica rarely displayed much emotion at all. She was normally as calm and relaxed as a person at a day spa, even in the midst of a gunfight. But now she was so upset, it felt as though the room was heating up around her.

"This decision was not made to be an insult to you," Cyrus informed her. "It was made because it is in the best interests of this country. If you can't handle that, I'm sure we could find another student willing to be Ben's handler."

Erica shifted her glare to her grandfather. "You know there's no one here better than me."

"Welcome aboard, then," Cyrus said. "Now, here's the skinny: In a few weeks, the Shangs are actually leaving China for the first time in as long as we've been tracking them. Better yet, they'll be coming to the United States. Jessica Shang wants to learn how to ski."

"They can't do that in China?" the principal asked. "They have snow there, don't they?"

"Of course they have snow," Cyrus said curtly. "However, their resorts aren't nearly as good as ours yet—so Jessica wants to go to Colorado. Vail, to be specific. They've already rented a hotel there and—"

"A hotel room," I corrected.

"What?" Cyrus asked.

"You said they rented a *hotel*," I told him. "Instead of a hotel room."

"That wasn't a mistake," Cyrus snapped. "They rented the entire hotel."

"For one family?" I asked, stunned.

"Actually," Alexander said, "Mrs. Shang isn't coming. We're not sure why, but we suspect that she's even more secretive than her husband. Or maybe she just doesn't like cold weather."

"So they rented an entire hotel for only two people?" I asked, even more stunned.

"Plus their security staff, which is quite large," Alexander explained. "Leo Shang doesn't like being around strangers. And like we said, he's very rich."

"Still," Erica said, "if he's so cautious, why's he coming to America at all? He must suspect the CIA is tracking him."

"We've been wondering that ourselves," Cyrus replied. "Our best guess is that the ski vacation is a cover for Operation Golden Fist."

"So this doesn't have anything to do with SPYDER?" I asked.

"Why should it?" Cyrus replied, in a way that suggested my question had been idiotic.

"Er . . . ," I stammered. "Well . . . SPYDER's kind of our main enemy, isn't it? I mean, every time I've confronted an evil organization, it's been that one. . . ."

"The United States has *lots* of enemies," Cyrus informed me. "Including hundreds you've never heard of. And we haven't heard a peep out of SPYDER since their headquarters blew up. That was a huge setback for them—financially and organizationally. So perhaps there's a chance they're out of the game."

"I guess," I said, though I didn't believe it. SPYDER wasn't the type of evil organization that quit being evil after a few setbacks. And we'd never captured most of the high-ranking members. Or even figured out the real identities of any of them.

"Now, Leo Shang might be only one man," Cyrus told me, "but he controls an empire that appears to be just as powerful and dangerous as SPYDER. Perhaps even more powerful and dangerous. If he is truly plotting something with a Level Eleven potential for danger and destruction, there are many possible targets in the Rocky Mountains. The U.S. government has dozens of extremely critical facilities there: the headquarters for North American Aerospace Defense, Strategic Missile Command, the Air Force Academy. . . ."

"The Central Food and Seed Reserve," Alexander suggested helpfully.

Cyrus frowned disdainfully at this, but he didn't discount it, either. "Shang could be targeting any one of them. Or something else entirely. It is imperative that we find out what—and that we do it quickly. Which is why you need to get close to Jessica Shang, Benjamin."

"How am I supposed to do that?" I asked, unable to hide how daunted I felt. "I won't even be able to get into her hotel."

"You'll be attending ski school with her," Alexander explained. "Leo Shang originally enrolled her in private lessons—but those were recently changed to group lessons. We're not sure why, but we assume that was Jessica's doing."

"That doesn't make any sense," Erica muttered. "Why would anyone *not* want private lessons? In public lessons, you have to be around other people."

"We suspect that might be the whole idea," Cyrus said. "Leo has kept Jessica very cloistered her whole life, so perhaps she's chafing at that." He gave Erica a pointed look. "Sometimes teenage girls like to challenge authority."

Erica rolled her eyes.

"Whatever the case," Cyrus went on, "we have an opportunity here. We've already been in touch with the Vail Ski School, and they've agreed to enroll both of you in the same class as Jessica." He turned to me. "Do you have any experience snow skiing?"

"Uh . . . no," I conceded.

"Excellent!" Cyrus said, to my surprise. "Neither does Jessica. You'll both be beginners. That will give you something to bond over right there. Erica will also be enrolled with you, as she's never skied either."

"Really?" I asked, stunned. Erica could do everything from martial arts to safecracking to infiltrating enemy compounds; it was hard to believe there was anything she hadn't tried, let alone mastered.

"It hasn't been a priority," Erica explained, then turned to her grandfather. "And what happens if Jessica decides to bond with someone else in the class other than Ben?"

"We've already taken that into account," Cyrus replied. "The other students in the class will be under orders to not befriend her."

"How?" I asked. "You can't give a bunch of random kids orders like that. . . ." As I spoke, however, I noticed Erica sighing, as though I was being dense. It took me another moment to realize what she had figured out instantly. "Unless they're not a bunch of random kids."

"Exactly," Alexander said. "Some of your classmates are going to be activated too."

"Now, wait one second!" the principal barked. "Even more of my students are being put in the field?"

"Who else is coming?" I asked.

"We haven't decided yet," Cyrus told me. "We'd like input from both of you before building the team. We want to make sure you're surrounded by people you trust."

A smile spread across my face. Not only was I being acti-vated as a primary agent for an official mission, but I'd get to bring some of my friends along as well. And Erica would be there too. Sure, she was upset at the moment, but once she cooled down, I was looking forward to working with her. And at a ski resort, no less. I'd heard those places were chock-full of hot tubs and roaring fireplaces, all of which sounded very romantic. "When does this mission begin?"

"Leo Shang scheduled the vacation over his daughter's

winter break," Cyrus reported. "That coincides with our winter break as well. You'll be enrolled in ski school at Vail for a week, beginning the day after Christmas."

My smile spread even further. My family hadn't made any plans for winter break; I'd feared I was going to spend it stuck at my house, staring at the walls. A ski vacation sounded a thousand times better.

"It's not going to be a vacation," Erica said, reading my thoughts.

I turned to her, trying to conceal my surprise. "That's not what I was thinking."

"That's exactly what you were thinking," she said testily. "You were smiling like you just won the lottery. Well, this isn't going to be fun. It's going to be dangerous. *Extremely* dangerous. Grandpa and my father have been sugarcoating things. Leo Shang is far more vicious than they've let on. I know all about him."

"How?" Alexander asked.

"I'm studying to be a spy. It's my job to know things." Erica turned back to me. "The reason Leo Shang is so hard to get close to is that he tends to *kill* anyone he's suspicious of. Like the poor sap who learned about Operation Golden Fist. The reason that mission was terminated was because the *agent* got terminated. And he probably wasn't the first we've lost." She looked to Alexander and Cyrus accusingly.

Cyrus held her gaze, not giving anything away, but Alexander averted his eyes, indicating Erica had guessed the truth.

Erica returned her attention to me. "So while this might *sound* like a dream vacation, we're being sent into the lion's den here. And believe me, Leo Shang's going to be doubly suspicious of anyone trying to get close to his only daughter. I'll do all I can to protect you as your handler, but you better bring your A game to this mission. Because if you screw this up, you're gonna end up dead."

With that, she stormed out and slammed the door behind her.

I looked back to the others in the cramped room. Cyrus simply nodded his agreement, displeased that Erica had spoken the way she had but not about to lie to me either. Alexander gave me an apologetic shrug.

Now the principal was the one smiling. Apparently, he was quite pleased by the thought that I might die.

Suddenly, being part of Operation Snow Bunny no longer seemed like such a great idea.

MEMORIZATION

The National Zoo

Washington, DC

December 9

1630 hours

"That stinks," Mike Brezinski said.

"I know," I admitted. "It does."

"Not for you, it doesn't," Mike argued. "You get to go skiing. For the whole winter break. Meanwhile, I'm gonna be stuck here by myself. You said you were going to be around!"

"I thought I was. But something came up."

Mike angrily snapped a twig off a tree and threw it into the panda exhibit. You weren't supposed to throw things into the zoo exhibits, but Mike had never been one for following the rules. It probably didn't matter, though. The pandas were inside because it was freezing.

I had just told Mike about my ski trip. Or at least, I'd told him as much as I was allowed to: that my school had approved an all-expenses-paid trip to Vail over winter break. The CIA had told my parents the exact same story. Neither Mike nor my parents—nor any civilians—even knew that spy school existed. Instead, they believed that I attended the St. Smithen's Science Academy for Boys and Girls, an elite boarding school in Washington, DC. (For a few weeks, while I'd been undercover at SPYDER's evil spy school, everyone had been led to believe that I'd left St. Smithen's for Wiseman Preparatory Academy, but now that Wiseman was a smoking crater in the ground, I'd been "reaccepted" at St. Smithen's.)

We were at the National Zoo because it was close to my campus and it was free; neither Mike nor I had enough cash to even buy ourselves a slice of pizza. I'd hoped that breaking the bad news face-to-face would go over better than a call or a text, but that hadn't been the case at all.

"How does a smarty-pants science school score a ski trip anyhow?" Mike groused. "You guys don't even have any sports teams. And suddenly you're taking up skiing?"

"There's lots of science in skiing," I pointed out. "Friction. Wind resistance. Aerodynamics. Plus, we're participating in a survey of the snowpack to analyze climate change."

"Wow," Mike muttered. "You guys can even make something as cool as skiing sound dorky."

I sighed. Not being able to tell Mike the truth about my training was one of the worst things about spy school. (Although it wasn't nearly as bad as the fact that people had tried to kill me on a regular basis.) Throughout our lives, Mike had always been cool. I hadn't. And now I was doing amazingly cool stuff like thwarting evil plots and saving the president's life—but I had to keep it all a secret. I hated lying to my best friend. And I wasn't exactly thrilled he thought I was a dork.

"Maybe we can see each other on Christmas Day," I suggested.

"Ha. Like that'll happen." Mike threw another twig into the panda exhibit, then stalked off toward the elephant house.

I raced after him. "What's that supposed to mean?"

"You're never around anymore. First you transferred from our school to St. Smarties. Then, instead of coming home for the summer, you went to nerd camp. And after that, you said you were transferring back to our old school, but you were only there a few hours before you transferred back out again. Now you're ditching me over winter break, too."

"At least Elizabeth will still be around," I suggested, meaning Elizabeth Pasternak, Mike's girlfriend and the hottest girl at my old school.

"I broke up with her," Mike said.

"What? Why?"

Mike shrugged. "I just wasn't that into her."

That's how cool Mike was. *He* broke up with the most popular girl at school, not the other way around.

Or, at least, he was *claiming* he'd broken up with her. I wondered if Elizabeth had really ended it—and if Mike was actually angry about *that*, rather than me.

But then, there was a good chance he was truly angry at me. After all, if Mike had treated me the way I'd been treating him—even though I wasn't doing it on purpose—I would have been upset too.

We passed some of the only other people dumb enough to be outside on a freezing day: a young couple, probably in their twenties. The girl had green eyes and short dark brown hair, while the guy had brown eyes, blond hair, and a knit ski cap. Both were wearing blue jeans and snow boots. The girl's hands were tucked deep into the pockets of a pink winter jacket, while the guy had leather gloves with a white paint stain on the thumb.

Normally, I wouldn't have noticed any of this, but I was working hard to improve my memory skills. It had been three days since I'd been assigned my mission, and to my surprise, most of my prep work had been memory exercises. It wasn't nearly as glamorous as learning martial arts or bomb defusion, but the Hales claimed it was even more important. "A keen memory is the best weapon an agent can have," Alexander had explained. "Well, besides a gun. Or a knife. And maybe a hand grenade. Okay, technically, there's a *lot* of weapons that are better than your memory, but memory's still awfully important. Because . . . Oh, nuts. I forgot what I was going to say."

At this point, Cyrus had groaned and told me, "If you actually succeed in getting close to Leo Shang, you'll have to remember *everything* you see and hear."

"You can't just give me a little spy camera and some sort of recording device?" I'd asked.

"If Leo Shang catches you with either of those things, he'll kill you," Cyrus had told me.

This was a very convincing argument. I didn't want to be dead, so I was beefing up my memory. It had turned out to be far more work than I'd expected. I had been pulled out of my regular classes and placed in an intensive memory immersion course. For hours each day, I'd memorized random strings of numbers and decks of cards. My instructor, Professor Richmond, had walked me down the city streets and then peppered me with questions about everything I'd seen: What model car was parked closest to the corner? What type of earrings had a mail carrier been wearing? How many people had failed to clean up after their dogs? It had seemed almost impossible at first, but I was already getting better at it, picking up things I never would have noticed about my surroundings before. Like how everyone else at the zoo was dressed.

"Why are you staring at those people?" Mike asked me.

I still needed a bit of work on not being so obvious, however.

"I thought I recognized them," I said quickly.

Mike stopped walking near a park bench where an old woman sat (black overcoat, red earmuffs, big hairy mole on her chin) and fixed me with a hard stare. "Have you recognized a lot of people at the zoo today? Because you've been staring at everyone we've passed."

"No, I haven't," I said, even though I had. It occurred to me that Mike had quite strong powers of observation himself.

"You have so. You've been acting weird all day. Even weirder than usual."

"What do you mean, 'weirder than usual'?"

Mike began ticking things off on his fingers. "The last time you went to Adventureland Mini Golf, you took after some suspicious guy and ended up burning the whole place down. On the one day you were back at school with me, you beat up Trey Patterson and three of his buddies and then vanished. And the one time you told me to sneak onto St. Smithen's to spring you for a party, I got tackled by a commando squad. They claimed it was only a training exercise, but I *know* that was a bunch of bull."

"I realize that all *seems* kind of weird," I replied. "But there's a good explanation for everything."

"Yeah. Something strange is going on at that science school. And you're wrapped up in it."

"Er . . . ," I said, and then had no idea what to add. Mike had caught me completely off guard by nailing the answer.

Mike waited for two other zoo visitors to pass us—a mother (heavy tan parka, hiking boots, librarian glasses) and son (blue Batman jacket, snow boots, a river of snot running from his nose)—and then whispered, "They're experimenting on you, aren't they?"

I'd been preparing myself to be accused of being a spy, so now I was caught off guard again. "What?"

"I mean, it's a science school, but there's all this secrecy around it," Mike explained. "So whatever they're up to . . . it's not kosher, right?"

"Um," I said, not quite sure where this was going. "Maybe."

"So what do they do to you?" Mike asked, growing intrigued. "Inject you with all sorts of weird chemicals to give you incredible martial arts skills one day and hyperattentiveness the next?"

I was annoyed that Mike thought I was a human guinea

pig, but then I remembered what was known as "Delman's Law of Opportune Aliases": If someone mistakenly assumes something about you, it's much easier to simply let them believe it than to make up something else entirely.

So I said, "Yes. I'm a human guinea pig."

"I knew it!" Mike crowed, so loudly he startled a passing zookeeper (gray hair, bushy mustache, coveralls smeared with what looked disturbingly like animal poop). Then he lowered his voice again and said, "This explains everything. All your screwball behavior."

"I guess," I said.

"Even the commando squad," Mike pointed out. "Because all these experiments must be super top secret, right? I'll bet the Pentagon's involved, cooking up stuff that'll turn even guys like you into mega-warriors."

I should have just said yes. But I didn't. I was growing too upset with the direction this conversation had taken. Although I was under orders to protect the secrecy of spy school, I hated that Mike thought I needed a secret formula to turn me into a warrior. When I'd defeated Trey Patterson—and SPYDER—I'd done it all by myself.

So I asked, "You've suspected this the whole time I was at St. Smithen's?"

"Well, not the whole time. I thought it was just your standard dorky science school for a while. But after the commando attack, I got a little suspicious. Why do you ask?"

"Because when I came back to our old school a few months ago, you told all those girls I was training to be a spy."

"I did?" Mike asked blankly.

"Yes. You told Elizabeth and Kate Grant and Chloe Appel . . ."

"Oh, right! I did! To impress them. I mean, I couldn't tell them you were a human science experiment. That would have weirded them out. To be honest, *I'm* a little weirded out by it. You're not radioactive or anything, are you?"

"No," I said curtly. "So you *never* thought I was training to be a spy?"

Mike burst into laughter. "You? A spy? That's ridiculous!"

I decided not to push the issue any further. I'd already violated a dozen secrecy protocols. And frankly, the direction of the conversation had grown even more embarrassing. "Yeah," I said, faking some weak laughter myself. "Imagine *me* being a spy."

"You'd be the worst." Mike snickered. "If anyone gave you a gun, you'd probably shoot yourself in the foot."

I frowned. Not because Mike was being insulting, but because he was right. On my first day at the school artillery range, I'd almost blown off my own toes. I still didn't like carrying a gun on a mission. Luckily for me, no one else liked me carrying a gun either.

Mike's laughter died down as we reached the elephant house. One of the elephants was actually braving the cold (chipped left tusk, three notches in right ear, mud all over its legs). Mike stopped to watch it. "So what's this ski trip really about, then? Are you getting some sort of secret medication to improve your balance? Or to make you faster? Or to keep you from getting cold? That'd be pretty cool. You'd never need mittens!"

"I don't know," I said. "They never tell us anything ahead of time."

"Any chance I could tag along?"

"You mean, to ski with us?"

"Yeah. And to get superpowers."

I looked at Mike curiously. "You mean, you think being a guinea pig would be cool?"

"Better than cool! You wiped out Trey Patterson and all his pals at school. That was amazing! Can anyone get into this program, or does everyone have to be a genius like you?"

"I'm not a genius, Mike. . . ."

"Yes, you are. You're like Einstein when it comes to math. And I know no one gave you some super-secret formula to make that happen."

I found myself smiling. The direction of the conversation had gotten much better. "I don't know if that had anything to do with me being picked. . . ."

"Well, could you put in a good word for me, at least? So I could transfer?"

"You mean, you'd want to leave regular school?"

"Yeah. Middle school sucks."

"But you're popular!"

"Big whoop. It's still middle school. It's not like anyone's doing any top-secret experiments on me."

"That's not always so awesome. . . ."

"Are they working on anything with radioactive spiders? So that you'll be able to shoot webs out of your wrists like Spider-Man?"

"Er . . . no. And so you know, spiders don't shoot webs from their wrists anyhow. If someone really shot webs like a spider, they'd do it from their butt."

"Oh," Mike said, sounding daunted. But only for a second. "See? I said you were smart. I'll bet there's lots of other cool stuff they're working on. Like super-strength and X-ray vision and teleportation and the ability to stay clean forever and never have to bathe."

"Why would the government be interested in having people stop bathing?"

"Water conservation. Plus, it'd be awesome to never have to shower again. So win-win for everyone. Dude, you have to get me into this school. . . ."

"I'll try, but . . ."

"Or at least see if you can get me on the ski trip. If cost is an issue, I could maybe even work out my own place to stay. I have an uncle in Colorado. . . ."

"I'll see what I can do," I told him, although I didn't mean it. Because there was no way I could get Mike enrolled in a top-secret government program that didn't actually exist. I felt bad about lying to him, although part of me was strangely happy as well. Not about the lying, but the fact that for once, Mike was jealous of me, rather than the other way around. In our entire lives, Mike had been jealous of me only one other time, and that was when he had mistakenly believed I was dating Erica Hale. (A misunderstanding I had never bothered to set straight.)

I was so distracted by all this, I had forgotten about being hyper-attentive. Which was a big mistake. Because I'd missed something important.

And it was going to come back to haunt me in a big way on my mission.

ACCLIMATIZATION

The Ski Haüs
Vail, Colorado
December 26
1530 hours

The town of Vail sat at the bottom of a valley in the Rocky Mountains, smushed between the base of the ski mountain and Interstate 70. The small downtown had a German theme—probably to evoke the European history of skiing—with covered bridges, buildings straight out of a Grimms' fairy tale, and lots of businesses with unnecessary umlauts in their names. Around this was a sprawl of expensive luxury hotels with fancy spas and heated swimming pools and attentive staffs who catered to the guests' every whim.

Unfortunately, we weren't staying in one of those hotels.

Instead, we were staying in the only motel in Vail, the Ski Haüs. It was a ramshackle one-story building with a crooked line of rooms that all opened onto a parking lot, and it sat on the opposite side of the freeway from the ski area, so close to the on-ramp that the whole place shook when trucks rumbled past. The Ski Haüs had been built back when Vail was founded in 1969 and the owners hadn't sunk another penny into it since. The beds were lumpy, the pipes were balky, the bathrooms smelled funky, and cold air seeped through the cheap windows, rendering the entire place as cold as a meat locker. And yet it was still nicer than our dorms back at spy school.

The only real problem was that we had to share the rooms, rather than having them to ourselves. Which meant I had three roommates: Chip Schacter, Jawaharlal O'Shea, and Warren Reeves. Chip, being two years older, was the biggest, toughest, and sneakiest of us. Jawa was the smartest and the best athlete. Warren wasn't really a very good spy at all. I'd invited him along only because Zoe said that if I didn't, we'd never hear the end of it. (He *was* pretty talented at camouflage, though. It came naturally to him. He was wearing a white outfit that blended in with the snow so well, we'd already lost him twice in the motel parking lot.)

"I call one bed!" Chip exclaimed the moment we entered our room.

"You can't do that," Warren pointed out. "There's only two beds. We have to share them."

"Fine." Chip sighed. "I'll share with you. You can have it during the day and I'll use it at night."

"Deal," Warren said. It wasn't until they'd shaken hands on it that he realized what he'd just agreed to. "Hey! Wait a minute. . . ."

"Too late. You shook on it." Chip flopped onto the bed, staking his claim to it.

"Handshakes aren't legally binding!" Warren protested. "Tell him, Jawa!"

"Technically they are," Jawa said, then looked to me. "I suppose that means you and I are sharing the other bed."

"All right." I was pleased not to have to share with Chip or Warren. Chip was so big, he would have taken up the whole bed, and Warren smelled like old cheese. (Zoe claimed this was because he never did his laundry, but I suspected he had some sort of personal hygiene problem.)

None of us bothered to take off the heavy ski parkas we were wearing. It was too cold in the room for that. There was a small heater by the door, but despite clattering like a car that had thrown a rod, it seemed to be heating only the three inches of air surrounding it.

We'd been traveling the whole day. First we'd taken a plane from Washington to Denver. Economy class, of course, but I hadn't cared; it was the first plane I'd ever been on. Then we'd boarded a shuttle from the airport, which took us up the winding highway, through the mountains, to Vail. I had spent the whole time on both legs of the trip staring out the window. I'd been awed to see the country passing below me from thirty-five thousand feet above— and I'd been equally awed by the Rocky Mountains from ground level. The previous summer I'd thought that the mountains of West Virginia were impressive (although I'd been a bit too busy running for my life to fully appreciate them). However, those were mere speed bumps compared to the Rockies, which were far more massive and beautiful than I could have ever imagined. I'd seen plenty of pictures of them before, but those hadn't come close to doing the mountains justice.

Jawa set his suitcase on the bed and unzipped it, revealing a neatly arranged selection of ski clothes. Jawa was exceptionally well organized; he had separate, clearly labeled plastic bags for socks, gloves, sweaters, and thermal underwear.

Chip, on the other hand, appeared to have wadded all of his clothes into a ball and then crammed it into a duffel bag that was two sizes too small. Two of the seams had split en route, forcing Chip to repair them with duct tape.

"I can't thank you enough for inviting me on this," Jawa told me, carefully arranging his underwear in the bureau. "As if it weren't amazing enough to be on my first assignment, I also get a free ski vacation out of it!"

"Yeah," Chip echoed. "You wouldn't believe how jealous everyone else back at school was when I told them I was going."

I turned to him, aghast. "You weren't supposed to tell *anyone*. This mission is top secret!"

"Relax," Chip told me. "They already knew. It's a school for spies. Nothing stays a secret there for long." He rolled off the bed and unzipped his overstuffed duffel bag. Clothes erupted from it with such force that a pair of boxer shorts sailed across the room and nailed Warren in the face.

Warren screamed in horror, stumbled backward over his own suitcase, and collapsed on the floor.

"It's not really supposed to be a vacation," I warned them. "Erica says our lives could be at risk."

Chip laughed and shrugged this off. "Erica always thinks her life is at risk. Remember last year when she got all worked up about us having a mole in the school?"

"Um . . . there *was* a mole," I reminded him. "And our lives really were in danger. I almost got killed. Twice."

"Oh, yeah," Chip recalled. "That's right. Hey, I wonder if anyone will try to kill *us* this time."

"I hope so!" Jawa said excitedly. "That'd be amazing!"

"Assuming they're unsuccessful," Warren pointed out.

Chip pegged him in the face with another pair of boxers. "Well, duh. No one wants a *successful* attempt made on their life, you nitwit."

"What if it happened on the slopes?" Jawa asked, his excitement ratcheting up a few notches. "And we got to have an honest-to-goodness ski chase? How fantastic would that be?"

"It'd be the best," Chip agreed. "Warren, stop playing with my underwear, you pervert." He snatched the boxers Warren had just removed from his head and tossed them into a drawer, along with a handful of random socks and gloves.

"You really think you could outrun someone on skis?" I asked them.

"Definitely," Jawa replied confidently. "I've been skiing ever since I was a kid."

"Me too," Chip agreed. "Just let Leo Shang try to mow me down out there. I'll leave him in the dust."

"I'm pretty good on skis myself," Warren boasted.

I sighed. This wasn't the first time I'd found myself out of my league around my fellow students. Most of them had been training in various skills such as jujitsu or marksmanship their whole lives, which had been great assets when the CIA was looking for new recruits. Meanwhile, I hadn't really gotten into spy school on my own merits at all. Sure, I had strong math skills and some facility with languages, but in truth, I'd been recruited as a patsy. I had been bait to catch that mole and the school hadn't really expected me to survive. When I had, they'd realized they couldn't return me to normal life—I knew too many secrets—so I'd been allowed to stay. But while I'd proven myself on subsequent missions, I still didn't feel anywhere near as confident as Jawa or Chip did. The reason they were so bizarrely eager to confront danger was that, after years of training for it, they were convinced they could handle it easily. They were like minor league baseball players who'd finally been bumped up to the majors and couldn't wait for their first game.

Meanwhile, I was like someone who'd been plunked into the majors without ever being taught how to catch. I'd had to pick up almost everything on the fly. For example, I'd never skied a day in my life. While Chip and Jawa would be posing as beginners to blend in with the ski school, I really *was* a beginner. "If anyone tries to kill *me* on the slopes, I'm going to be a sitting duck." I sighed.

"Ptarmigan," Warren corrected.

"What?" I asked.

"There's no ducks in the mountains," Warren explained. "Whereas a ptarmigan is a bird found in cold climates like the northern tundra. So you wouldn't be a sitting duck. You'd be a sitting ptarmigan."

"Shut up, Warren," Chip threatened. "Or the next time

I throw a pair of boxers at you, they'll be the ones I've been wearing for the last sixteen hours."

Warren cringed in fear and stumbled over his suitcase once again.

"No one's really gonna try to kill us," Jawa told me reassuringly. "That's just wishful thinking on our part. Statistically, ninety-eight-point-five percent of CIA missions resolve without any action at all."

"Mine haven't," I reminded him. "So far, a hundred percent of my missions have ended with bad guys trying to kill me."

"That's great!" Chip exclaimed. "Then you're due for an easy one. But just in case this mission *does* have some danger . . ." He paused to share an excited glance with Jawa. "Don't sweat it. We've got your back."

"That's right," Jawa agreed. "You brought us in on this mission. We're gonna make sure you get out of it alive."

"Thanks," I said, hoping they were right.

Warren unzipped his luggage on the floor beside me. "So what does the CIA think Operation Golden Fist even is?"

"They don't know." I set my own suitcase next to Jawa's on the bed. "Though Cyrus thinks it might have something to do with one of the government facilities in the Rockies. NORAD, Strategic Missile Command . . ."

"The Cheyenne Mountain Complex," Jawa suggested.

"What's that?" I asked.

"Noah's ark for the Cold War," Jawa replied. "It was built during the 1950s to be able to withstand a nuclear attack. Thirty miles of tunnels, living spaces, and control rooms dug deep under the mountains. The idea was, should everyone actually launch their nukes, the president and a few thousand people could actually live down there for years so humanity would survive."

"Why would a bad guy want to access a bunch of old tunnels?" Warren scoffed.

"Because the complex is still active," Jawa replied. "It houses the emergency backup controls for everything from our defense systems to the entire U.S. power grid. If Shang got to it, he could cripple our entire country in one blow. Which would then set the stage for China to become the world's primary economic and military power."

Warren's smug expression vanished. "Oh."

"Of course, I'm just spitballing," Jawa admitted. "Maybe Shang has something even more sinister up his sleeve."

"Well, whatever he's plotting, I'm sure Ben will figure it out." Chip gave me a punch in the arm that was supposed to be supportive and playful but was actually strong enough to knock me into the wall. "Oops," he said. "Sorry about that."

"It's cool," I said, trying to act like it hadn't hurt—even though it had. I was also trying to act like I wasn't completely daunted by my mission. The idea that Shang could be plotting something so diabolical was terrifying to me, and I didn't have nearly the confidence in myself that Chip seemed to. I caught sight of myself in the slightly cracked mirror that hung over the lopsided dresser in the motel room. I didn't merely *feel* incapable; I didn't *look* capable either. But then, my pathetic clothing probably had a lot to do with that.

While Chip, Jawa, and Warren all wore brand-new ski outfits, I had cobbled mine together with hand-me-downs from my cousins. My parka was twenty-five years old, and my scarf had more holes in it than a piece of Swiss cheese. My gloves didn't even match.

In fact, now that I thought about it, I was missing one glove entirely. The first was still clipped to the zipper of my parka, but the other had gone AWOL. I tried to remember when I'd last had it. The lobby, I figured. I'd worn the gloves when getting off the shuttle in the motel parking lot but had removed them in the lobby to warm my hands by the fire. The fire had turned out to be a fake—some ceramic logs with cheap plastic flames dancing among them—but I hadn't seen my other glove since then.

"I'll be right back," I said.

"Where are you going?" Chip questioned. "To see Erica?"

"Why would I be going to see Erica?" I asked.

"Because you're madly in love with her," Chip replied.

Yet another piece of top-secret information that everyone at spy school knew anyhow. Although this wasn't really a testament to any great spy skills on Chip's part; practically every guy at spy school had a crush on Erica. "I'm not seeing Erica. I lost my glove."

"Ah, the old 'pretending to lose your glove so you can go see Erica' trick," Jawa teased. "Can't fool us with that one."

"I'll be right back," I said, then stepped through the flimsy door into the parking lot.

It wasn't much colder outside than it had been inside. The sun was already sinking below the mountains on the horizon, casting the valley in shadow, but the sky was still brilliant blue above. Across the highway, I could see the snowy slopes of Vail Mountain, giant white slashes through green forests with skiers wending their way down them.

Something suddenly nailed me in the head, just behind my right ear. For a moment I was terrified that I'd already been ambushed by the enemy, but then the sensation of cold wetness kicked in and I realized the weapon had merely been a snowball.

Hank Schacter, Chip's seventeen-year-old brother, emerged from around the side of the motel, smirking, two more snowballs at the ready. Hank was a meathead and a jerk. I never would have willingly invited him on a mission, but as my resident adviser at spy school, he'd been brought along as a chaperone. Somehow, he'd scored his own space—albeit an extremely cramped one that barely had room for a twin bed. "We're on a CIA mission, Ripley," he scolded. "You can't drop your guard like that. We can't have anyone making dumb mistakes."

"Like announcing that we're on a CIA mission in a public space?" I asked.

Hank tried to think of a response, failed, and then threw another snowball at me.

I tried to dodge it, but wasn't fast enough. It thwacked me in the chest.

"Lousy reflexes, too," Hank chided. "You better hope the heat doesn't come down on this operation, or you're gonna be dead meat."

I looked around for cover, but there wasn't any in the parking lot. The few cars were too far away. And there wasn't any snow nearby to fight back with; it had all been pummeled into slush.

The third snowball smacked me in the face. Snow cascaded down into my jacket.

"You're pathetic!" Hank snarled. "If you want to survive, you need to think! You need to keep your guard up at all times. If you allow yourself to be distracted for so much as one second, you're gonna end up in serious trouble."

"Like you?" a voice asked.

Hank spun around, startled, to find Erica fifteen feet away, standing next to a large pile of snowballs. Meanwhile, Hank had thrown his last one at me and was unarmed. Instantly, his demeanor changed from cocky to weaselly. "Hold on, Erica," he pleaded. "I was just trying to teach Ben a lesson. . . ."

"So now I'll teach you one," Erica said. "Don't be a jerk, or *this* will happen." With that, she unleashed a fusillade of snowballs, moving so fast Hank might as well have been shot with a snowball machine gun. Hank ran, but Erica predicted his every move, pegging him repeatedly, until he finally escaped into the safety of the lobby.

"Nice work, roomie!" Zoe cheered, emerging from a motel room. Zoe tended to be unnaturally cheerful most of the time, but being on her first mission—and at a ski resort—had made her almost manic with glee. She'd been smiling constantly since the moment we'd met at the airport that morning. "You sure showed him!"

Erica regarded Zoe curiously, thrown by her enthusiasm. "Yes," she said finally, "I did."

Zoe came to my side to help me scrape the snow out of my hair. "How's your room?"

"Crowded," I said. Zoe and Erica had lucked out; as the only two girls on the trip, they got a whole room and separate beds to themselves. "How's yours?"

"Great!" Zoe chirped, and then lowered her voice to even

below a whisper. "Although it's kind of freaky being with Erica. Half her luggage was ammunition. Who brings grenades on a ski vacation?"

"I can hear you," Erica said, even though she was still fifteen feet away.

Zoe grimaced, alarmed that she'd been overheard.

"And it's not a vacation," Erica pointed out. "It's a top-secret CIA mission."

"Why does everyone keep saying that out loud?" I asked.

"Because the only people close enough to hear me are also on the mission," Erica explained. "I've already cased the area. All the other residents of this fleabag motel are out skiing, housekeeping has gone home for the day, and the guy running the desk has the stereo in the lobby jacked up so loud playing Christmas music he can barely hear anything over the jingle bells. So the only humans around are either fellow spies or shams."

"Shams?" I asked.

"Hello!" Alexander Hale cried, exiting his room.

"Case in point," Erica told me, indicating her father.

Erica and Alexander had the most dysfunctional family relationship I'd ever encountered. And I came from a family where my cousins had gotten into three different fistfights at our Christmas party. Erica absolutely resented her father—though, in her defense, for much of his life, Alexander hadn't been a model parent. For example, six months before, he'd accidentally left a piece of information crucial to national security in a public bathroom and then covered for himself by blaming the mistake on Erica, resulting in a black mark on her permanent record. Alexander had ultimately admitted to the truth—and ever since, he'd been desperately trying to prove his worth to Erica every chance he got, but she rejected each attempt he made.

"How are my little agents doing?" Alexander asked. He was wearing a ski outfit that appeared to be custom-tailored. Zoe and I looked round as Butterball turkeys in our parkas, but Alexander looked stylish as could be in his. "Having a good time so far?"

"Hardly," Erica replied, before Zoe or I could. "This place is a dump."

Alexander's good cheer faltered. When he smiled again, he looked far more apologetic. "Ah, yes. Well, there's been quite a bit of belt-tightening at the Agency lately. We have to keep an eye on the budget for missions now. Not like the good old days. Once, when I was on a mission in Gstaad, I rented the executive suite of the Hotel Beauxville for six weeks. . . ."

"And he wonders why the CIA doesn't have any money anymore," Erica muttered.

"But this place isn't so bad," Alexander said spiritedly.

"Sure, it's a little cramped. And it's cold. And it's unlikely that the sheets have been washed in the last few weeks. And there's barely any water pressure in the showers. And . . ." Alexander frowned. "What was my point again?"

"This place isn't so bad," I reminded him.

"Oh! Right you are, Benjamin! The fact being that sometimes, struggling against adversity is the best way to build friendships. Why, I can remember one mission in Siberia, when I was subjected to simply the worst ordeal known to man. I was on the run from the Russians with Agent Johnny Cliff. We were off in the most hostile wilderness you can imagine, miles from civilization, with no food, no shelter, and half the KGB on our tail. But while the experience was miserable, it brought Johnny and I together in a way like no other. We were as close as brothers after that. Closer, maybe."

"Didn't you take all the responsibility for the success on that mission?" Erica asked. "After which Johnny never talked to you again?"

Alexander smiled weakly. "Er, well . . . all brothers have their differences."

Erica sighed with disgust and then started across the parking lot toward me. "Well, Dad, this has been extremely enlightening, as usual, but I'm afraid Ben and I have something to take care of right now."

"I've lost a glove," I said.

"No, you haven't." Erica pulled my glove from her pocket and slapped it into my hand. "I found that in the lobby."

"Hey, thanks!" I told her, then added, "Um . . . if you had this, what do we have to take care of?"

"Reconnaissance." Erica grabbed my arm and led me across the parking lot, toward a pedestrian bridge that crossed over the highway to connect us with Vail Village. "We're on a mission, remember? It's time to get to work."

RECONNAISSANCE

Lionshead Village

Vail, Colorado

December 26

1630 hours

Thirty minutes later, I got my first glimpse of my target.

Erica and I were casing the Shangs' hotel, the Arabelle. It was five stories tall and located in an area of Vail known as Lionshead Village. Lionshead was mostly free of roads, with wide-open concourses for tourists to walk on. The Arabelle had a prime position in the center of it, right at the base of Vail Mountain, closer to skiing than any other hotel, and it was incredibly luxurious. For example, there were "ski valets" whose job it was to carry guests' skis to the lifts for them, even though the lifts were less than a minute away. Renting one small room for a week there cost more than my father's car. And yet Leo Shang had rented out the entire place, top to bottom, on the busiest ski week of the year for only himself, his daughter, and their security staff.

One side of the Arabelle faced a public square with an ice-skating rink, some fancy restaurants, an ice cream parlor, and a pizza joint. Erica had treated me to a slice of pepperoni and grabbed one for herself as well. We ate them as we walked around the hotel. "We'll look less suspicious if we're eating," Erica explained. "Like two kids who just went out for pizza, rather than two spies on a recon mission. Plus, I'm starving."

I didn't question this. I was starving too. Between the plane and the shuttle, we hadn't had a chance to eat much that day except airline peanuts.

It didn't seem as if we needed much of an excuse to be walking around, though. There were hundreds of other people walking around too. The ski lifts had just closed for the day, and skiers were pouring down the mountain in droves. An area the size of a soccer field in front of the Arabelle was crowded with people unclipping their skis and snowboards and heading off to their hotels. The ice rink was packed with parents and children. The line for pizza had taken fifteen minutes. Everyone seemed to be in an extremely good mood, jazzed after their day of skiing, sharing stories about their best runs. For a brief period, I forgot all about my mission and began to grow excited about learning to ski the next day.

I watched a crowd of snowboarders not much older than me skid to a stop after their last run, beaming with excitement. "Looks like fun," I observed.

"I suppose it could be," Erica replied.

I took a bite of my pizza; the cheese was already congealing in the cold weather. "I can't believe you've never skied before."

"Why not?"

"It just seems like something you would have done. I mean, you know fourteen different styles of martial arts. I figured you would have mastered skiing somewhere along the line."

"I haven't had the chance," Erica said. "I'll master it tomorrow."

I smiled, amused by her attitude. "It's not supposed to be that easy. I read that it can take a few days before some people even learn how to turn."

Erica shrugged. "I taught myself how to be a world-class fencer in one morning. It won't take me more than a day to get good at skiing."

I wondered if Erica was right. At the moment, the nearby slopes were full of evidence that skiing could be difficult.

For every skier who came down the mountain well, there were many others coming down badly. I could see a dozen people who'd wiped out at the base of the mountain. As I watched, one poor soul shot off the run entirely and fell into Vail Creek. And things didn't get much better once everyone had taken their skis off. Ski boots seemed to have been designed to make walking as difficult as possible. Everywhere I looked, people were wobbling about in them like toddlers taking their first steps. One person crashed to the ground right in front of us, his skis and poles flying every which way.

Erica stepped right over him, leading me toward the front doors of the Arabelle.

I hustled after her, feeling strangely out of breath. "Hey. Can we slow down a bit?"

"Getting winded?" Erica asked.

"Yes."

"It's the altitude. We're more than eight thousand feet above sea level here. There's far less oxygen. Your body isn't used to it yet. It might take a day or two."

"You don't seem to be affected."

"I'm using ashanti-veda yogic breathing techniques to modulate my oxygen intake. And, of course, I'm in much better shape than you are."

"You can actually control how much oxygen you're breathing? How?"

"It's very complicated. You have to harness your chi energy, align your chakras, and then—" Erica stopped so suddenly I almost slammed into her from behind. "The target is approaching," she whispered.

I glanced around me, trying to pick up on what Erica had. But everything looked completely normal. We had now reached the front of the Arabelle, where a semicircular driveway passed the main doors. Skiers were streaming across the road, returning to other hotels that were farther from the slopes. "How did you . . . ?" I began.

"Check the front doors," Erica hissed.

I looked that way. Some very large Chinese men had exited the Arabelle. Of the dozens of people within view, they were the only ones who weren't wearing ski clothes. Instead, they wore three-piece suits, each of which had the telltale bulge of a weapon under the jacket. Bodyguards. "Oh," I said, feeling like an idiot for missing them before.

Two of the bodyguards, each the size of a professional linebacker, stepped into the path of the skiers, holding up their hands to stop the crowd, like extremely well-dressed crossing guards. They didn't say a word, but something ominous in their demeanor froze everyone in their tracks. Both guards had radio wires curling from their ears. One said something in Chinese into his.

"That's the 'all clear,'" Erica informed me.

A second later, three vehicles came down the road. I'd never seen anything like them. Each looked like someone had crossed a car with a tank. They were big and boxy, with all-terrain tires and what appeared to be armor plating. The windows were heavily tinted, so we couldn't see a thing as they rumbled past us.

The first looped past the front doors of the hotel and stopped, blocking the exit of the driveway. The second parked in front of the hotel doors. The third stopped short, blocking the driveway's entrance. No one got out of the first or third car-tank.

Jessica Shang got out of the second.

Leo Shang also got out of it, but I didn't see him. In the first place, he had exited on the far side of it, closer to the hotel doors, so the car-tank was blocking my view of him. And after that, he was instantly surrounded by a scrum of bodyguards.

But the *real* reason I didn't see him was that I couldn't take my eyes off Jessica.

The single picture I'd seen of her before hadn't done her justice. Either it had been too grainy, or she'd blossomed since it was taken. Probably a bit of both. Whatever the case, she was equally as beautiful as Erica—only, there was something different about her. Erica always had an aura of danger about her that made her alluring but also incredibly intimidating.

Meanwhile, Jessica, despite being surrounded by armored vehicles and menacing guards, appeared to be completely the opposite. As opposed to Erica she seemed . . . friendly. I couldn't explain how, but I immediately got the sense that she'd be extremely kind and good-natured. She had wide, luminous eyes and an endearing little smile, and she was wrapped in a big, fuzzy pink parka that made her look like she was wearing a giant Hostess Sno Ball.

Jessica quickly slipped around the car-tank and disappeared into the pack of bodyguards before being shunted through the doors of the hotel. My entire glimpse of her had lasted five seconds. If that.

I kept my eyes locked on the hotel doors, hoping she might exit again.

"Oh, great," Erica muttered. "One look at the target and you already have a crush on her."

"No, I don't," I said, way too defensively.

Erica heaved a disdainful sigh. "The moment you saw her, you stopped breathing."

"It wasn't because of her. It was because of the lack of oxygen up here."

"Well, you're definitely not getting enough oxygen to your brain. You can't develop feelings for the target. She's the enemy. If you bring emotion into this, you'll screw everything up."

"I'm not going to get emotional," I said heatedly.

"You're getting emotional right now," Erica pointed out.

I started to argue that I wasn't, then realized this would be exactly what Erica was talking about. So I fell silent, embarrassed and annoyed.

The bodyguards in the street in front of us seemed to have received a new message over their radios. They stood down at the same time, allowing the crowd of skiers to cross the street again. Every single person around us was now talking about the Shangs, impressed by their car-tank convoy and wondering who they were. Even in a community as wealthy as Vail, they had just made a very big impression.

Erica fell in with the flow of tourists and I followed her. As we neared the guards who'd stopped traffic, Erica instantly changed her entire demeanor, shifting from spy surveillance mode to behaving like an actual teenage girl. Even her voice changed, ratcheting up a few octaves. "I am so psyched to hit the slopes tomorrow!" she exclaimed, taking a bite of pizza. "Aren't you?"

"Definitely," I replied, trying my best to play along.

"I hear there's some major freshies coming in this week," Erica proclaimed, leading me between the guards and across the street. "Maybe a foot. Twelve inches of pow-pow! How radical is that?"

"Er . . . very radical." I had no idea what Erica was talking about, but suspected it was skier-speak for something to do with snow.

Erica shot me a peeved glance, as though she was annoyed I wasn't holding up my end of the charade very well, and then decided to handle everything herself. She launched into a long, purposefully vapid diatribe about how much she loved skiing while we continued our circuit around the hotel.

A pedestrian walkway cut past the lobby, heading back toward the ice rink again. One of Shang's guards remained in position at the front doors as we wandered past. Unlike the others, he was Caucasian, with pale skin, bright blue eyes, and a white-blond mullet. He was one of the largest human beings I'd ever seen in my life. His arms were so muscular, he'd had to rip the sleeves off his suit to accommodate them. Apparently, the cold didn't bother him. He stood still as stone as we passed, although his eyes followed us suspiciously.

Erica acted as though she didn't even see him, rambling on about hucking off ledges and pulling kangaroo flips in the terrain park, until we were well past him and at the ice rink again. Then she turned to me, fluttered her eyelashes, and announced, "Let's go ice-skating!"

I stared at her, thrown. There weren't any bodyguards around for her to be acting in front of, and yet "Let's go ice-skating!" was one of the last things I would have ever expected to hear Erica Hale say, along the lines of "I love scrapbooking," or "Unicorns are awesome."

"Ice-skating?" I repeated. "You mean, like, for fun?"

"Of course for fun, sillypants," Erica chirped, giving me a playful swat on the shoulder. "Why else would we do it?" Then she took me by the hand and led me into the skate-rental area.

I stopped breathing again. Only for a second, but I was aware of it this time. This was the first occasion in months that Erica had touched me in any way that didn't involve demonstrating martial arts. I was relatively sure she was merely playacting, but still, it was human contact. Between this and my glimpse of Jessica Shang, I was a mess.

We wound through a few benches where people were in the various stages of putting on or taking off rental skates. As we passed among them, I leaned in close to Erica and whispered, "You don't do *anything* for fun. Are Shang's men around?"

"Check out the ice cream parlor," she whispered back, finally sounding like herself again.

I glanced back the way we had come. The ice cream parlor looked perfectly normal, though. There were no hulking men in suits there. Only a long line of families with small children and a guy reading a newspaper on a bench. "What do you mean?"

"Who reads a newspaper outside when it's twenty-two degrees?" Erica asked.

I looked back, feeling like an idiot again. Now that I knew what to look for, the guy didn't appear to be reading his newspaper at all. He was only pretending to read it, while really keeping his eyes on the crowd, carefully assessing anyone headed toward the hotel lobby. Thankfully, he didn't seem interested in us. Between the pizza place, the ice cream parlor, and the ice rink, there were dozens of other kids our age around and we were blending in perfectly.

"There's another guy by the pizza place," Erica informed me. "And a third by the skate-rental booth. I clocked them all the first time we came through." Rather than waiting in the long line for rental skates, she plucked a pair off the ground that a kid my size had just changed out of and shoved them into my arms. "Here, put these on."

I instantly did as she'd ordered, figuring that questioning it would only annoy Erica. I sat and yanked my shoes off. "Aren't you going to skate too?"

Erica didn't answer me. Instead, she looked up at the Arabelle and said, "Looks like Shang's staying on the fifth floor."

I looked up too. Sure enough, on the top floor, high above us, lights were flicking on in several rooms.

"Nice recon." I slipped my foot into an ice skate and started lacing it. "So what's the plan?"

Erica sat beside me and looked at me adoringly, which made me stop breathing again. Then she tenderly ran her fingers through my hair, which nearly gave me a heart attack. And after that, she secretly slipped a radio transmitter into my ear, confirming yet again that the only reason she ever touched me outside of a dojo was as part of an act.

We had used the radios on missions before; I could hear anything Erica said to me, while no one else could—and mine could pick up anything I said and transmit it back to her. At the moment, though, we were close enough not to need them. "You're going to be my lookout," Erica told me. "If you see any sign of trouble, let me know."

"Trouble?" I repeated, slipping on my second skate. "What are you planning to do?"

"Find out what Shang's up to."

"Now? How?"

"I'm going to infiltrate his hotel room."

"What?" I gasped. "You can't do that!"

"Sure I can. I'm good at this stuff."

"I meant, you're not *supposed* to do it. The mission is for *me* to befriend Jessica and use that connection to get close to her father."

"The mission is for *us* to find out what Operation Golden Fist is, period." Erica was back to her normal, cool self; only somehow, she seemed even cooler than usual. Her attitude was icier than the skating rink. "The other plan is too complicated, the other students aren't ready for activation yet, and like I said, you're too emotionally involved where Jessica is concerned."

"Emotionally involved? I saw her for five seconds!"

"It was enough. Your ability is compromised. I'm going with Plan B. Which should have been Plan A all along. If you just do your part, this will all be over within ten minutes." Erica stood again and started toward the ice cream parlor.

I followed her. Only, since I now had ice skates on, I couldn't follow very quickly. "Wait!" I called.

Erica stopped by the entrance to the ice rink. We were now close enough to the guy with the newspaper that she had to resume her teenage girl act again. "What is it, pumpkin?"

I lowered my voice. "The hotel is crawling with guards. You'll never be able to get into Shang's room."

Erica smiled at me in a way I knew was pretend but that still melted my heart. "Oh, sweetie." She sighed. "You're so cute when you worry about me. But I'll be fine. They won't see me because of the diversion."

"What diversion?" I asked, suddenly feeling very worried.

"This one," Erica said, and shoved me onto the ice.

I had ice-skated a few times before, so I might have been all right if Erica hadn't caught me so off guard.

Or shoved me so hard.

Or sent me onto the rink backward.

But the combination of all three was impossible to overcome. I sailed out onto the ice in reverse and completely out of control. The first thing I did was give out an involuntary yelp of surprise, which drew the attention of everyone around—including the three undercover guards.

The second thing I did was slam into another skater. And after that, I slammed into three more people. I sent each of them careening wildly across the ice, where they promptly slammed into other skaters, who slammed into still others, sparking a chain reaction of wipeouts all around the rink. Adults face-planted. Teens crashed. Small children caromed off the railing. I tried to stop myself before I caused any more trouble, digging a skate into the ice, but succeeded only in tripping myself. I swiveled around, landed flat on my stomach, and promptly cut a rather large father off at the knees. He landed right on top of me. And then his entire family landed on top of *him*. I was pancaked beneath all of them. For the fourth time in the last few minutes, I stopped breathing, but this time it wasn't due to a girl. It was because the air had been crushed out of me.

I could no longer see what was happening on the rink, as I was buried beneath a pile of humanity and my face was smushed into the ice. But I could still *hear* what was going on, and it didn't sound good: a cacophony of crashes, thumps, yelps, and screams.

It took me a while to wriggle out from under the pile. The rink was now strewn with upended skaters; it looked as though an earthquake had struck in the middle of the Ice Capades. Lots of children were crying, although thankfully, none appeared to be seriously hurt. Around them, their parents and the other skaters were struggling to get back to their feet and wiping ice shavings off their parkas. Most were glaring angrily at me.

The guy with the newspaper was watching us all, completely distracted from his job. So were the other two guards, both of whom were laughing at me. The diversion had worked perfectly.

In the midst of the chaos, I glanced upward, toward the fifth floor of the Arabelle. Each floor had a balcony on the corner, overlooking the ice rink. To my astonishment, Erica was already to the fourth. The building had provided little challenge for her incredible rock-climbing skills. Within another two seconds, she nimbly scrambled up to the fifth floor and swung lightly over the railing onto the balcony.

No one but me was looking up. Everyone else was still focused on the carnage I'd caused. I was the only one on the ground aware that Erica was high above us.

There was a sliding glass door leading from the fifth-floor

balcony into the Shangs' suite. Erica quickly flattened herself against the wall. I could hear distant voices speaking Chinese, filtering through the glass door, then through Erica's radio and into my earpiece.

Someone suddenly grabbed me from behind. It was the big father I'd knocked over. He was now back on his feet and hopping mad. "What the heck were you thinking?" he demanded. "You could've killed someone!"

"I . . . ," I began.

"Shhhhh!" Erica hissed over the earpiece. "Your radio is live! I'm trying to listen to Shang!"

I clammed up, not wanting to interfere with the mission.

The angry father took this as insolence. "Well?" he demanded. "Don't you have anything to say for yourself?"

"No hablo inglés," I told him.

"Shhhh!" Erica hissed again.

A lot of other angry skaters were coming toward me. So I did the only thing I could think of: I skated away from them as fast as I could. I shot across the ice, managing not to knock anyone over this time, and scrambled back through the gate into the prep area.

The angry skaters seemed pleased with this. At least I couldn't cause any more damage off the ice.

I chanced another look upward. Erica was now tucked against the wall of the building by the sliding glass door, almost hidden from sight. Unless they knew where to look, no one down on ground level could see her. Shang's three guards around the ice rink obviously had no idea she was up there.

Unfortunately, there was also someone on the roof of the Arabelle, crouched right above the balcony. He was dressed completely in black, and he was obviously aware of Erica's presence, as he was staring right at her.

"Erica!" I said.

"Shhhh!" she snapped.

"There's—"

"What part of 'shhhh' don't you understand?"

"Someone's above you on the roof!"

By the time I said this, though, the guard wasn't on the roof anymore. He had dropped to the balcony behind Erica.

Through my earpiece, I heard her gasp in surprise.

Which was followed by the sound of her being knocked unconscious.

PUNISHMENT

Lionshead Village

Vail, Colorado

December 26

1700 hours

There was only one person I could trust in this situation: Cyrus Hale.

Unfortunately, he wasn't answering his phone.

This wasn't really surprising. Cyrus hated cellular phones. He also hated computers, e-mail, and pretty much any technology invented over the last thirty years. "Takes all the sport out of spying," he often grumbled. "In the good old days, we didn't need cell phones. If we got into trouble, we didn't call for backup. We just knocked a few heads together and then ran like hell."

I tried Jawa next. He answered on the second ring. "Ben! Where are you?"

"In Lionshead Village. Do you know where Cyrus is?"

"Back at the motel, I think. But I'm not sure. We're all out at McDonald's."

"Who's 'we'?"

"Everyone."

"Even Alexander?"

"Yes. We were all starving. Do you want us to grab you something?"

"No, thanks. I've got to go." I yanked off the ice skates, pulled my shoes back on, and raced back to the Ski Haüs as fast as I could. It wasn't that far away—a few blocks through Lionshead, then across the pedestrian bridge over the highway—but it took longer than usual for me to cover the distance. It turned out that running at high altitude before you've fully acclimatized is really difficult. In fact, it can make you sick. I puked three times. Twice in the village and once over the railing of the pedestrian bridge. On the last one, I painted a minivan on the highway below me.

I ignored the pain and the nausea and kept going, though. Erica's life depended on it. I staggered through the parking lot of the Ski Haüs, my stomach cramping, my lungs on fire, and pounded on the door to the room Cyrus shared with Alexander. "Cyrus? Are you there? It's an emergency!"

I heard footsteps from inside. Then the door opened a crack and Cyrus peeked out, looking annoyed.

"Erica's been captured!" I told him.

"I know," he said.

"We were at the Arabelle . . . ," I began, and then realized what he'd just said. "You know? How?"

"Because I'm the one who captured her." Cyrus opened the door a little more, allowing me to see Erica, sprawled on his bed. Then he yanked me inside and locked the door behind us.

Now that I was in the room, I could see he was still wearing the black outfit. Erica was slowly waking, groggy from being unconscious. "Why did you capture your own granddaughter?" I asked.

"To keep her from getting captured by Shang," Cyrus said.

"I wasn't going to get captured," Erica told him, already awake enough to be annoyed.

"You were darn close," Cyrus shot back angrily. "That stunt you pulled was reckless and insubordinate. I am extremely disappointed in you."

Erica cringed. "But I thought . . ."

"No," Cyrus said curtly. "You didn't think at all. Because if you had, you would have followed my orders and done things the way I told you to. Instead, you decided to disobey me—and the entire CIA—and do things your own way."

"My way was working!" Erica exclaimed. "I could hear Leo Shang and his men talking inside the room! They were discussing their plans! I might have learned everything we need to know if you hadn't interfered!"

"You would have been caught if I hadn't interfered!" Cyrus yelled. He held his fingers a millimeter apart. "You were this close to getting busted! Which would have torpedoed this entire operation! You're doggone lucky I was there doing recon myself and was able to bail you out!"

"How *did* you get back here so quickly?" I asked Cyrus, trying to change the subject before things got even further out of hand. "I mean, you beat me here, even though you were carrying Erica. And you had to get down off the hotel first."

"I had my grappling hook at the hotel," Cyrus explained. "I dropped down the far side while you were taking your skates off. And then I beat you here because, well"—he flexed an arm, displaying his bulging muscles—"I'm in much better shape than you are."

I sighed. "I've been hearing that a lot lately."

Erica sat up on the bed, pulling her phone out of her pocket. "By the way," she told her grandfather, "I recorded the tiny bit of Shang's conversation I overheard. I would have gotten more, but you knocked me unconscious. Me. Your own granddaughter."

"I did that for your own good," Cyrus told her. "It was

the only way to get you out of there quickly. I couldn't risk starting an argument out on that balcony. Or having you struggle against me."

"Maybe you should listen to this before you start accusing me of being reckless again," Erica said, then pressed play.

The conversation wasn't easy to hear, as Erica had recorded it through a glass door. And it was impossible for me to understand, since it was in Chinese. Cyrus apparently knew the language, though. Despite his annoyance with Erica, he still listened to the recording intently.

Two men were talking, sometimes at once. They seemed to be having a heated discussion about something.

There were a few times when Erica's "Shhhh!" cut into the conversation. "That was for Ben," she explained to her grandfather. "He wouldn't stop talking."

"Only because the people you'd shoved me into were angry at me," I pointed out. "And then I was trying to warn you that you were about to be attacked."

"Shhhh!" Cyrus hissed at me, trying to listen.

On the recording, I heard a new voice. It was stern and commanding, and the other two people stopped speaking immediately to listen to it.

"Leo Shang," Erica mouthed to me.

Leo continued a bit longer, but he was cut off by Erica asking me, "What part of 'shhhh' don't you understand?"

And then there was the sound of Erica being knocked unconscious. After that, Leo Shang's voice faded away as Cyrus spirited Erica off.

"What did he say?" I asked.

"'I want a helicopter tomorrow,'" Erica translated, then gave Cyrus a hard stare. "Obviously he's planning some sort of aerial reconnaissance."

"Or he just wants to go helicopter skiing," Cyrus replied, unimpressed.

"What's that?" I asked.

"Skiers can have a helicopter take them out into the wilderness for the day," Cyrus explained. "No lift lines, plenty of untracked snow. It's quite popular with those who can afford it."

"That's not all Shang said," Erica went on. "He also said, 'If all goes well, everything is on track for the thirtieth.'"

"You think he's planning Operation Golden Fist for that day?" I asked.

"It seems pretty obvious," Erica replied. "Only, I don't have any idea what Operation Golden Fist is, because somebody knocked me unconscious before I could hear about it." She glared at her grandfather.

If Cyrus felt bad about this, he didn't show it. Instead, he returned Erica's glare. "For all we know, he was making further ski plans."

"The whole point of this mission is to find out what Shang's plotting," Erica growled. "Based on *your* intel that he's plotting something. And now you're telling me that he's not plotting anything at all? He's simply here to go skiing?"

"All I'm saying," Cyrus growled back, "is that you're jumping to conclusions based upon an insufficient amount of information."

"Well, I would have had a lot more information if it hadn't been for you!" Erica yelled. It was the first time I'd ever heard her raise her voice in my life.

"Use that tone with me again," Cyrus warned, "and you're grounded."

Erica lowered her voice but remained impertinent. "What are you gonna do? Send me to my room?"

"Worse. I'll boot you off this mission."

Erica's eyes widened in surprise. "You wouldn't. This mission would be a disaster without me."

"It was almost a disaster tonight *because* of you," Cyrus retorted. "Ben's the primary agent on this. He's the one who's crucial here, not you."

"That's a mistake," Erica said coldly. "He's not ready for this. He's already showed feelings for Jessica Shang."

Cyrus wheeled on me, concerned.

Suddenly, the frigid room seemed like it was a hundred degrees. I could feel my face turning red in embarrassment.

"That's not true," I stammered. "I've barely even seen her. I just thought she was cute is all."

"Ben gets flummoxed around girls he's attracted to," Erica told Cyrus.

"I do not," I said.

"You get flummoxed around me," Erica pointed out.

"That's because you're always doing things like shoving me onto a crowded ice rink to create a diversion for you without telling me first," I shot back.

Erica started to say something else, but Cyrus held up a hand, silencing her. He kept his gaze locked on me, though, carefully assessing me. Finally, he said, "There's another reason we selected Ben as the primary agent on this mission, Erica: He's a team player. He follows orders, he works well with others, and he doesn't go running off half-cocked anytime an idea pops into his head. Now, you might have tons more raw talent than he does, but you could still learn some things from him." He turned back to face her. "If you pull one more stunt like you did today, I will deactivate you and ship you home faster than you can say 'jackrabbit.'"

Erica didn't say anything in response. She just gave Cyrus a stare so cold it seemed to lower the temperature around us.

Right at this moment, Alexander Hale returned. He barged through the door, whistling happily, and completely failed to pick up on the tension in the room. "Great news!"

he cried, holding up a grocery bag. "I got everything we need to make s'mores!"

Cyrus squinted at him crankily. "Now, where the heck do you expect to do that?"

"The fireplace in the lobby," Alexander suggested.

"The fire in the lobby's a fake," Cyrus informed him. "Boy, your observation skills stink on ice."

"That's right," Erica told Cyrus tartly. "Everyone in this family's a lousy spy except you. And no matter how hard we try, we'll apparently never be good enough." With that, she stormed out of the room and slammed the door behind her. A cheap framed ski poster fell off the wall and busted on the floor.

Cyrus rolled his eyes and muttered, "Teenagers."

Alexander glared at him, still smarting from his insult. "See if I ever buy you campfire treats again," he said, and then stormed out himself.

Somehow, with them gone, there was even more tension in the room. Cyrus was prickly on his best days, but now he seemed ready to blow. I edged toward the door, desperate to get out of there, hoping he might simply ignore me and let me go.

He didn't. His angry gaze now fell on me.

"I should probably be going too," I said as cheerfully as I could. "I've got a big day tomorrow with the mission and all, so I want to turn in early and get a good night's sleep. . . ."

"Do you have the hots for Jessica Shang?" Cyrus asked accusingly.

"No!" I lied, selling it as hard as I could. "I don't even think she's that attractive. In fact, to be totally honest, she's kind of ugly. I actually feel sorry for her. . . ."

Cyrus didn't buy this for a moment. "Erica may have made a lot of mistakes tonight," he told me, "but she was right about one thing: If you want to succeed on this mission, you need to keep your heart out of it. Once you let your emotions get involved, it's trouble. And I don't want any trouble. Is that understood?"

"Yes, sir."

"Dismissed."

I slipped out the door as fast as I could.

The parking lot had filled up with the cars of returning skiers, but Erica was nowhere to be seen. Neither were any of my fellow spies-in-training. As I passed the lobby, though, I could hear Alexander speaking to the guy who ran the motel. "I understand the fire's electric, but it still generates heat, right? I promise not to get any melted marshmallow on it. And I'm happy to share."

I headed back through the frigid night to my room, worried about the mission. I was afraid that I really did have a crush on Jessica Shang—and that Erica was right that it would compromise my abilities. I was concerned that I might fail to befriend Jessica, dooming our operation. I feared that Erica might go off and do something dangerous on her own, just to prove she was right, and get herself in trouble. The only thing I knew for sure was that things had gotten off to an extremely rocky start. If they continued like this, Operation Snow Bunny was going to be a catastrophe.

CONNECTION

Schüss Ski Rental

Lionshead Village

Vail, Colorado

December 27

0830 hours

"**According to Ostby's *Manual of Practical Under-cover Work*,** there are four steps to proper acquisition of information," Zoe said, trying to cram her foot into a ski boot. "What are they?"

"Introduction, ingratiation, inquisition, and deflection," I rattled off.

"Meaning . . . ?"

"Introduction is making the first connection with the

target. Ingratiation is making them want to be friends with you. Inquisition is subtly getting them to tell you what you need to know. And deflection is convincing them that you've never done any inquisition at all."

Zoe beamed at me. "That's exactly right!"

At normal schools, kids quizzed each other before their exams to make sure they were prepared. We were prepping for our mission the exact same way, only instead of algebra or Shakespeare, we were reviewing the finer points of espionage. And the penalty for failure wasn't an F. It was death. After which, we would also get an F, posthumously. So I was a bit more nervous than I had been before tests back at normal school.

Zoe and I were at the ski rental, getting our equipment before beginning our mission. Erica, Chip, Jawa, and Warren were also there, but we had lost sight of them. The room was a sea of people. The week between Christmas and New Year's was the busiest of the ski season, and everyone appeared to have shown up at once. Our fellow renters stood in long, snaking lines, waiting for equipment, or clogged the benches, trying said equipment on. All around Zoe and me, people were desperately trying to wrestle their ski boots on. Many were losing the battle. I had managed to wedge my feet into mine, but it had taken five minutes to figure out how to do it.

As far as the mission was concerned, we were on our own. Cyrus and Alexander were busy tailing Leo Shang, who was helicopter skiing. His caravan of car-tanks had left the Arabelle a half hour earlier. Cyrus and Alexander had followed in a rental car, while Hank had remained at the Ski Haüs to coordinate the mission with CIA headquarters. That left the rest of us without any adult supervision for the day, which was both liberating and daunting.

The harried rental room employee who'd given us our boots stopped by to check on us. He was a young guy with a tan line where his ski goggles normally would have been, making him look kind of like a reverse raccoon. "How do those boots feel?" he asked me.

"Way too tight," I replied. "Like they're two sizes too small."

"Perfect," the guy said. "That's exactly how you want them to feel."

"Really?" I asked skeptically. "They're pretty painful."

"It takes a little getting used to," the guy told me. "You want them nice and snug, though." Before I could protest any more, there was a clatter as Warren knocked over a dozen sets of rental skis across the room. "Nuts," said the rental guy, and ran off.

"Snug?" I muttered, trying to wiggle my toes inside my boots. "When I fail to get Jessica Shang to give me the info, maybe we can just use some ski boots and torture it out of her." I probably wasn't supposed to say things like that out loud, but the room was so packed, it was like being in a train station at rush hour. I could barely hear myself over all the other voices.

Zoe gave me a hard stare. "What's wrong?"

"My feet hurt."

"Besides that. You just said '*When* I fail.' Not '*If* I fail.'"

"Did I?"

"Yes. You're not going to fail, Ben. You know your stuff backward and forward. You haven't gotten one of my quiz questions wrong all morning."

I sighed. "That doesn't necessarily mean I'll succeed. There's a big difference between knowing what I'm supposed to do and actually being able to do it."

"You've succeeded against the enemy before."

"This time is different."

"Why?"

I hesitated for a moment, then owned up to it. There wasn't much point in keeping secrets at spy school; everyone would find them out soon enough anyhow. "This time I'm supposed to get a girl to like me. I don't know if I can do that."

Zoe giggled.

"What's so funny?" I asked.

"You are. You're actually worried about getting a girl to like you? Last time you went on a mission, the bad girl totally fell for you. What was her name? Ashley Spritz?"

"Ashley *Sparks*," I corrected. "And she didn't fall for me. She only liked me as a friend. Which didn't mean anything because there hadn't been anyone else for her to hang out with for the past year. She would have made friends with a baked potato."

"You're an idiot," Zoe told me. "She totally liked you. Like, *liked* you liked you. She invited you to go to Disney World with her, for Pete's sake! You don't invite someone to go to Disney World with you unless you're really into them."

"Not necessarily," I said. "I'd go to Disney World with you. But that doesn't mean I'm into you."

Zoe stopped smiling, like I'd said something wrong. "C'mon," she said coldly. "Let's go get our skis." Then she clomped away in her ski boots.

"Wait up!" I called, then tried to run after her.

Running in ski boots was even more difficult than I expected. In addition to being exceptionally tight, the boots were also heavy and oddly balanced. I got exactly one step, then pitched forward and landed on top of two small children, knocking them flat. Just my luck, it turned out to be the same family I'd wiped out on the ice rink the day before. "You again!" the father snarled, while his kids started crying.

Several other adults glared at me accusingly. Behind them all, I caught a glimpse of Chip and Jawa, laughing hysterically.

"No hablo inglés," I said to the father. Then I hurried off before he could pound me, doing my best not to crush any other preschoolers.

I found Zoe at the ski counter, trying to act like she didn't know me in front of everyone else. I wasn't sure if this was because she was angry at me—or embarrassed to be seen with me after I'd just made a scene. "That was smooth," she said under her breath.

I glanced around the rental area, examining all the other faces as carefully as I could.

"What are you looking for?" Zoe asked.

"Jessica Shang. If she saw me wipe out like that, it'll be a hundred times harder to win her over."

"Relax," Zoe told me. "She's not here. When you're as rich as Jessica Shang, you don't rent skis. Your daddy just buys you a pair. Heck, she probably has a different set for every day of the week. I got yours, by the way." She pointed to a pair leaning against the counter next to hers. They were slightly shorter than I was, chipped and scarred from the abuse of a few hundred previous renters, and they were a disturbing fluorescent green.

"Do you have anything less bright?" I asked the girl behind the counter.

"You're lucky we have anything left in your size, period," she told me. "Besides, you want bright skis as a beginner. It makes them easier to find again after you wipe out."

"You mean *if* he wipes out," Zoe corrected.

"No. I mean *when*," the ski girl said. "You're beginners. You'll wipe out. In fact, you'll wipe out a lot. And you'll wipe out big. Everyone does. That's skiing. Take your boots off."

"Why?" I asked. "It just took me five minutes to get them on."

"I need to adjust the bindings on the skis, and I need your boot for that. It's about a million times easier to do if your foot isn't still in it."

Zoe and I both sat and pried our boots off. The ski girl adjusted our bindings and then we had to go through the agony of forcing the boots back on. After that, yet another ski rental employee gave us poles and helmets, and then we finally emerged from the shop.

If it had been hard to walk in ski boots to begin with, it was even harder to do while carrying a set of skis, which were extremely unwieldy. I felt like I might topple over at any moment.

Chip and Jawa were waiting for us outside, examining their rental gear with disdain.

"I miss my real skis," Chip grumbled. "This stuff is garbage."

"You're supposed to be a beginner," Zoe pointed out. "Beginners don't have their own skis."

"I'll bet Jessica Shang does," Chip argued.

"We're not even supposed to know the name Jessica Shang," Jawa hissed under his breath. "So stop talking about her before she overhears us and you blow the whole mission."

"Jessica's not going to overhear you," Erica said.

She had seemingly appeared out of nowhere. It was something she did all the time, and yet I had never gotten used to it. There was nothing magical about it; Erica simply moved with such stealth and grace that you never saw her coming unless she wanted you to. What made it all the more impressive was that, once I knew Erica was there, I found it almost impossible to take my eyes *off* her again. Not only was she beautiful, but she had a way of making everything around her look good too. Even things that weren't attractive. For example, her rental equipment. The rest of us, with our dented helmets and ill-fitting ski clothes, looked like we'd just been fired out of a cannon. Erica had the exact same stuff, but somehow looked like she should be on the runway at Fashion Week.

"Why won't she hear us?" Jawa asked, still keeping his voice low.

"Because she's way over at the ski school meeting area," Erica explained.

Everyone looked that way.

"Don't all look at once!" Erica snapped.

Everyone turned back to her at the same time, which was even less subtle.

"Try it again," Erica growled. Although she didn't actually add "you idiots," the tone of her voice indicated it was there. "Only this time, do it one at a time, and don't stare. Act like you're looking somewhere else."

We all did our best to casually glance over toward the ski school meeting area, one at a time. It was across a snowy plaza, a little beyond the boarding area for the gondola.

There were hundreds of other skiers in the plaza, but it wasn't hard to pick Jessica Shang out among them. She was the only one surrounded by bodyguards. There were four of them. They were doing their best to blend into the crowd, wearing ski clothes and dopey woolen hats, but it didn't work. They were all so big that they stuck out like islands in the sea of humanity around them. Each had a set of skis the size of a small tree. The scary one with the blond mullet was with them. His stringy hair poked out from below his hat behind his ears.

I couldn't actually see Jessica. She was too short to make out in the crowd. But I could see the tip of a pink ski helmet between all the guards and figured it had to be hers.

"We'd better get over there," Erica said. "Lessons start at oh-nine-hundred hours. We will all approach the target separately. And remember, none of us are supposed to know each other. So don't act too familiar and blow our cover."

"Know what else might blow our cover?" Chip asked. "Saying things like 'oh-nine-hundred hours.' The only people who talk like that are spies and the guys in charge of launching rockets. Normal people say 'nine o'clock.'"

Erica fixed him with a stare sharp enough to bore holes through him. "I'm not a moron. When the time comes, trust me, I can be in character."

"Sure you can," Chip said dismissively.

I was about to tell Chip to back off—I'd seen Erica in character before, and she was staggeringly good at it—but before I could, Warren walked out of the rental shop. Or at least, he *tried* to walk out of it. The problem was, he was carrying his skis sideways across the front of his body, the way one might carry firewood, which didn't work very well when trying to go through a doorway. The tips of his skis caught on both sides of the doorframe, stopping Warren so abruptly that he clotheslined himself and collapsed to the ground.

Erica groaned in disgust and turned to me. "Ben, you head over first. We'll all give you a little time to get to know Jessica solo."

"All right." I took a deep breath to gather my nerve.

Zoe pulled me aside. "One last quiz. What's the best way to establish a rapport with a target?"

"Find an area of common interest."

"Exactly! And that's already done for you: You're both beginner skiers. Easy peasy lemon squeezy. Start with that and just be yourself. She'll like you. I promise." She gave me a big smile that actually made me believe her. If she'd truly been upset with me before, it seemed to have passed.

I took another deep breath, grabbed my skis, and plunged into the crowd, stumbling through the mass of fellow skiers to the ski school meeting area. A dozen blue signs ringed it, each marked with the ages of the kids who were supposed to meet there: 5 AND UNDER, 6–7, 8–9, and so on. There was a surprisingly large crowd around the sign marked SKIERS 12–15. Some seemed to have come with friends, or had made friends quickly, while others looked kind of lost and lonely. Despite this, no one had attempted to talk to Jessica Shang yet. The bodyguards surrounding her were too intimidating.

Jessica stood in the center of the four big men, wearing a stylish ski outfit and—as Zoe had predicted—holding a set of brand-new skis. She looked a bit self-conscious, like she was unhappy to be cut off from everyone else her age. I decided to play to that.

I wandered up to the bodyguard with the mullet and asked, "Do you know if this is where ski school for ages twelve to fifteen meets?"

"What's the matter?" Blond Mullet asked gruffly, nodding toward the blue sign. "Can't you read?"

"Oh," I said. "I didn't see that. Sorry. It's my first day."

"Now you've seen it," Blond Mullet said dismissively. "So go read it." He had a deep, imposing voice, but also a singsong Scandinavian accent that made him sound ridiculous.

I was still cowed by him, though, and almost shrank away. But then I noticed Jessica. Although she hadn't said a word, she seemed upset at Blond Mullet for trying to run me off so quickly. So I steeled myself and decided to ignore the bodyguard. I looked right at Jessica, as if Blond Mullet hadn't even spoken, and asked, "Is it your first day too?"

She gave me a shy smile. "It is."

"I'm Ben," I said. "Ben Coolman."

The name had been devised for me by a team of CIA analysts. I'd been allowed to stick with my own first name so that I wouldn't forget it. And I'd been given the name "Coolman" because, well, it had the word "cool" in it, which a million dollars' worth of CIA research said made me sound cooler.

Jessica's smile widened, like she was thrilled someone had actually braved her bodyguards. "I'm Jessica."

I started to say "It's nice to meet you," but I barely got through the first syllable before Blond Mullet stepped between Jessica and me and pointed a finger the size of a kielbasa at my face. "I told you to go," he warned. "If you don't, I will rip your arms off."

I might have backed off right then and abandoned the mission—after all, I liked having my arms attached to my body—if Jessica hadn't intervened. She stepped around the bodyguard, placed her hand on his, and said, "Dane, there's no need for that." Her voice remained soft and sweet, but there was a firmness beneath it that unnerved the big man. Even though Jessica's hand was dwarfed by his, he lowered it obediently.

"But . . . ," he began.

"He's only a boy," Jessica said. "And he was just being friendly." She then turned to me, looking embarrassed about the whole ordeal. "Sorry about that."

I glanced at Blond Mullet—Dane—warily. "Did I do something wrong?"

"Not at all," Jessica replied. "Dane overreacted. He wouldn't have really hurt you, I promise; he just likes to act tough."

If Dane was upset by this comment, he didn't show it. Instead, he kept his stony gaze fixed on me.

"He's good at it," I said.

To my surprise, Jessica giggled.

Dane's gaze grew even stonier.

The other three bodyguards were acting like I wasn't even there. They were staring off in other directions, watching the crowd. With so many people around, keeping an eye out for potential threats was a big job.

"Where are you from, Ben?" Jessica asked.

"Near Washington, DC." The CIA had advised me to use my real hometown, rather than a false one, because I'd never really lived anywhere else and wasn't ready to fake it. (I would have needed more research for that, and we hadn't had the time.) "How about you?"

"Shanghai."

I did my best to act surprised, like this was news to me. "Shanghai, China?"

"No, Shanghai, Nebraska," Jessica said sarcastically. However, she did it in an inoffensive way that made me laugh. Her sense of humor caught me pleasantly by surprise.

"Sorry," I said. "It's just that . . . well, you speak English like someone who's actually from Nebraska. Actually, probably *better* than most people from Nebraska."

Now Jessica laughed. "Thanks. I ought to speak it well, though. My father has taught it to me ever since I was a baby. Though I've never had the chance to speak it to anyone from the United States before."

"No way," I said.

"Well, I got to say a few sentences to the customs agent at the airport," Jessica admitted. "But other than that, you're my first."

"You're doing great," I said, genuinely impressed—and Jessica seemed pleased by the compliment.

I thought about asking her about her father then and there—who he was, what he did, and so on—but decided against it. Kids didn't usually ask other kids about their parents right off the bat, and I didn't want to make Jessica suspicious. Or make her think I was a weirdo. As it was, she seemed surprisingly happy to talk to me, so I figured I'd just go with it. "So you came all the way here from Shanghai just to ski?"

"I've always heard Colorado was the best. So here I am." Jessica looked around excitedly. "I wonder how many different classes there'll be. Looks like there's a lot of kids our age here."

"Yeah," I agreed, taking the opportunity to look around as well. My fellow spies had all come along by now, blending in with the other kids and doing their best to look normal—except for Warren, who had clonked several other people in the head with his skis. "They're not supposed to put too many kids in each class, though."

"It'd be cool if we were in the same one."

I turned to Jessica, unable to hide my shock that she'd said this. "Really?"

"Of course," she replied shyly. "You're the only person I know here. So it'd be nice to get to stay together."

"It would," I agreed, pleased with how well things were going.

"All right, kids!" yelled a pretty blond woman in a blue Vail Ski School outfit. "Gather 'round! It's time to meet your instructors!" Several other adults in matching blue outfits stood behind her. The blond woman checked a clipboard and began to rattle off names. "Ben Coolman, Jessica Shang, Chip Stonehill, Zoe Kinsler, Warren Tinkleberry, and . . . Oh boy, I know I'm going to mess this one up . . . Jawhortlelal?"

"Jawaharlal," corrected Jawa. "But you can just call me Jawa."

"Jawa, right," said the blond woman. "You guys and Sasha Rotko are all in a class together."

Erica stepped forward with the rest of us. She was Sasha Rotko, the only one of us the CIA trusted to be able to use a completely fake name.

She had once again shifted out of her normal personality, just as she had around the Arabelle the day before. "Sasha Rotko" was nothing like the normally cool, calm, hyper-intelligent Erica Hale. Instead, she was an awkward, fatuous, gum-smacking ditz. Erica made everything about herself different, from the way she walked to the vacant look in her eyes to her voice, which was now high and squeaky. If they gave Oscars for undercover work, Erica would have won in a landslide.

"Hey, Ben!" she said to me. "We're in the same class! Super-coolness!"

"You two know each other?" Jessica asked warily.

"Not really," Erica told her. "We just met at the pizza place yesterday. I was getting a slice and Ben was getting a slice, and both of us wanted to walk around town, so I was like, 'Hey! Let's walk around town together!' So we did!"

She was telling the story for the benefit of Dane, who'd seen us together the day before. Despite how well Erica sold it, though, it was hard to tell if Dane was convinced. His stony gaze remained exactly the same, giving no indication of what was going on in his mind.

I wish I could have said the same for my fellow students. None of them had ever seen Erica transform herself like this before, and they all did a lousy job of hiding their astonishment. Chip, who had been so dismissive of Erica's ability to act a few minutes earlier, now appeared completely dumbfounded by her performance.

Luckily, before Jessica, Dane, or any of the other three bodyguards could notice this, the blond ski school woman intervened. She waved us all over to her and said, "Okay, kids, your instructor is going to be Woodchuck."

My friends, who had finally recovered from the shock of seeing Erica morph into Sasha, now struggled to hide their surprise at the identity of our instructor. (Erica, of course, registered no surprise at all.) Their reactions were subtle, though, so no one probably noticed but me. There was a good chance I showed some surprise myself, figuring it was unlikely that there were two people in the world who actually went by the name "Woodchuck."

"Hello, future skiers!" a big voice boomed behind me. Sure enough, it was Woodchuck Wallace, the CIA's expert outdoorsman. Normally, Woodchuck ran our academy's summer facility for outdoor training—also known as spy camp—so I'd never seen him in winter clothing before. Or really, much clothing at all. He'd made most of his own clothes at camp, usually out of buckskin. So he looked a bit odd in a ski suit. But he was still the same burly, incredibly athletic, exceptionally confident guy—although he pretended that he didn't know us. "It's nice to meet all of you. I know it's only your first day, but I promise you, if you're ready to learn, I'll have all of you blazing down this mountain in no time!"

All my friends responded with enthusiasm, though Erica was the most enthusiastic of all. "Sounds great!" she whooped. "Let's do this!"

Woodchuck grinned and pointed at her. "I like that spirit!" He checked his roster and asked, "You're Sasha?"

"That's right."

Woodchuck turned to the rest of us. "Take a lesson from

Sasha, gang. Skiing is ten percent physical ability and ninety percent attitude. If you *want* to do it, you can do it. So who's ready to ski?"

All of us whooped excitedly now. We weren't faking. Woodchuck's energy was infectious.

"Excellent!" Woodchuck cried. "Now, the ski school for kids is up at the top of the mountain. We've got an awesome setup there to teach you everything you need to know. So let's head over to the gondola right now and get to know each other on the way up." With that he hoisted his skis onto his shoulder and led the way.

The rest of us grabbed our skis as well. Dane the bodyguard reached for Jessica's, but she made a point of taking them herself. Warren managed to bonk three more innocent bystanders in the head while starting out. Fortunately, they were all wearing ski helmets, so no one got hurt.

Jessica's bodyguards tried to stay around her as she walked, but she sideslipped them and dropped in next to me. "I'm excited we get to be ski buddies," she said.

"Yeah," I agreed. "Me too."

Dane didn't seem too happy about this, though. Instead, he sized me up suspiciously, his gaze so cold that it made me shiver.

"And I'm excited to get out there and finally ski," Jessica went on. "This is going to be more fun than a bucket of weasels!"

"Bucket of weasels?" I repeated.

Jessica frowned. "Oh, shoot. I got that wrong, didn't I? I always have trouble with your idioms. They're so strange."

Understanding came to me. "You meant 'more fun than a barrel of monkeys.'"

"Yes! That's it!" Jessica agreed brightly. "See what I mean? Honestly, would a barrel of monkeys be that much fun?"

"More fun than a bucket of weasels," I pointed out.

"No way. Have you ever been around monkeys? They smell and they throw poo at you."

"Are you two talking about monkeys?" Erica asked, slipping in between us. "I loooove monkeys! They're so cute! Especially lemur-monkeys!"

Jessica shot me a sideways "get a load of this airhead" glance. "There's no such thing as lemur-monkeys," she said. "There are lemurs and there are monkeys. They're totally different species."

Erica shrugged, unfazed, then looked to me. "Ben, you didn't tell me you had a friend here with you."

"Actually, Jessica and I just met this morning," I told her.

"Get out!" Erica cried. "Because it seems like you two are total besties. I was getting this vibe that you'd known each other since you were kids or something."

Jessica smiled, seeming to like something about this. "We've only known each other about ten minutes."

"Seems more like ten *years*." Erica whipped out her cell phone and stiff-armed it to aim it back at us. "Selfie time!" she announced.

Jessica and I obediently looked at the camera.

"No photos," growled Dane.

Erica turned to Jessica, a perplexed look on her face. "Who's this guy? Your dad?"

"My bodyguard," Jessica said, like it was embarrassing.

Erica's eyes widened in fake shock. "You have bodyguards? No way! Are you, like, famous?"

"No," Jessica said. "My dad's just kind of important. So he thinks I need them."

"Who is he?" Erica asked bluntly. "Like an actor or a singer or something?"

"No, he's only a businessman," Jessica replied, in a way that indicated she didn't really want to talk about her father at all.

Erica pretended not to sense this. "What kind of business is he in?"

"He's in the 'none of your' business," Jessica said curtly.

Erica screwed up her face in confusion, then faked a flash of understanding and burst into laughter. "None of your business! You're funny, Jessica! Really funny!"

We arrived at the gondola, which was kind of like a normal ski lift on steroids. Each gondola cabin was surprisingly large, the size of a small bathroom, and able to hold up to nine people at a time. The cabins all dangled from a thick wire that would whisk us up to the top of the mountain. A line of several hundred skiers waited for it, but as ski school students, we were allowed to cut. There was a separate entrance for us. Woodchuck waved us all through, but then held up a hand to Jessica's bodyguards. "Gentlemen, I believe the ski school made it clear that having all four of you along is unnecessary—as well as detrimental to providing Jessica with the optimal ski school experience."

The bodyguards all frowned at this, but then nodded grudgingly. Dane stepped forward. "I will be staying close to Jessica today," he announced.

"All right," Woodchuck said, looking him up and down. "But you're so big, you're gonna take up almost the whole cabin." He turned back to the rest of the class. "We'll need to split up, gang. Jessica, you go with your guard here and . . ."

"Ben?" Jessica suggested.

"Sure!" Woodchuck agreed. "You guys take one cabin. The rest of you, come with me." With that, we entered the loading area and Woodchuck led the rest of the group into a waiting cabin.

Zoe looked back at me and gave me a subtle thumbs-up, indicating that I was doing a good job so far.

I had to admit, I felt awfully good about the way things

were going. I couldn't believe Jessica had taken a shine to me so quickly. I still had a long way to go on my mission, but I'd apparently taken care of the first two steps—introduction and ingratiation—without any trouble at all.

The next gondola cabin came along and the doors slid open for us. Dane stepped inside first. As Woodchuck had suspected, he took up a good deal of the tiny room himself. A small bench wrapped around three sides of it. Dane plopped himself down on it. Jessica and I sat across from him, side by side. Jessica gave me an excited smile that made my heart start thumping so loudly, I was worried she'd hear it.

"How long are you here for?" Jessica asked.

"A week," I replied.

"Me too!" Jessica exclaimed. "This is great! We're going to have so much fun together!"

I grinned at her, unable to believe my luck.

And then, just like that, everything went wrong.

"Ben!" a familiar voice yelled. "Hey, Ben!"

Someone bolted from the front of the line for the gondola and slipped into our cabin right before the doors shut. He slid onto the bench, then removed his helmet and ski goggles to reveal his face, the face of the last person I needed to see:

Mike Brezinski.

COMPLICATION

Eagle Bahn Gondola

Vail Mountain

December 27

0915 hours

"I *told* you I had an uncle in Colorado," Mike explained.

"No," I said. "You didn't."

"I *did*," Mike insisted. "The other day at the zoo."

I thought back to our conversation, wondering if that was true. To my annoyance, I realized I could remember the clothing that every random passerby had worn but not that important detail. Apparently, I'd been too focused on the wrong things. "Okay, maybe you did. But I didn't know he lived in Vail."

"He doesn't!" Mike exclaimed. "He lives down in Denver, but it turns out, some friend of his has this condo here in town and he said my uncle could use it whenever he wants. So after you said you were coming here, I called my uncle up to say hi, and he said why didn't my brother and I come on out to ski? So we did!"

"Why didn't you tell me you were coming?" I asked.

"I wanted to surprise you," Mike replied. "And boy, did I. You should have seen your face! Total and complete shock." He turned to Jessica and asked, "Am I right?"

"Oh, yeah," Jessica agreed, then told me, "You went as white as a skeet."

"You mean 'white as a sheet'?" I asked.

"Yes! That's what I meant!" Jessica agreed. Then she turned back to Mike. "I'm Jessica, by the way."

"Mike Brezinski. Ben's best friend. It's nice to meet you." Mike flashed a perfect smile.

Jessica smiled back, blushing a tiny bit.

Which confirmed all my worst fears. Mike being there was an absolute disaster. Because Mike was a really great guy. Everyone liked him. Especially girls. He wasn't the most handsome kid at my old school, but he was close—and he exuded this sense of confidence and fun that attracted girls like flies. Now that he was there, in Vail, I *knew* he was going to divert Jessica Shang's attention from me. Which would throw a massive wrench into my ability to complete my mission.

Plus, there was also a good chance that Mike would blow my cover and get me killed. He didn't know I was a spy, of course, but he knew I went to a top-secret academy—and he'd at least joked that I was training to be a spy in the past. Plus, he knew me as "Ben Ripley," not "Ben Coolman." I'd completely lucked out that the CIA had let me keep my real first name. But even so, there were plenty of ways Mike could reveal I wasn't exactly who I said I was. And if he did, I figured there was a decent chance Dane might get suspicious and throttle me.

We were halfway up the mountain in the gondola. It was hard to imagine anyplace more unnerving to be cooped up in with a professional thug like Dane than a tiny room dangling from a wire a hundred feet above the ground. I was doing my best to keep smiling at everyone and act happy, like Mike's being there was the greatest thing that could have ever happened, but in truth, I was sweating buckets despite the cold temperature.

Mike had been so focused on me, he hadn't paid much attention to Jessica until that point. But now that he'd finally taken a good look at her, I could tell he liked what he saw. His smile jacked up another few notches. "Where are you from?" he asked her.

"Shanghai."

"That's awesome!" Mike exclaimed. "I hear that Shanghai's excellent."

All of which was a much better response than my stupid "Shanghai, China?" had been.

"It's nice," Jessica replied. "So are you in ski school too?"

"Nah," Mike said suavely. "I've been skiing since I was three. I'm going with my brother and my uncle today. We were all waiting in the line down there, but when I saw Ben, I had to come say hey. They're in the next gondola back."

"So, are you super-good?" Jessica asked, growing even more interested.

"I'm okay," Mike said, in a humble way that meant he was really extremely good. "Though I've never skied out here before. I've only done Vermont and the Poconos." He peered out the gondola window, taking in the whole expanse of the mountain. "This place is enormous compared to there. It makes the Poconos look like a bunch of bunny slopes."

I looked out the window with him. Vail was much bigger than I'd expected. For well over a mile to the east of us, the white slashes of its ski slopes cut through the trees.

"This sure beats spending winter break hanging out in my basement, doesn't it?" Mike asked me. "I can't believe we ran into each other right off the bat!"

"Neither can I," I said, trying my best to remain upbeat.

"Sounds like we won't see much of you, though. If we're in school and you're out with your family . . ."

"That's only during the day," Mike informed me. "The slopes close at four. You guys want to meet up after that?"

"I don't know . . . ," I began.

"That'd be great!" Jessica exclaimed, grinning at Mike in a way that said she'd already forgotten all about me.

Dane grunted disapprovingly. "Jessica, your father wants you to come right back to the hotel after school today."

Jessica huffed, annoyed. "Why? He won't even be there."

Mike seemed to notice Dane for the first time, despite the fact that the man was taking up half the gondola. "Who are you?" he asked, nice and friendly. "Jessica's brother?"

Mike certainly knew this wasn't true. For starters, Dane was such a freak of nature, he and Jessica barely looked like they were the same species. Mike was only goofing around for Jessica's benefit.

Dane grunted again. "It's my job to make sure Jessica doesn't get into any trouble."

"Really?" Mike asked, then gave Jessica a sly smile. "You must misbehave a lot to need someone like this to look after you."

Jessica giggled. "Oh, I don't get into any trouble at all. My father's just really overprotective." She gave Dane a pointed stare.

"That's a shame," I said quickly. "But if he wants you at the hotel, I guess you should go there." I couldn't believe it, but I was actually in agreement with Dane on something: I wanted to keep Jessica and Mike as far apart as possible too.

Mike shot me an angry glance, annoyed I was messing things up for him. But then he brightened. "Hey! What if we just hung out at your hotel? There must be a place we could grab a bite, right?"

Jessica brightened as well. "There is! There's a whole restaurant."

Dane grunted a third time, but before he could say anything, Jessica cut him off. "All Daddy said was that he wanted me back at the hotel. He didn't say I couldn't have anyone visit me there. And he's paying for the whole restaurant anyhow. We might as well use it."

Mike looked at me, wondering what Jessica meant by all this. I shrugged, pretending that I had no idea her father was rich enough to rent out an entire hotel.

Dane shook his head. "I don't like it."

"Well, it doesn't matter if you like it or not," Jessica countered. "Because I'm doing it. You're only supposed to protect me from trouble, not keep me from having any fun." She shifted her attention back to Mike. "And you're not going to be any trouble, are you?" she asked, in a way that indicated she kind of hoped he would be.

"No," Mike replied, grinning wolfishly. "I'm a regular Boy Scout."

As he said this, we arrived at the top of the mountain. A three-story building was perched there, housing restaurants, the ski school, and the gondola station. Our gondola cabin shuddered as it plunged into the building and then slowed down so we could get out. The doors slid open, allowing an icy blast of air inside, and we all got to our feet.

"I'm staying at the Arabelle," Jessica told Mike. "It's the one right by the ice rink."

"I know it," Mike said. "I walked right past it this morning. Very snazzy."

"We'll meet you in the hotel restaurant after ski school gets out," Jessica told him.

"Sounds great!" Mike said. "See you then!" He grabbed his skis and headed for the slopes.

My fellow spies were already out of the gondola ahead of us, holding their skis. Mike had to walk right past them to get to the exit. No one else took notice of Mike—except Erica, who knew exactly who he was. Her jaw dropped slightly at the sight of him. It was as close as I'd ever come to seeing her express surprise.

"That is so insane," Jessica told me, watching Mike saunter out the door. "To run into your best friend like that?"

"No kidding," I agreed, still stunned it had happened.

"He seems really nice."

"He is," I said, then thought to add, "His girlfriend's crazy about him."

"Girlfriend?" Jessica asked, surprised. "He's only, what, thirteen?"

"Yeah." I felt kind of bad telling a lie about Mike, but national security—and my own life—was at stake. "But he's pretty serious about her. They've been together for a whole year already."

"Hmmm," Jessica said thoughtfully. She didn't seem as discouraged by the news that Mike had a girlfriend as I'd hoped. Instead, it kind of seemed like this made him even *more* interesting to her.

By now everyone else had shouldered their skis and was moving out of the gondola station. Jessica and I followed them, and Dane followed us. We emerged onto a snowy, windblown plain. Despite being high up on the mountain, the slope here was surprisingly gentle. There was a wide beginner run with its own small ski lift, as well as two "magic carpets." These were basically moving sidewalks designed for the outdoors, which worked as conveyor belts to move beginning skiers who couldn't handle the lifts yet up the hill. They were practical, although the sight of skiers being ferried along like groceries on a giant supermarket checkout belt was kind of ridiculous.

All around us, hundreds of other ski school students were gathered in clumps, beginning their day of lessons. Some were going over the basics with their instructors, while others were already beginning to edge out onto the snow.

"This way, gang!" Woodchuck called to us. He pointed to a tree about thirty yards down the slope. "Let's walk over there and have a little talk about fundamentals, then see if we can get up on our skis."

We started across the snow, wending through the clumps of other skiers. Erica dropped in beside me and, without any warning at all, kicked my feet out from under me.

I gave a squawk of surprise and landed hard on the packed snow, my poles and skis scattering everywhere.

All the other beginners laughed.

"Whoopsie!" Erica exclaimed. "Careful there, clumsy!" Then she knelt by my side to help me up and instantly dropped the airhead act. "What is your friend Mike doing here?" she hissed.

"It's a coincidence," I hissed back. This wasn't exactly true—after all, I'd told Mike I was heading to Vail, and he'd decided to come here as a result—but I wasn't about to tell Erica that.

Erica didn't buy it. "Boy, you really screwed up this time," she said, gathering my ski poles.

"It's not my fault," I informed her, struggling back to my feet. "I had no idea he was going to be here!"

Erica looked ready to argue this, but before she could, Jessica came over. Dane followed behind her. "Are you all right?" Jessica asked.

"He's fine," Erica told her, transitioning right back into dingbat mode. "He just needs to watch his step better. This snow's really slippy." She handed my poles back to me, gave me a meaningful stare that Jessica couldn't see, and warned, "You'd better be extra careful now."

"I will," I said. The rest of the group was well ahead of us by now, gathered by the tree Woodchuck had pointed out. I started toward them, wondering how to get Mike out of the picture. I couldn't believe I was even thinking of trying to ditch my best friend over winter vacation, but he'd already screwed things up plenty as it was. I was going to have to step up my game if I wanted to win back Jessica's attention. Only, keeping girls interested in me wasn't exactly my strong suit. After all, I'd been trying to get closer to Erica for nearly a year and she'd just tripped me on purpose.

I hadn't *completely* lost Jessica's attention. Unfortunately, all that was keeping her interested in me was that I knew Mike. She came up alongside me as I trudged downhill and asked, "So, this girlfriend of Mike's . . . Is he *super* into her, or just kind of into her?"

"He's mentioned marriage," I lied.

Jessica frowned, not liking that at all.

Suddenly, Erica shot past us. Instead of walking over to the tree Woodchuck had pointed out, she had clipped on her skis and was poling over. "See ya, slowpokes!" she taunted.

"Hey!" I shouted after her. "Woodchuck told us to walk!"

"I can handle this!" Erica shouted back, a bit of her real, über-confident self slipping through. "It's easy!" She jammed her poles into the ground again, pushing herself forward, gaining speed.

By the tree, Woodchuck noticed her coming and yelped in alarm. "Sasha! You're not ready to start skiing yet!"

"Sure I am!" Erica yelled. Even though the slope was gentle, she was picking up speed, quickly closing the gap on the rest of the gang.

It was at this point when Erica discovered that, while she knew how to *start* skiing, she didn't actually know how to *stop*. And now she was heading right for everyone else.

They all leapt out of the way as Erica barreled toward them. Except Warren, whose reflexes weren't quite up to snuff. Erica clipped him as she shot past, knocking him into a snowdrift.

Beyond the tree, the incline of the slope increased quickly—and so did Erica's speed. She began cannonballing downhill.

"Sasha!" yelled Woodchuck. "Just fall down! That'll stop you!"

I'm sure Erica heard him, but falling down simply wasn't her style. It would have made her look foolish and it would have been admitting defeat, two things Erica simply didn't do. Instead, she stubbornly stayed upright, determined to solve this problem with her usual finesse. And so she only made things worse, gaining more and more speed.

The slope below her was crowded with skiers, many just learning how to ski. Erica sliced right in front of one group, forcing them to wipe out, then bowled another group over like tenpins. She began making a noise I'd never heard from her before—although one I'd made myself quite a lot at spy school—a kind of uncontrollable, panicked scream: "Aaaaaaaaaaaaaaaaaa!!!!" Her arms were pinwheeling wildly as she tried to figure out a way to stop.

She couldn't, though. Despite the large number of skiers on the slope, Erica seemed to be on a path to hit nearly every one of them. She cut some off, making them wreck, and caromed off others, knocking them down. One skier crashed into a tree trying to avoid her, while yet another clanged into a ski-lift pole. Several others went sprawling and ended up spinning down the slope on their bellies, taking out still more skiers on the way. A line of small children in a ski class toppled over like dominoes. And yet, somehow, Erica stayed upright through it all, gaining even more speed.

And then she hit the jump.

It wasn't a huge jump, like in the Olympics. It was really only a medium-size lump of snow to the side of the run. But it did the trick. Erica launched into the air and flew several feet.

It turned out, in addition to not knowing how to stop, Erica also didn't know how to land.

Her skis bit into the ground and came to a sudden stop—but Erica didn't. Instead, she sailed right out of her bindings and began tumbling down the mountain. Her equipment flew off her as she went, leaving a trail of belongings strewn across the slope. (Later, I learned skiers referred to this as a "yard sale.") One pole landed high in a tree. The other nearly impaled a passing snowboarder. One ski ended up embedded in the ground like a fence post—and yet another unsuspecting skier promptly crashed into it.

Eventually, Erica stopped tumbling and started sliding, her arms and legs stuck out around her like she was a giant starfish. She took out a few more skiers this way until she finally sailed off the run into the woods and plowed headfirst into a snowbank, hitting so hard that she wound up embedded all the way to her shoulders.

"Whoa," Woodchuck gasped. "That was the most epic wipeout I have ever seen."

I nodded agreement. My wreck at the ice rink the day before had been embarrassing, but it was a mere ripple compared to the tsunami of destruction Erica had caused. On the slope below me, skiers and snowboarders were strewn everywhere, groaning in pain or shouting after her in anger. Luckily, no one had been badly hurt, but there were plenty of sprains, sprawls, and busted ski equipment. It looked as though a panzer tank division had come through, rather than only a teenage girl. Far below us, Erica extricated herself from the snowbank, saw what she had done—and turned so red with embarrassment that we could see it all the way uphill.

Beside me, Jessica was laughing so hard, she could barely breathe. So were many of my fellow spies. Even Dane—who had seemed genetically incapable of even smiling—seemed to find the whole thing funny. But then, I couldn't blame any of them; I was having trouble keeping a straight face myself.

"Man, oh, man," Jessica gasped. "That Sasha is a case of baskets."

"You mean 'a basket case'?" I asked.

"That's it! She's . . . uh, is 'nuts' the right term?"

"Yeah. She's nuts, all right," I agreed.

Jessica gave me a conspiratorial grin in response.

I found myself smiling back. Mike might have really messed things up for me, but for the moment, Jessica and I had at least one more thing in common.

REASSESSMENT

Eagle's Nest Dining Area
Vail Mountain
December 27
1200 hours

Three hours later, when we broke for lunch, Jes-sica was still laughing about Erica's wipeout. "Did you see her when she slammed into that snowbank?" She snickered. "She practically buried herself alive!"

Jawa, Chip, Zoe, and Warren cracked up along with her. The dining area was a large, serve-yourself cafeteria, and Erica was still off getting her food. My fellow spies-in-training were just as amused by Erica's disastrous run as Jessica was—if not more. After all, while Erica had let her guard down with me only on rare occasions, she'd *never* done it with any of them. All they'd ever seen of her was the icy, distant, perfect Erica who was constantly making everyone else look bad, so it was a thrill for them to witness her actually failing at something for once—and failing spectacularly, at that.

To make things even better, Erica hadn't improved much at all during the next few hours of ski school, while the rest of us had. (The rest of us who weren't faking being beginners, at least.) I had actually turned out to be pretty good at skiing—"a natural," according to Woodchuck—but everyone else was getting better as well. Even Warren had made progress. He had obviously lied when he'd boasted that he wasn't so bad at it the night before, but then, he wasn't terrible, either. Meanwhile, skiing was like Erica's Kryptonite. She couldn't seem to do anything right. When she was supposed to turn, she'd go straight. When she was supposed to go straight, she'd turn. And she'd been falling constantly: on the slopes, on the magic carpet, even while merely standing still. According to my calculations, she'd actually spent more time on her butt that morning than on her feet.

All of which made her more frustrated, which made her more determined to show us up, which made her take more chances, which made her crash even more. She didn't even have to be on skis; she'd wiped out three times so far in the cafeteria alone.

"She must have taken out fifty people on that first run." Jessica laughed. "She was like a cow in a Chinese restaurant."

"You mean 'a bull in a china shop'?" I asked.

"Right! That's what I meant!" Jessica agreed.

"Can you believe she honestly thought she could ski right off the bat?" Zoe giggled. "Without even a single lesson?"

"What a nut job," Chip said, and Warren and Jawa chimed in with agreement.

Then Erica emerged from the cafeteria line and everyone immediately stopped laughing. Erica seemed fully aware of what had been going on, though. Behind Jessica's back, she narrowed her eyes at everyone else for a split second, but then fell right back into character. She stumbled over to the table with her salad and hot tea, collapsed into a chair, and heaved a sigh of relief. "Whew! Made it! These ski boots sure are hard to walk in!"

"And even harder to ski in," Jessica whispered to me.

Even though we were on the opposite side of the table from Erica in a very loud room, Erica turned our way anyhow, like she'd heard this.

Jessica instantly grew uncomfortable. "I, uh . . . need to visit the ladies' room," she said, then stood and headed that way.

Dane dutifully rose from his seat and followed her.

Jessica grew embarrassed. "I can handle this on my own," she told Dane.

"Father's orders," he insisted.

Jessica groaned and headed off to the bathroom with him in tow.

The moment both were out of earshot, Erica returned to her normal self. "First off," she told the table, "I admit, I'm having a bit of trouble skiing, but it's only temporary. You're not going to be laughing so much tomorrow when I put you all to shame. Second, we need to figure out this Mike Brezinski situation *now*."

"Now?" I repeated, glancing back toward the bathroom warily. "Jessica might not be gone that long."

"Yes, she will," Zoe informed me. "She's wearing a one-piece ski suit and she has at least three layers on under it. It's going to take her five minutes just to get her pants down, let alone go to the bathroom."

"Plus, I spiked her drink with a laxative," Erica added. "So tack a few extra minutes on to that estimate."

I swung back to Erica, stunned. "You drugged her?"

"Only a little," Erica replied. "What was I supposed to do, *wait* for her to have to go to the bathroom?"

I started to argue that this wouldn't have been such a bad idea, but then realized no one else seemed to have a problem with it, so I kept silent.

"Now, then," Erica went on. "Mike's presence here is a huge problem. Something that could derail this entire mission."

"Not necessarily," I pointed out. "I've been thinking about it. If Jessica likes Mike and I'm her connection to him, she still has to keep me in the picture, right?"

"Wrong," Erica countered. "Jessica will only keep you around as long as it takes her to cozy up to Mike, and my bet is that won't be long at all. If you and Mike drop by for hot cocoa with her this afternoon, within thirty minutes she'll be asking him to take her on a date, just the two of them—and you'll be tossed aside like a used Kleenex. Once that happens, you won't get diddly-squat out of her, and Operation Snow Bunny will be dead."

Everyone else nodded agreement with this.

"Leo Shang is plotting Operation Golden Fist for December thirtieth," Erica continued. "That's only three days from now. Ben, you need to find out what it is as soon as possible. Which means we need to get Mike out of the picture."

"You mean, like, kill him?" Warren asked.

Chip whacked him on the back of the head with an open palm. "We're not gonna kill an innocent kid," he chided. "We only have to maim him a little."

I gagged on my soda. "Maim him?"

"Nothing permanent," Chip assured me. "Just enough to send him off to the hospital for a few days."

"You can't maim Mike," I pointed out. "He's my best friend."

"He's a threat to this operation," Jawa said pointedly.

"We don't need to maim Mike at all," Erica said. "There's a much simpler way to get rid of him."

"Poison him?" Warren asked.

This time Zoe whacked him on the back of the head.

Erica sighed, disappointed the rest of us hadn't figured out the answer. "We make sure Mike isn't interested in Jessica anymore."

"How?" I asked.

"By giving him someone even more interesting to fall for," Erica replied.

It took another few moments for us all to realize who she was talking about. "You mean *you*?" I asked.

"Of course." Erica took a sip of tea. "I tag along for hot cocoa with you guys today. Mike falls for me instead of Jessica. Then we take off, leaving the two of you alone. . . ."

"Just like that?" Jawa asked skeptically.

"Just like that," Erica said.

"And then," Zoe joined in, "Jessica feels rejected by Mike, so she's more vulnerable, which makes it easier for Ben to connect with her and win her affection."

Erica seemed slightly confused by this line of thought, as it concerned human emotions, but she nodded agreement anyhow. "Exactly."

"It might not work out so easily for you," Chip warned.

"Jessica Shang has a lot going for her. She's pretty, she's nice, she's fun—and she's rich."

"Yes," Erica agreed. "But I'm *me*."

Chip laughed dismissively. "I'm just saying, given the choice between two girls, if one of them's a billionaire, that's gonna mean something. This Mike character's gonna show up to the hotel, find out Daddy Shang rented the whole darn thing, and be gobsmacked. And once Jessica starts batting her eyes at him, he's gonna think he hit the mother lode."

"Mike's not that shallow," I argued.

"We're *all* that shallow," Chip retorted. "Whether we want to believe it or not. Mike's on a weeklong vacation. He's not looking to fall in love. He's looking to have fun! And who's he gonna have more fun with? The girl he can only afford to take to McDonald's—or the girl who has an entire hotel and a private jet and all the free food they can eat?"

"Good point," I conceded.

"I can compete with that," Erica said confidently.

"How?" Jawa asked. "No offense, but you're not exactly the warmest person in the world. Your own family doesn't even think you can make friends with Jessica. So what do you know about winning over a boy's affection?"

"I know it's easy," Erica replied. "Much easier than making friends with someone. To make friends with another girl is *work*. You have to be nice and pretend to like the same things and have all these excruciatingly dull conversations about your feelings. To get a guy to fall for you, you barely even need to use your brain."

"That is not true," Jawa argued, offended.

"Really?" Erica came around the table to Jawa, kneeled close to him, batted her eyelashes, and purred, "Would you like to go somewhere quiet and explain why you're right to me?"

Jawa looked as though his brain had shorted out. Face-to-face with Erica, his fourteen-year-old mind was completely overwhelmed by her beauty. "Sure!" he said eagerly. "Let's go right now!"

Erica pulled away from him, dropping any hint of interest she'd just shown. "And that's how you win over a boy," she said.

Jawa sagged as he realized he'd allowed Erica to toy with him so easily.

Zoe shook her head, looking disgusted.

I couldn't judge Jawa too harshly, though. I'd been close to Erica like that several times and been just as smitten. In fact, only a few seconds before, even though I'd been fully aware that Erica was simply leading Jawa on, I'd still felt jealous of him—and a glance at Chip and Warren confirmed they'd felt the same way.

Erica returned to her seat, sat down, and dug into her

salad. "So it's settled, then?" she asked me. "I'll come with you today, distract Mike, and get this mission back on track."

I hesitated before agreeing, because I wasn't very happy with this plan.

First, I wasn't pleased that, after I had been doing so well with Jessica on my own, Mike had come along and messed things up, forcing Erica to intervene and bail me out on yet another mission.

Even more importantly, I didn't like the idea of Erica flirting with Mike. Because I was afraid that once she got to know Mike, the flirting would stop being pretend. Erica had never seemed like the type of girl who'd fall for a guy easily, but I knew that she *had* developed a crush on someone once before. (Someone who'd turned out to be evil, no less.) Which meant it could happen again. And it seemed to me that if anyone could charm the Ice Queen, it was Mike. I'd already had him steal one girl's attention from me that day, which was rough enough. To have him win over Erica would be devastating.

There was, however, one legitimate argument against the plan. So I put it on the table. "There's a chance Mike might recognize you," I told Erica. "He's seen you before."

"When?" Zoe asked.

"Back when I first got to spy school," I explained. "While we were investigating the mole. Mike spotted Erica and me sneaking back onto campus at night."

Erica waved this off. "It won't be an issue. That was nearly a year ago, it was dark, and he was really far away."

"Mike never forgets a girl," I pointed out.

"He won't make the connection," Erica said. "He saw Erica Hale. But today he's going to meet Sasha Rotko. They're two entirely different people."

She was so confident, I knew I wasn't going to convince her otherwise. And to be honest, I believed her. There were a few times that morning when *I* had forgotten that Sasha Rotko was actually Erica Hale. I considered making another argument against the plan, but I couldn't really come up with one. Plus, I was forced to admit there were bigger things at stake here than my schoolboy crushes. My life, for one thing. I didn't have a better plan—and I didn't want to say what my problems were with Erica's proposal—so I gave in. "Sounds great."

"Good. Now, there's also *this* to deal with." Erica slid her phone across the table to me.

The selfie she'd taken of herself with Jessica and me was on the screen.

"Nice picture," Warren remarked. "Are you gonna post that?"

"I don't post," Erica said coldly. "That's a surveillance photo, you moron."

Warren shrank back in his seat while I took a closer look

at the photo. I now realized what Erica was talking about. She hadn't really been taking a selfie at all. Her real target was behind us: Dane the bodyguard.

I picked up the phone and zoomed in on him.

"I sent that to Hank while we were on the gondola," Erica went on.

"Not your grandfather?" Chip asked.

"He was busy tailing Leo Shang," Erica replied. "Anyhow, Hank got some intel for us. This guy's no mere bodyguard. His name's Dane Brammage. He's Danish, and he's a real piece of work. The CIA didn't even know he was working for the Shangs until Hank sent this over. Last they knew, he was working for an international arms dealer named Paul Lee."

"Polly who?" asked Zoe.

"No," Erica corrected. "Paul Lee. Two words. 'Paul' as in 'McCartney.' 'Lee' as in 'General Robert E.'"

"What kind of arms does he deal in?" Jawa asked.

"You name it, they move it," Erica replied. "The badder, the better. Bombs, tanks, torpedoes, rocket launchers. Everything. If you're wondering where SPYDER got all those Russian missiles they had, there's a good chance Paul Lee was the middleman. Real scum of the earth, that guy."

I looked back toward the bathroom, making sure Dane Brammage wasn't on his way back. "What did Dane do for him?"

"Bad stuff," Erica said. "Sometimes he moved weapons, but he mostly worked as muscle. If Paul Lee had a problem with someone, Dane made that someone disappear."

I swallowed hard. "And now he's working as a bodyguard for a thirteen-year-old girl? Why?"

"Because she's not your normal thirteen-year-old," Erica replied. "No one in that family is to be trusted, including her. Your sweetheart probably knows a lot more about Operation Golden Fist than she's letting on."

From the direction of the bathroom, I caught a glimpse of Jessica on her way back to the table. She hadn't been delayed as long as we'd thought. Dane was lumbering along behind her.

"She's not my sweetheart," I said.

"Point is, she's dangerous," Erica told me. "The whole Shang family is dangerous. And Dane Brammage is *really* dangerous. The moment he suspects you're not just a normal kid in ski school, you're in serious trouble. So we'd all better keep our guards up."

Jessica and Dane were almost back to the table now.

"This isn't a game," Erica warned all of us. "Our lives are at stake here. And maybe a lot of other people's as well." She slipped back into her fake persona just as Jessica came within earshot, acting like she was in the middle of the story. ". . . and then Maya laughed so hard, the soda came right out of her nose. It was dis-gust-ing!"

Everyone made an appropriate "ewwwww" in response. Except Jessica, who looked around at all of us, seeming upset she'd missed something good. "What are you guys talking about?"

"Sasha's trying to make us all lose our lunch," Zoe said.

"Yuck," Jessica declared, now seeming happy she'd missed the whole story. She looked a bit pale after her trip to the bathroom, like maybe she'd lost her lunch herself. Erica's cover story had worked, though; Jessica didn't seem suspicious of us at all.

Unfortunately, I couldn't say the same for Dane Brammage. He sat down heavily, staring hard at all of us. This was pretty much the same stare he'd been giving us all day, but now that I knew how dangerous he was, it was even scarier than before.

I really hoped he didn't suspect us of anything, because I didn't really need a deadly thug on my bad side.

I had enough problems as it was.

DISTRACTION

Schnitzengrüben Tavern

The Arabelle Hotel

Vail, Colorado

December 27

1630 hours

The rest of our ski lesson was actually fun and productive. As Woodchuck had told us, skiing had a great deal to do with our attitude, and since we were all determined to get better, most of us progressed well. (For Chip and Jawa, this wasn't an issue; since they already knew how to ski, they only had to *pretend* to get better.) Zoe, Jessica, and I mastered skiing down a beginner run slowly without falling, as well as getting on and off the ski lift without gravely injuring ourselves. Erica, to her chagrin, didn't improve quite as much, but she managed to stay upright most of the time. Meanwhile, Warren had somehow managed to actually get *worse* during the day. He'd started with at least an idea of how to ski, but by the end of the class, he was spending most of his time splayed out on the snow.

As enjoyable as the lesson was, though, I was exhausted and chilled after our day on the slopes. By the time we took the gondola down to the mountain base (we weren't quite good enough to ski all the way back down yet), the idea of grabbing a hot chocolate with two beautiful girls in a nice warm restaurant seemed like it should be a dream come true.

Instead, it was closer to a nightmare.

For starters, Jessica was extremely unhappy when Erica tagged along. Erica had suspected this would be the case, so she didn't even ask if she could join us. Instead, she blatantly invited herself. She did it when we were back in the ski rental, where we were allowed to store our equipment for the night. I was reveling in the feel of having normal shoes on my feet again, rather than ski boots, while Jessica was giddily pressing me to text Mike and see how long it would be until he could join us. Then Erica walked up in full Sasha mode and asked, "What are you two doing now?"

Jessica gave me a subtle signal not to tell Erica, but I

pretended not to notice. "Getting a hot chocolate," I said, nice and friendly.

"Oooh! That sounds dee-lish-ous!" Erica crooned. "Count me in!" Then she followed us to the Arabelle, blindly ignoring Jessica's many hints that she didn't want Erica around.

The three of us headed to the Schnitzengrüben Tavern to have a hot chocolate and await Mike's arrival. The Schnitz-engrüben was supposed to be the less fancy but more cozy of the two restaurants at the Arabelle. Unfortunately, it didn't feel cozy there at all.

This was partly because the restaurant was empty, reserved entirely for the Shangs, and being there felt eerie—like there'd been a zombie apocalypse or something. It was oppressively quiet, there were way too many vacant chairs around us, and the single waitress who'd been kept on staff solely to serve the Shangs seemed ill at ease. She hovered around us like a vulture, unsure what was expected of her.

The presence of Jessica's bodyguards made things worse. Now that we were back off the mountain, we had reunited with the three enormous Chinese men who'd been protect-ing Jessica that morning. They were all posted at the doors of the tavern, making sure no random people wandered in or out. Meanwhile, Dane Brammage sat at the next table over, glaring at us. It seemed to me that he was doing his best to make sure Erica and I felt uncomfortable, hoping we would leave—and it was working. On me, at least. His steady gaze was so unsettling, I was having trouble stomaching my hot chocolate.

I wondered if he was simply protecting Jessica by trying to keep everyone away from her, or if he had actually grown more suspicious of me that day. Either way, he certainly wasn't happy to have me around.

I was also worried about Mike's impending arrival. There were so many ways he could blow my cover: calling me by my real last name, for example, or mentioning there were strange things going on at my school—or deciding to once again joke that I was training to be a spy. Erica was unfazed by this, however, believing that she could handle Mike and lure him away from Jessica before he screwed anything up.

The biggest cause of tension, however, was Erica herself. Jessica was obviously angry at her for crashing our party. Thus, instead of being her normal, cheerful self, Jessica was now dour and gloomy, taking every opportunity to subtly let Erica know she wasn't wanted there, which forced Erica to act staggeringly oblivious.

"Mmmmmmm!" Erica exclaimed, sipping her hot chocolate and rubbing her stomach. "That is yummy in my tummy! It was soooo nice of you to invite me along!"

"I didn't," Jessica said coldly.

Erica giggled in response to this, like it had been a joke. "You're so funny! Is everyone in China as funny as you?"

Jessica glanced toward Dane. It seemed to me that she was considering the manners of simply having her bodyguard toss Erica out of the restaurant.

Before this could happen, there was a commotion by one of the doors. I could hear Mike trying to talk his way past the bodyguard stationed there. "I swear, I've been invited. A girl who's staying here asked me to come over after skiing. Her name's Jessica."

Jessica's foul mood immediately lifted. She lit up, thrilled that Mike had finally shown. "It's okay, Zhou!" she yelled to the bodyguard. "He's with me! Let him in!"

The bodyguard grudgingly stepped aside. Mike slipped through the door, red-faced from the cold. "Hey!" he called to us, then paused to look around the empty restaurant, confused. "Is this place even open?"

"Just for us," Jessica replied proudly.

"Really?" Mike seemed like he was about to ask *why* this was the case, but then he spotted Erica with us. Her presence immediately derailed his train of thought. Attracted to her, he flashed his standard wolfish grin—which Jessica didn't appreciate—and said, "I didn't realize there were going to be four of us. Hi, I'm Mike. Ben's best friend."

"I'm Sasha," said Erica.

"It's a pleasure to meet you," Mike said suavely. Just as Erica had predicted, he didn't recognize her. Even so, I was thankful Erica was using an alias. Mike might not have known exactly what Erica Hale looked like, but he certainly knew her name, as I had told him Erica was my girlfriend. To make things worse, I had kept that lie going for months, until finally claiming we'd broken up. Erica had found out all about it, of course, which was embarrassing enough. But having Mike put everything together would have been deadly.

Erica went right to work flirting with him, wanting to get him away from Jessica as quickly as possible. To this end, I had unwillingly briefed her on a few things that would pique Mike's interest, like his favorite movies, video games, and hobbies—and how he liked girls who were really good at sports—although Erica had insisted that she could probably get by with the basics from Flirtation 101. Like simply batting her eyes.

She did this now, and Mike was drawn toward her like a moth to a porch light.

"I'm in ski school with Jessica and Ben," she said, flipping her hair for good measure.

"Cool," Mike said. "Where are you from?"

"Baltimore," Erica replied.

Mike's smile grew. "Hey! Ben and I are from outside DC! We're not too far from you."

"I know," Erica purred. "Not even an hour apart."

I could already see Mike doing the math in his head. Jessica was attractive, but she was from China. Erica was *really* attractive and lived much closer, which gave her an edge.

Jessica seemed to be doing the math as well. She quickly tried to shift things in her favor. "Would you like something to drink?" she asked. "Or to eat?"

The waitress rushed to Mike's side, relieved to finally have something to do. "A hot chocolate, perhaps?" she asked. "Or a sandwich? Or pasta? Or a burger?"

"You can have anything you want," Jessica offered. "My father's paying."

"That's not necessary," Mike said graciously. "I can cover myself."

"No, I insist," Jessica said. "Trust me, Daddy can afford it." She waved a hand to the empty restaurant.

Mike shifted his attention from Erica to Jessica, intrigued. "Does your father own this hotel?"

"No," Jessica said. "But he's renting the whole place out for the week."

"He's renting the entire hotel?" Mike echoed. "Just for your family?"

"Yes," Jessica replied proudly.

Mike whistled, then warily scrutinized the bodyguards

around the room. "What exactly does your father do?" he asked.

I shot a glance at Erica, intrigued. It had never occurred to me that Mike might actually *help* us interrogate Jessica about her father.

"He's in business," Jessica said coyly.

"My dad's in business too," Mike said, "but he's not renting out entire hotels in Vail. What's your dad do, own companies or something?"

"Yeah," Erica chimed in. "How *does* he afford this whole place?"

At the next table, Dane Brammage stiffened, not liking where this conversation was going. Jessica didn't seem to notice. She was too happy to have Mike's attention again. "He does own a few companies in China."

"Like what?" Mike asked.

"I don't know," Jessica admitted, and it sounded like the truth. Given that she was trying to impress Mike, it seemed she would have told him if she'd known.

"You don't know what companies your father owns?" Erica taunted.

Jessica shrugged. "He doesn't like to talk about work much. Whenever I ask him about it, he's quiet as a louse."

Mike looked at me, confused by this.

"I think you mean 'quiet as a mouse,'" I told Jessica.

"That's the expression?" Jessica asked. "Really? Because lice are really quiet. They don't even have vocal cords. While mice are all squeaky."

Realizing we'd gotten off track, Erica tried to switch things back to Leo Shang. "If you don't know what companies your father owns, then maybe he *does* own this hotel. Is that why you're here?"

Jessica shook her head. "I think Daddy would have told me if he owned this place. And he *swore* he wasn't going to do any business this vacation. He works so much, I almost never get to see him. We're just here to go skiing."

"Only you and your dad?" Mike asked. "Or is there other family here too?"

"No, it's just me and Daddy," Jessica said. "I'm the only child—and my mother doesn't like the cold. She went to our island instead."

"Your family has a whole island?" I asked, stunned. It was off topic, but I couldn't help myself. "Where?"

Jessica actually had to think about this a while before answering. "Fiji, maybe? Somewhere warm."

"So where's your dad now, then?" Erica asked, trying to get the conversation back to Leo once again.

"He went helicopter skiing today," Jessica replied.

"No way!" Mike gasped. "That's supposed to be awesome."

"I know," Jessica agreed. "Daddy says that if I get good

enough over the next few days, he'll take me. Maybe he could take me and a friend." She looked at Mike meaningfully.

I could now see Mike mentally recalculating. An exceptionally rich attractive girl from China who could take him helicopter skiing was slightly better than an attractive girl from Baltimore.

Erica realized she was losing her edge, so she decided to shift the conversation—even if it meant getting off the subject of Leo Shang. "So, Mike, Ben says you're a really good skier."

"I'm okay," Mike said, in the exact same fake-humble way he had in the gondola that morning.

"Where'd you ski today?" Erica asked, shifting closer to Mike. She did it subtly, though, so that it didn't appear she was throwing herself at him.

"In the back bowls," Mike replied. "There was tons of untracked snow. It was pretty epic back there."

"Speaking of epic," Jessica interjected, not liking the attention Erica was getting, "Sasha had an epic wipeout today."

"Oh, that's not a big deal," Mike said. "Everyone wipes out when they first start skiing."

"Not like this," Jessica pressed. "This was a mega-wipeout. She took out everyone on an entire run."

Mike shrugged. "I've had worse. Once, on a massive

powder day, I biffed a jump and ended up buried in the snow all the way to my knees."

"That's not so bad," Erica said.

"Well, I'd landed headfirst," Mike explained. Then he broke into laughter.

Erica laughed too. "Oh, you're hilarious!" she said. "I like you."

Jessica joined in the laughter as well, not wanting to be left out, though it didn't sound very natural.

"I really have wiped out plenty," Mike told Erica reassuringly. "It's part of skiing. It's good that you didn't let it discourage you."

"Thanks," Erica said, looking truly flattered by this compliment. "I guess I thought it was going to be more like waterskiing. I'm pretty good at that."

"Really?" Mike asked, suddenly growing more intrigued. "Do you go a lot?"

"All the time," Erica said. "My folks have a vacation house on Chesapeake Bay. It's not far from DC. We have a couple ski boats out there—and some Jet Skis, too." This was all a lie. Erica was actually relying on my intel now to win Mike over; I'd told her that he loved waterskiing. It worked like a charm, quickly ramping up his interest in her.

"No kidding?" Mike was once again recalculating. An attractive girl with a vacation house and Jet Skis close to where he lived was better than an extremely wealthy rich girl who lived halfway around the world from him.

Erica scooted a little closer to Mike. "I usually don't have any problem with sports. I can ride a horse and throw a baseball and sink a layup and all that stuff. So I guess I figured it'd be easy to take up skiing. But it's not. I'll get the hang of it, though."

"I'm sure you will," Mike said. I could see he was starting to fall for Erica. All the references she'd just made to being good at sports had done the trick.

"Know what I'm *really* good at?" Erica asked. "Ice-skating! Does anyone want to go ice-skating?"

"I'd love to!" Mike said.

"Great!" Erica sprang to her feet and grabbed her coat.

"I thought we were all going to have hot chocolate together," Jessica insisted. She seemed stunned that Mike had been won over so quickly. "They make a really good hot chocolate here. With whipped cream and little chocolate shavings on top."

Mike shrugged. "I'm not that into chocolate. And it's kind of weird being all by ourselves in here. Why don't you guys come with us?" He gave me a sly wink, then nodded toward Jessica, indicating I should make a move with her.

"You know what'd be more fun?" Jessica asked. "We could all go up to my suite! There's a private Jacuzzi right out on the balcony up there!"

At the mention of this, Dane stiffened, not liking the idea of us visiting the suite at all.

Mike glanced his way, seeming to sense this. "I don't have a bathing suit," he said.

"You could borrow one of my dad's," Jessica said.

Mike made a face, disturbed by the thought of wearing a strange man's clothes. "Er . . . thanks," he said, "but I think we're gonna skate."

Erica had already slipped her coat on. "See you guys tomorrow!" she told us, and then she and Mike hurried out the door.

I watched them go, trying not to be overwhelmed by jealousy. There were only three days until Operation Golden Fist. I had a job to do and, as Erica had pointed out, I couldn't let emotion get in the way of it. I returned my attention to Jessica, expecting her to be feeling rejected and vulnerable, like Zoe had predicted.

She wasn't. Instead, she was really, really angry. "You should probably go," she told me, and then stormed out of the restaurant.

"Wait!" I yelled after her, leaping off the couch. Dane snapped out of his seat, trying to block me, but I slipped past him and chased after Jessica. "I thought we were going to use your Jacuzzi. . . ."

"I don't feel like it anymore." Jessica didn't even look

back at me as she spoke. She continued on into a hallway where the hotel elevators were.

Dane lumbered down the hall behind me. He was so big, I didn't even have to look back at him. I could feel his presence.

At the far end of the hall, beyond Jessica, was the hotel lobby. To my surprise, Leo Shang was coming through the doors. He was back from helicopter skiing. Through the windows behind him, I could see his caravan of car-tanks parked in the roundabout. Leo himself was surrounded by a cluster of bodyguards. All of them appeared unhappy to see me in the hotel—although none seemed as unhappy as Leo Shang himself.

Everything around me was indicating I should leave, but I felt I still had to make one last attempt to get back into Jessica's good graces. It wasn't going to be easy, though; she was so angry, she hadn't even noticed her father yet.

"I don't understand," I told her. "Did I do something wrong?"

"You invited *her*," Jessica spat.

"No, I didn't! She invited herself!"

"Which she wouldn't have done if you hadn't told her what we were doing. You might as well have given her an engraved invitation." Jessica stabbed the button for the elevator.

"Jessica," Leo Shang said sternly.

Jessica froze. She turned to him, startled he was there, then looked back at me. Her anger shifted into something closer to worry. "Hi, Daddy," she said. "How was your skiing?"

Leo pointed toward me and demanded, "Who is this?" As he came closer to us, I got a better view of him. He looked like a Chinese version of Alexander Hale. He was handsome and suave, wearing a designer ski jacket over an expensive button-down shirt. His attitude was extremely different from Alexander's, though. Alexander had always been friendly and charming, while Leo Shang appeared forbidding and mean. He stared at me with disdain, like I was a rat that had somehow gotten into his hotel, rather than a fellow human being.

Although every fiber of my being wanted to shrink away from Leo, I knew that probably wasn't the best choice. Instead, it seemed that I should behave exactly how Mike would in my situation. Mike would be confident and brave, like he had every right to be there.

"I'm Ben Coolman," I said, extending my hand toward Leo. "I'm a friend of Jessica's from ski school."

Leo Shang made no attempt to shake my hand. Instead, he recoiled from it in disgust, as though I had just blown my nose in it. Then he looked back at Jessica. "I thought I made myself clear: You are not to have any visitors at the hotel."

"I didn't invite him into the hotel," Jessica said. "I invited him into the restaurant. He followed me into the hotel just now."

"Don't split hairs with me," Leo said through gritted teeth. "The restaurant is part of this hotel and you know it."

"I can't go out anywhere *and* I can't have anyone visit me here?" Jessica asked petulantly. "That's not fair! This is my vacation too!"

"Your daughter only invited me over for hot chocolate," I said, as charmingly as I could. "That's not a crime, is it?"

Leo ignored me and shifted his attention to Dane. "This is unacceptable."

The big blond man actually cowered under Leo's gaze. "I'm sorry, sir. It won't happen again." With that, he clamped a massive hand on my shoulder and said, "You heard him. Let's go."

I raised my hands in mock surrender. "No need to rough me up. I'm leaving."

Jessica stared bullets at her father. Even though she'd been angry at me not long before, her anger at her father had trumped that. "You can be a real jerk sometimes," she said, then stepped into the elevator and let the doors close on Leo Shang.

I let Dane lead me back down the hall, trying to make sense of everything that had happened. Two minutes before, Jessica had wanted me to get out of her sight, and now she was mad at her father because he wanted the exact same thing.

I could feel Leo Shang's eyes on me the whole way to the restaurant, but I didn't look back. I returned to my table, grabbed my ski parka, and slipped it on.

As I did, though, something occurred to me. My memory lessons were paying off. I'd observed something about Leo Shang that was important.

He was wearing a button-down shirt under his ski jacket.

I'd been out on the mountain only one day, but I'd had the opportunity to observe thousands of fellow skiers. Under their jackets, they had worn thermal underwear or fleeces or sweaters or combinations of all three, but not a single one of them had worn a button-down shirt. Button-down shirts were what people wore to business meetings, not to go skiing.

Which meant Leo Shang probably hadn't gone helicopter skiing at all. And he'd either lied to his daughter about it—or she'd lied to me. Either way, it indicated he was up to something.

"See you tomorrow," I said to Dane, trying to appear unfazed by my unsettling encounter with Leo Shang. As though it were perfectly normal to meet a mean, insensitive billionaire who treated me like pond scum and then had his Danish thug evict me from his private hotel. I quickly slipped out the door to the ice-skating plaza.

Erica was already out on the rink with Mike. To my surprise, she didn't seem to notice me. Normally, Erica was so attuned to her surroundings that nothing got past her, but at the moment, her eyes were locked on Mike's. And his were locked on hers. Each had a dreamy smile on their face that I found almost as disturbing as the disdainful glare Leo Shang had given me. I hoped it was all part of her act—but worried that it wasn't.

Unfortunately, I didn't have time to deal with Mike and Erica. I hurried through the plaza, heading back to the Ski Haüs.

I had to talk to Cyrus Hale.

ANALYSIS

The Jackalope Cantina

Vail, Colorado

December 27

1730 hours

Cyrus, Alexander, and all my fellow students weren't at the motel, but Zoe had left a note in a simple arabesque code that I easily translated. It informed me they were at a restaurant down the street.

The Jackalope Cantina, being on the wrong side of the highway from most of Vail, wasn't designed in the same fake-Tyrolean style as the rest of town—and it didn't have a random umlaut in its name either. Instead, it was a standard, blocky strip-mall restaurant on the outside, with a cheesy

Western theme on the inside. The walls were lined with neon beer signs and the mounted heads of local wildlife: deer, elk, peccaries—and lots of jackalopes. Jackalopes were fake animals: stuffed rabbits with antlers grafted to their heads, apparently some sort of joke cooked up by Rocky Mountain taxidermists.

I found everyone in a private back room, where they could eat and talk without worrying about anyone spotting them or overhearing them. The kids, including Hank, were all seated at one table, scarfing down burgers and fries. Cyrus and Alexander were at the next table over. Even though it seemed like a breach of protocol, I sat with the adults, wanting to lay out my case against Leo Shang as quickly as possible.

Cyrus barely looked up from his food, but Alexander welcomed me heartily. "Hello, Ben! How did things go with Jessica today?"

"All right," I said, not wanting to admit that they'd really been disastrous. "But then Leo Shang showed up and ran me off."

Now Cyrus looked up. "You interacted with Shang?"

"Yes," I said, and quickly filled them in on the entire encounter, proudly explaining how I'd deduced Leo hadn't really gone helicopter skiing that day.

Unfortunately, Cyrus wasn't as impressed by it as I'd hoped. "I saw him get on that helicopter," he told me.

"But you didn't see him actually *ski*, right?" I countered. "Because you didn't have your own helicopter to follow him. This is proof he was doing something else. . . ."

"A button-down shirt isn't proof," Cyrus said dismissively. "You're making wild speculations based upon scant evidence."

"It's not a wild speculation, Dad," Alexander argued on my behalf. "There's sound reasoning behind it. No one likes a nice, well-tailored button-down shirt more than I do, and even *I* wouldn't ski in one."

"What's to say Shang skied in it at all? He could have easily changed clothes after he landed." Cyrus sank his teeth into his double bacon cheeseburger. He was very old-fashioned when it came to food. I'd never had a meal with him that didn't involve red meat. His burger was so rare, I was afraid it might walk off his plate.

Alexander, on the other hand, wasn't used to places like the Jackalope Cantina. His taste ran toward expensive five-star restaurants, and he'd made the mistake of ordering as though he were in one: French onion soup, braised salmon, and oysters, even though we were a thousand miles from the nearest ocean. The food obviously didn't look anything like what he'd hoped. The oysters had actually been deep-fried, the salmon was greenish, and the cheese atop the soup had congealed into the dairy equivalent of a hockey puck.

Alexander was poking at it all gingerly with a fork, as though afraid of it.

"Would you bring a button-down shirt to change into right after skiing?" I asked Cyrus. "You wouldn't just wait until you got back to the hotel?"

"We're not talking about what *I'd* do," Cyrus pointed out. "We're talking about what Leo Shang might do. For all we know, Shang's the kind of guy who wears button-downs every chance he gets. Maybe he even went skiing in one today."

"I doubt that," I said.

"But you can't prove it's not true," Cyrus countered. "Meanwhile, here's what I *know* to be facts, because I observed them myself: One, Leo Shang had his men drive him to the helipad of the Epic Heli-Skiing Company this morning. Two, Leo Shang brought his skis with him and loaded them into the helicopter. Three, the helicopter remained in the backcountry ski area all day."

"How can you be so sure if you couldn't follow him?" I asked.

Cyrus sighed, as though he was growing annoyed with me. "I had the Agency track the chopper via GPS. Its pattern of movement was consistent with helicopter skiing: It landed on mountaintops for several long stretches, which is exactly how a ski copter would set down to allow its clients to ski. And it never ranged out of the designated backcountry ski area in the White River National Forest. No side trips over to the North American Aerospace Defense Command or the Cheyenne Mountain Complex or any of the other strategic military facilities in Colorado."

The kids' table perked up at the mention of this.

"You think that's what Golden Fist might be?" Chip asked. "Leo Shang is really targeting one of those places?"

"I *thought* that's what Golden Fist might be," Cyrus corrected. "But I don't anymore—as he didn't go anywhere near any of those places. They're all at least sixty miles from where he was."

"Well, maybe he was doing reconnaissance on something else," I suggested.

"Yeah. Snow," Cyrus grumped. "And rocks and trees. That's all there is to see back where he was today. If the CIA learns he was only skiing, they're gonna think this whole operation's a bleeding snipe hunt."

"What's that?" Warren asked.

"A 'snipe hunt' is Agency terminology for a mission which is investigating a plot that doesn't actually exist," Alexander explained helpfully. "Sort of like a wild-goose chase. There's a very interesting story behind the name. You see, back in the early days of the Agency, under Roscoe Hillenkoetter, a lot of the first agents were avid hunters. . . ."

"No one wants to hear a damn history lecture," Cyrus

snapped, even though everyone else probably did.

Alexander clammed up and sullenly dug into his deep-fried oysters.

"I don't think it's a snipe hunt," I said quietly. "I've seen Leo Shang twice now, and I definitely think he's up to something."

"Well, your hunch and a penny are worth a penny." Cyrus crammed the last of his french fries into his mouth. "The point of an operation is to obtain solid evidence. So you'd better step up your game and get me some."

"I don't think Jessica knows anything about Golden Fist," I pointed out.

"Well, we never expected she would. Kids are rarely the brains of the operation," Cyrus told me, in a way that made no secret he was talking about me, too. "The idea here was never to shake *her* down. It was to *use* her to get close to her father and find out what Operation Golden Fist is. So get to work. You've already been on the case a day and all you've got for me is a button-down shirt." He shoved away his empty plate, stood, and grabbed his coat, ready to go.

I frowned, frustrated with Cyrus—and myself. I was annoyed that he hadn't given my report on Leo Shang more credit, but I also realized he had a point. I hadn't brought him much. And to make matters worse, I didn't know if I could get any more. Jessica had seemed pretty much done with being friends with me.

"Ben's doing his best," Zoe told Cyrus as he headed for the door. "But there was a complication today."

Cyrus froze in his tracks and wheeled on her. "What kind of complication?"

I desperately signaled Zoe to be quiet. I knew she was only trying to help, but I also knew Cyrus much better than she did. Telling him about Mike's presence in Vail would only make things worse.

Zoe noticed me and got the picture. "Um," she said, trying to think on her feet. "Jessica Shang's really mean. Very hard to get to know."

"So?" Cyrus asked.

"She has terrible breath, too!" Warren added, trying to be helpful. "Like, the worst breath ever. It smells like dirty diapers."

Cyrus glared at everyone. "What's the *real* complication?" he demanded.

"Ben ran into his best friend from back home while he was with Jessica on the gondola today," Hank reported.

Chip turned on his brother. "Hey! I told you that in confidence."

"Yeah. That was stupid of you," Hank said, then returned his attention to Cyrus. "In addition to potentially blowing Ben's cover, this kid also attracted Jessica Shang's affection, which has threatened the objective of the mission."

Cyrus shifted his angry gaze back to me. "This is your friend Mike Brezinski?"

I gaped in surprise. "You know who Mike is?"

"Of course I know who Mike is!" Cyrus snarled. "This wouldn't be the first time that friend of yours has compromised one of our missions. How on earth did he end up here?"

"It was a coincidence," I said weakly.

"There's no such thing," Cyrus informed me.

"Well, to be honest, that's not true," Alexander put in helpfully. "Once, when I was undercover in Istanbul, I ran right into my third-grade teacher, Mrs. Jenkins, at a falafel stand. Luckily, I was disguised as a nun, so she didn't recognize me. . . ."

"Shut up," Cyrus ordered.

Alexander clammed up again and resumed eating his oysters.

"You don't need to worry about Mike Brezinski," Jawa told Cyrus. "We developed a plan to distract him so that he won't be a problem anymore."

Cyrus took a step back, growing even more concerned, putting things together before we could explain them. "Where's my granddaughter?" he demanded.

"I'm right here," Erica said.

We all spun around to find her leaning against a stuffed

grizzly bear nearby. Once again, she'd managed to arrive without anyone noticing. Even Cyrus seemed surprised to see her there.

"You were the distraction?" Cyrus asked.

"Yes," Erica answered.

"And were you successful?" Cyrus added.

"Mike Brezinski is no longer going to be an issue where Jessica Shang is concerned. He has set his sights on someone else." Erica slipped past her father, took a seat at the junior spies' table, and began perusing the menu.

"But he could still blow Ben's cover?" Cyrus asked.

"Yes, *that's* still an issue," Erica said. "But I have it under control. He's skiing with his family during the day, and in the afternoons, I can divert him so that he doesn't go anywhere near Jessica."

"How are you going to divert him?" Alexander asked suspiciously, more like a worried father than a spy.

"I'm going to invite him to be lots of places where Jessica is not," Erica replied calmly, then asked her father, "How's the French onion soup?"

"Inedible," Alexander replied.

"I figured as much." Erica sighed.

"I don't like this," Cyrus muttered. "I don't like it at all. Erica, you're supposed to be Ben's handler on this operation, not running around with some hoodlum."

"First of all," Erica said, "my ability to handle Ben hasn't been compromised. And second, not every teenage boy is a hoodlum. Mike's not so bad."

Zoe dropped her fork into her mashed potatoes in shock. "Oh my gosh," she gasped. "You *like* him."

Erica recoiled as though Zoe had just electrocuted her. "I do not!"

"You just said he's 'not so bad,'" Zoe informed her. "That's the nicest thing I've ever heard you say about a boy. Or anyone. In fact, it's the nicest thing I've ever heard you say, period."

"Erica," Alexander said, intrigued, "if this fellow is special to you, do you think I ought to meet him?"

"No!" Erica gasped, horrified. "I don't like him! Any interest I have shown him is solely acting, and once this mission is over, I will have no interest in ever seeing him again!"

"You sure *sound* like you like him," Chip taunted.

"Well, I don't!" Erica snapped. "Not one bit!"

This was about the most emotionally worked up any of us had ever seen Erica, which only seemed to confirm that she really *did* like Mike. Normally, I would have loved to see Erica unsettled like this, especially when she was being subjected to almost the exact same grilling she'd given me about Jessica Shang the day before. But this was different. Because *I* liked Erica. The last thing I needed was her developing a crush on someone else. Especially my best friend.

Everyone else seemed just as unconvinced by Erica's arguments, but for the moment they all let it slide. Cyrus returned his harsh gaze to me. "Seems my granddaughter is really putting herself out to fix this trouble you've caused. . . ."

"I had no idea Mike was going to be here," I reiterated.

Cyrus snorted disapprovingly. "Point is, she's going way out on a limb to get this mission back on track. Now, are you prepared to do your part? Can you get to Leo Shang?"

I hesitated before answering. The truth was, I felt I had almost no chance of getting to Leo Shang. The man was surrounded by bodyguards trained to kill, and I'd be lucky if Jessica ever talked to me again.

But then I thought about my encounter with Leo Shang that day. Even though Cyrus said my hunch wasn't worth anything, I *knew* I was right. The man was up to something. Whatever Operation Golden Fist was, it wasn't good. And if I was the CIA's only route to finding out what was going on, then I couldn't back down. Yes, it would be dangerous. Yes, it would be scary. And yes, it would force Erica to flirt with Mike even more. But there was a job to be done, and I was determined to figure out a way to do it.

So I looked Cyrus right in the eye and said, "Yes. I can get to Leo Shang."

Cyrus held my gaze for a long time, as though trying to

determine whether he believed me—and whether I believed myself. "All right," he said finally. "We'll move ahead. But if this mission goes to pot, you're the one who'll take the fall for it." With that, he slipped into his parka and headed out into the cold, stiffing all of us with the check.

"I hope you're not saying you can get to Leo just to please my father," Alexander said to me quietly. "You can never please him. Trust me, I've spent my whole life trying."

There was a sadness in his eyes as he said this, and I suddenly had a revelation about Alexander. The man had built his reputation on hundreds of lies about how successful his missions had been. I had always assumed that he'd done this to further his career, but now I wondered if it had all simply been a desperate attempt to impress his father.

"I'm not sucking up to Cyrus," I said. "I can do this."

"Well, you're going to have to do it fast," Erica told me. "There's only three days left until Golden Fist goes down."

"Erica and Mike, sitting in a tree," someone at the other end of the table sang under their breath, "K-I-S-S-I-N—"

Erica suddenly lunged out of her chair, grabbing Warren by the hair and slamming him face-first into the remnants of his dinner. "Say one more letter," she growled, "and I will gut you with a steak knife."

"It wasn't me!" Warren whined. "It was Chip!"

"I don't care if it was the Queen of England!" Erica

warned us all. "I am not interested in Mike Brezinski. And the next person who makes a joke about it ends up in the hospital."

She released Warren, who collapsed back in his chair, gasping for breath, pulling french fries out of his nostrils.

Erica calmly returned her attention to me, as though she hadn't done anything out of the ordinary. "So, how'd things go with Jessica after I got Mike out of there?"

"Um . . . We have some problems," I reported, then looked to Zoe. "She didn't get vulnerable after Mike left like you said she would."

"She didn't?" Zoe asked.

"No," I replied. "Instead, she got angry. *Really* angry. And then she told me to leave."

"Oh boy," Zoe said. "I was hoping that wouldn't happen."

"You mean you knew it *might*?" Erica snapped at her.

"You didn't?" Zoe shot back. "You're a teenage girl! You've never had your emotions get all out of whack?"

"No," Erica said, without any emotion at all.

"Well, it happens to normal people sometimes," Zoe replied. "Normal people aren't robots. They have feelings, and I can't predict every possible one of them. So I went with what I thought would be the most probable outcome."

"Sadly, that wasn't the case," I said. "Jessica went totally cold on me. So now I have to figure out a way to get her interested in me again."

"Lucky for you, you've come to the right place," Alexander said suavely. "When it comes to piquing a woman's interest, I'm an expert."

"Dad, please don't say things like that in front of me," Erica said, looking nauseated. "I'm going to lose my appetite."

"Now, then," Alexander went on, oblivious to his daughter, "the best way to win over a woman is with good manners and charm. You invite her out to a delicious meal, then order something special, like a nice bottle of champagne. . . ."

"I'm only thirteen," I pointed out.

". . . or beluga caviar . . . ," Alexander went on.

"That's a hundred and forty dollars an ounce," Jawa told him.

". . . or perhaps some oysters," Alexander continued, indicating the ones on his plate. "Normally, you'd want them raw, of course. I prefer Kumamotos, myself. They have just the right hint of brininess and a certain je ne sais quoi, but these local ones are surprisingly tasty."

Erica cocked an eyebrow at him. "You ordered the Rocky Mountain oysters?"

"Yes. They're quite flavorful, although they don't taste much like other oysters. . . ."

"That's because they're bull testicles," Erica told him.

"Don't be ridiculous," Alexander chided. "They wouldn't make something like that at a restaurant like this!"

Erica handed him the menu and pointed to the small print he'd overlooked that indicated exactly what Rocky Mountain oysters were.

"Oh dear," Alexander gasped. He promptly turned green and ran out the door to throw up in the parking lot.

Hank slid into the seat next to me and put an arm around my shoulder. "Don't listen to Alexander. When it comes to women, he's way too old-school. But me . . . I'm a regular Casanova. You have any questions about chicks, I can answer them."

Chip burst into laughter. "You? You don't know anything about women! That's why Claire dumped you!"

"She didn't dump me," Hank retorted. "I dumped her!"

"Then why did you spend the next three days crying about it?" Chip asked. He then performed an overblown imitation of Hank, bawling into the telephone. "Please, take me back, Claire! I'm nothing without you. I promise, I can change!"

"Stop it," Hank warned.

Chip didn't. Instead, he amped up his imitation even more. "You can't dump your little Hanky-Wanky. I love you!"

"That does it!" Hank launched himself at Chip, knocking

him out of his chair. They proceeded to roll around on the floor of the restaurant, trying to pound each other.

Jawa gingerly stepped over them and took the chair Hank had just vacated. "I might be of service where women are concerned," he said. "I have read Agent Percival Perry's *Manual to Seducing Women in the Field* a hundred times."

"Agent Perry was a hack," Erica said coldly.

"He was?" Jawa asked.

"Yes," Erica replied. "He was actually terrible with women in the field. They stopped using his manual thirty years ago."

"So the 'Red Rose Rendezvous Ruse' . . . ," Jawa began.

"Never works," Erica finished. "All it will get you is a slap in the face and a knee in the crotch."

"Oh," Jawa said, turning red. "Apparently, I may not be of service after all."

"Well, *I* know all about women," Warren said, grinning at Zoe slyly. "If you want to win a girl over, the first thing you do is slip up behind her and give her a nice, soothing massage." He tried this on Zoe, digging his fingers into her shoulders.

"Ouch!" Zoe screamed. "Stop that, you moron!"

Warren cringed. "But it's shiatsu!"

"It's painful," Zoe snapped. "And disgusting. Your hands are all clammy. Ugh. I need to go home and shower."

Warren wilted and sat back down.

Chip and Hank rolled past us, still trying to clobber each other.

Erica sighed. "Looks like we're pretty screwed where relationship advice is concerned."

As she said this, however, I had a flash of insight. Maybe things weren't quite as bad as Erica thought. When it came to women, I knew exactly who to turn to for help.

ASSISTANCE

Simba ski run

Vail Mountain

December 28

1600 hours

"I need some advice," I said to Mike.

"Sure," he replied. "You're dragging your left ski when you turn."

"Really?" I made another turn, taking care to not drag my left ski. Mike's advice was spot-on. I moved much more naturally.

"There you go!" Mike exclaimed proudly. "Nicely done!"

Since my lessons had ended before the lifts closed, Mike had agreed to meet me for one last run at the end of the day.

(To give us some time, Erica had told him she needed an hour to change and do her hair before she met up with him for another ice-skating date.) We had taken the gondola up to Eagle's Nest Ridge and were now coming down a wide intermediate run called "Simba." (Why anyone had named a ski run in the Colorado Rockies after the Swahili word for "lion" was something no one could explain to me.) It was the toughest run I'd ever attempted, a huge challenge for me— while it was so easy for Mike, he was skiing backward down it. This allowed him to talk to me as we went.

"Actually," I said, "I need advice about something besides skiing."

"Cool," Mike said. "Because, to be honest, you're skiing's coming along great. You've got a lot of natural talent for this."

"I do?" I asked, getting distracted from the topic once again. I couldn't help it. In my entire life, Mike had never given me a compliment like that. Well, he *had*, but I knew he hadn't really meant any of the others. With those, he was merely being a good friend and trying to bolster my spirits, like when he said "You're getting a lot better at basketball" after he'd just creamed me in a game of one-on-one. Or "You've got a great swing" after I'd just whiffed at thirty straight baseballs in the batting cages.

This was different, though. I could tell Mike was being honest, which meant a lot to me.

I'd pushed myself hard in my ski lessons that day, determined to improve as quickly as possible. Woodchuck had been impressed enough to put me at the top of the class. (Well, not quite the top. Jawa and Chip were the best skiers, but then, they had been good to start with. I could tell it was driving them crazy to have to keep pretending to be beginners when they could have been off skiing the fun runs like Mike all day.) I had gone from the beginner's wedge turn (known as "making a piece of pizza" because of the angle you formed with your skis) to the more advanced turn, where I kept my skis parallel to each other (known as "making french fries.") This allowed me to go faster and take on tougher runs.

"Keep going like this," Mike said, "and you'll be able to ski almost anything by the end of the week." He skidded to a halt with a deft spin.

I stopped right next to him. We were now perched at a lip where the run got steeper. The entire Vail Valley was spread out far below us, while low-slung gray clouds covered the mountaintops not far above our heads. It looked like someone had installed a ceiling over the earth.

"Looks like snow," Mike said eagerly. "I heard we might get twelve inches tonight."

"Is that good?"

"No. It's *great*. If we get a foot of fresh powder, it's gonna be epic tomorrow." Mike shifted his gaze from the clouds to me. "So, what do you need advice about?"

"Jessica."

"Ah! You have chosen wisely, my friend. She's cute. And loaded."

"And into *you*," I pointed out.

"Oh." Mike seemed genuinely upset. "Sorry about that. I got that vibe, but I also sensed she might like *both* of us. I thought maybe she'd shift to you once I took off with Sasha."

"She didn't. Instead, she got all annoyed and she's been cold to me ever since."

I had tried to talk to Jessica plenty of times during ski lessons that day, but she hadn't been very interested. The sweet, approachable girl I'd met on the first day had been replaced by a sullen loner. What made everything even stranger was that Erica—who was usually the sullen loner—was stuck pretending to be nice and friendly all day for Jessica's sake. It felt like the two of them had switched brains.

"Well, now," Mike said confidently, "that doesn't mean she's not into you at all. She might just be embarrassed by the idea of making an obvious rebound to you."

"You really think so?"

"She *was* awfully friendly to you at first, right? When I found you two in the gondola, it looked like you were getting along great."

"We were."

"So, there you go: She likes you. I think we can still get you back in the game."

"You do? That's awesome! Thanks!"

"And I only need one thing from you in return."

"Oh," I said, growing concerned. I assumed Mike wanted my help getting closer to Erica in some way—and I was going to have to give it, no matter how much I didn't want to. "What is it?"

Mike raised his ski goggles, then fixed me with a hard stare. "Tell me the truth about this school you're going to."

This caught me by surprise so badly, I pulled away from Mike, lost my balance, and fell on my butt. Which then made it very hard to pretend like nothing was wrong. I gave it my best shot anyhow. "What are you talking about?"

"You said you were coming out here on a class trip. So where's your class?"

"They're all in different lessons from me."

"Oh, come on!" Mike snapped. "Give it a rest, will you? I'm not an idiot."

"I know that. . . ."

"Then stop treating me like one. You're not out here doing snowpack research. I want to know what's really going on. And don't give me that garbage about you being a human guinea pig."

"*You* were the one who guessed I was a human guinea pig," I pointed out.

"Yeah. That's why I know it's garbage. And you actually played along. No one would ever willingly admit to being a human guinea pig! Not unless they were trying to cover up something else that they couldn't admit to!"

"That's not true," I said, struggling back to my feet.

"You're training to be a spy, aren't you?" Mike asked.

He caught me so off guard, I promptly fell over again. This time I made a valiant attempt to cover my surprise, laughing like this was the funniest thing I'd ever heard. "C'mon, Mike! That's crazy. You said it yourself the other day: I'd be the worst spy of all time."

"I was trying to get a rise out of you so you'd admit the truth."

I looked around the ski run nervously, worried someone else might be listening in on our conversation. Luckily, it was late in the afternoon and most other skiers had already gone in for the day. Those still out on the slopes were a good distance away and focused on getting down the mountain.

"Being a spy explains everything," Mike continued, ticking things off on his gloved fingers. "Your strange behavior. The commandos around your school. How you could beat up Trey Patterson and three other guys. Plus, when I told a bunch of cute girls that you were training to be a spy, you denied it."

"How on earth does that prove I'm a spy?" I asked.

"The only reason a thirteen-year-old boy would deny he was training to be a spy in front of three cute girls is if he actually *was* training to be a spy. Anyone else would have totally lied about it."

"I'm not training to be a spy," I said.

"There!" Mike cried. "You're doing it again!"

I struggled back to my feet again. "If you're going to take my denial of training to be a spy as proof that I'm actually training to be a spy, then if I say I *am* training to be a spy, won't that be proof that I'm *not* training to be a spy?"

Mike paused a moment to make sense of that, then said, "It's different with me. I'd know if you were telling the truth."

I glanced around the ski run again. I now had the eerie sensation that we were being watched. None of the other skiers were paying any attention to us—but when I looked toward a grove of aspen trees to my right, I thought I caught a glimpse of something moving among them. However, whatever it was seemed to disappear the moment I looked that way.

"Come on," Mike pleaded. "I know there's probably a ton of rules against admitting this, but I'm your best friend. It's not cool to lie to your best friend. And you've been lying to me for months." He then fixed me with a mournful, wide-eyed stare.

It suddenly started to snow. Hard. Like the clouds had ripped open and everything was falling out of them. Big, wide flakes came down in sheets. The grove of aspens—and whoever might have been watching us from it—vanished behind the white curtain. The snow made the world quieter, too. It swallowed up the conversations of all the skiers near us, meaning that they would have trouble hearing anything I said too.

If I was ever going to tell Mike the truth, this seemed like as good a place as any to do it.

And I was tired of lying to him. It wasn't simply because it made me feel like a bad friend. It was because he already *knew*. Like Mike had said, he wasn't an idiot. He'd stumbled upon too many things that were too hard to explain away, and the more lies I piled up on top of one another, the worse things would get.

And yet I lied to him anyhow. I'd been sworn to secrecy; if I spilled the beans without permission, I could be expelled from school. And kicked out of the CIA. And Erica would never talk to me again. And, for all I knew, Cyrus might order a hit on Mike and me. So I looked Mike right in the eye, doing my best to seem believable, and sold the lie as hard as I could. "For the last time: I. Am. Not. A. Spy."

Mike held my gaze for a moment, then huffed in disgust. "Fine. Be that way. Some friend you are." With that, he stabbed his poles into the ground, starting down the hill.

"Wait!" I yelled, unable to hide my panic. I didn't want Mike upset with me—and I didn't want him to strand me up on the mountain, either. I still hadn't solved my problems with Jessica—and I wasn't sure I could get back down without him.

Mike skidded to a stop a few feet down the slope. "What?"

"I still need help . . . ," I began.

"You're unbelievable," Mike sneered. "First you lie to me—and then you still ask for a favor?"

"I'm not lying," I lied.

"Whatever." Mike looked like he was about to start downhill again but couldn't bring himself to ditch me. He groaned and turned back. "Fine. I'll help you. Because that's what friends do. Even when their friends are being jerks. If you want to get back in with Jessica, just make her jealous of you."

"How?"

"Have Sasha act interested in you. Jessica's already annoyed at her. If she thinks Sasha likes *you* and not me, she'll shift right back to you again."

"Are you sure?"

"No," Mike said pointedly. "I'm not sure of anything. Not even who my friends are." With that, he turned and shot downhill, vanishing into the snow.

"Mike!" I yelled after him. "Don't leave me here!"

There was no answer. The snow was coming down even harder now. I was surrounded by white. There still might have been other skiers close by—or an enemy lurking in the trees next to the run—but I couldn't see any of them. I was all alone.

I called for Mike a few more times, but heard nothing. So I angled my ski tips at each other, making a piece of pizza, and pushed forward.

It turned out, skiing in fresh powder was much harder than skiing the groomed runs I'd been on so far. I promptly pitched forward, snapped out of my skis, and face-planted in the snow.

It was going to be a long way down.

INFORMATION ACQUISITION

Lionshead Village
Vail, Colorado
December 28
1800 hours

It took me more than an hour to get down the mountain.

I wiped out in every way possible. I had slips, skids, slides, stumbles, tumbles, sprawls, splats, topples, crumples, and collapses. I had little falls where I landed on my rear and big ones where I ended up somersaulting down the slope, shedding ski gear the whole way. The falling snow was so thick, I could barely see anything in front of me until I was about to run into it—and thus, I ran into plenty: two ski-lift poles, four fellow skiers, and six trees. At one point, I somehow veered onto a mogul run, which was so difficult to traverse, it seemed as though SPYDER might have designed it. Instead of being nice and smooth, it was full of tiny hills; it was like trying to ski over a herd of Galápagos tortoises. I fell over and over and over again. I ended up with snow in my jacket, my gloves, my ears, my nose, and—by far the worst—down my pants. There were a dozen times when I wanted to simply chuck my skis into the woods and just walk the rest of the way down the mountain.

But I didn't.

I stuck it out, figuring out what mistakes I'd made and correcting them, pushing myself harder and harder. And I improved. It was baptism by fire—or ice, really. I got better at keeping my skis parallel and started to make tighter turns. Every now and then, I'd link two or three turns together, carving through the powder like a pro, and it would feel absolutely amazing.

And then I'd wipe out again.

I got back up every time, though. By the time I finally made it back to the base of the mountain, I was a significantly better skier than I'd been when I'd gone up. I was also a significantly colder, wetter, and more exhausted skier. I staggered into the ski rental to store my equipment for the night, wanting only to get back to the motel, take a hot shower, and crawl into bed.

Erica had other plans, though. She ambushed me the moment I exited the ski storage area and said, "Come with me. I need your help."

"Doing what?"

"What do you think? Investigating."

"I thought you might need to meet up with Mike today."

"This is much more important. I texted him to say I had a headache."

We walked through the wide pedestrian concourses of Lionshead Village, which were almost empty. The snow had chased everyone inside—except for a few kids who had come out to have snowball fights. Erica led me away from the Arabelle into an area devoted to shopping. Strangely, every store seemed to sell either ski equipment or T-shirts, as though there were nothing else to buy in the entire world.

"Where are we going?" I asked.

"To get some answers. Speaking of which, was Mike any help?"

"I think so." For now I decided to leave out the part where Mike had figured out I was a spy. "He said that if I wanted to win Jessica back over, you need to pretend as though you really like me in front of her."

Erica gave me a sidelong glance. "I'll bet."

"He did. I swear. He says that once Jessica sees that *you* like me, that will make *her* interested in me again."

"If Jessica doesn't like you now, why would she like you more once she realizes that I'm interested in you?"

"Because she *did* like me before. But then she liked Mike. Only Mike liked *you* instead of her. Which is why she doesn't like you. So now, if she thinks you like me, she'll want to make me like her again to get even with you for making Mike like you instead of her."

Erica shook her head, dumbstruck. "The mind of a teenage girl is the most complicated thing I've ever encountered. And I know how to defuse a nuclear bomb."

"*You're* a teenage girl," I pointed out.

"So I've heard. Here we are." Erica stopped in a small public square and pointed to a doorway wedged between two ski equipment shops. The name on the door said Epic Heli-Skiing. Erica yanked me toward it.

I dug my heels in. Or at least, I tried to. The ground was slippery with new snow, and Erica ended up dragging me across the pavement. "Hold on," I said. "This is the company Leo Shang used."

"Yes."

"So you want to find out where he went in the helicopter yesterday?"

"Yes."

"Well, don't you think we ought to have a plan first?"

"I *do* have a plan."

"Is it a plan where you create a diversion by knocking me over or shoving me down a flight of stairs or something else painful like that while you break in and hack the computer?"

"Yes."

"That's a lousy plan."

"No, it's not. It works all the time."

"I mean it's lousy for *me*," I said. "Isn't there some sort of diversion that doesn't involve me getting hurt?"

Erica sighed like I was being unreasonable. "Fine. But I'm going to need you to cry."

"Why?"

"I need you to pretend that you're a lost and scared kid, and while they're diverted with that, I'll hack the computers."

This didn't sound much better than the previous plan. "Um, Erica . . . I'm not six years old. I'm thirteen."

"Yeah, but you can act younger. And a crying kid is a crying kid. Now, can you fake tears—or do you need me to hurt you?"

"I can fake them!" I said quickly. Erica was the school expert at producing pain. Before I could protest any more, she'd yanked me through the door into Epic Heli-Skiing.

Even though heli-skiing was expensive, it didn't look like much money had been spent on decorating the offices. A long, dingy hallway led between the ski shops toward a room tucked behind them. The walls had ancient wood paneling, the floor was cement—and though there were lots of framed photos of people going heli-skiing, they were all dusty and hanging askew. I could hear a male voice on the phone at the far end of the hall, selling the experience. "Dude, you don't even have to come here. We'll pick you up at your hotel and take you right to the helipad."

"Start crying," Erica whispered to me, in a way that indicated she'd make me cry if I didn't obey her.

I did my best, sniffling quietly.

Erica frowned, unimpressed. "I need *major* crying. Like a kid who's lost and frightened. Not a kid who just bit his lip."

I gave it another shot, bawling loudly.

The guy on the phone in the office paused in mid-sentence. "Uh . . . Hold on," he said.

Erica morphed from her normal, cold self into a surprisingly concerned persona. "That's all right," she cooed in a soothing tone. "We'll find your parents, I promise. I'm sure someone here can help us."

We entered the main office. If anything, it was less impressive than the entry hall had been. Apparently, most clients never visited the offices of Epic Heli-Skiing. Most of the room was used for storage. The walls were lined with high-performance skis and boots, as well as some high-tech black vests that looked like something commandos would wear. In the middle of it all was a single desk piled high with medical release forms. A guy who looked like he'd barely graduated from high school sat at it, the phone cupped to his ear, gaping at us as if he wasn't used to seeing people there. He wore an official Epic Heli-Skiing parka with a name patch that said SLEDGE. There was a vacancy in his gaze that indicated he wasn't the brains of the operation. "Hey, guys," he said. "Something wrong?"

Erica gave me a hard stare, indicating it was time for me to start playing my role. "I lost my mommy!" I bawled.

"I found him wandering by the gondola," Erica told Sledge, speaking as though she were fifteen years older than me, rather than merely two and a half. "I'd have called his mom myself, but the battery on my phone died."

"Aw, man, that stinks," Sledge said. "I hate when my phone dies."

It was evident that Sledge found Erica attractive and that he was far more interested in trying to connect with her than he was in trying to help me.

"Could we use *your* phone?" Erica asked.

"Uh, yeah. Sure." Sledge returned his attention to his call and said, "Can I ring you back in a few? Thanks." Then he hung up and started to hand the phone to Erica, although he got distracted by her beauty. "So . . . how long are you in town for?"

I was forced to kick things up a notch to get him back on

track. I started crying even harder, making a scene. "I want my mommy! I want my mommy!"

Sledge turned back to me, making a show of being cool for Erica. "Don't worry, little dude," he said. "We'll find her. How old are you?"

"Nine," I said, hoping that wasn't too much of a lie.

Apparently, it was. "Nine?" Sledge asked. "You look pretty old for nine."

"He obviously has some sort of gland problem," Erica whispered to him. "Don't rub it in. He's upset enough as it is."

"Oh," Sledge said, worried he'd just made an awful mistake.

"Do you know your mom's phone number?" Erica asked me. Behind Sledge's back, she nodded, indicating what my answer should be.

"Uh-huh." I sniffed. And then I rattled off a phone number I knew wouldn't be answered by a person. One of the perks of being extremely gifted in math is that I never forget a phone number. Like the information line for the Smithsonian's National Air and Space Museum.

Erica took the phone from Sledge, dialed it, and let it ring until the automated voice came on. She allowed Sledge to overhear just a second of this—enough to recognize it was a recorded message, rather than a human being—then hung up. "She's not answering," Erica told me.

"Oh no!" I cried. And then I pretended like I was on the

verge of completely freaking out, whimpering and hyperventilating.

Sledge stepped away from me warily, as though I might explode. "What's wrong with him?"

"He's panicking," Erica said. "We need to calm him down. Can you get him a glass of water or something?"

"Uh . . . There's no bathroom here," Sledge said. "We have to use the public one by the gondola."

I saw my opening and went for it. "I think I'm gonna throw up," I wailed.

"No!" Sledge yelped, far more worried about me puking in his office than he had been about me being lost. "I don't want to clean that up! Can you hold it?"

I slapped my hands to my lips and bulged my cheeks out, as though I were trying to hold the vomit inside at that very moment.

Sledge leapt into action, grabbing me by the arm and racing me back down the hallway. "Keep it in! Keep it in!" he ordered, close to panic himself.

We barged back outside. Rather than lead me to the bathroom, Sledge aimed me directly for a decorative planter. In the summer, it probably held flowers, but now it only had a few inches of snow piled up in it. "There you go," he told me. "Puke away." Then he quickly backpedaled away from me, like he was allergic to vomit.

He gave me plenty of room and was desperately trying to look anywhere but at me, so I figured he'd never notice if I actually threw up or not. I bent over the planter and pretended to barf, nice and loud for him. "Bleeeeeeaaaarrrr-ghhhhh."

"Are you done?" Sledge asked hopefully.

I shook my head no, wanting to buy Erica as much time as possible. I stayed hunched over the planter, clutching my stomach. Then I waited, letting the seconds tick by.

Eventually, Sledge edged a little closer to me. "You sure that wasn't it?"

"Bleeeeeeaaaarrrrghhhhh!" I gagged, pretending to throw up again.

Sledge scrambled away from me once more. A few passing tourists did the same, giving me a wide berth.

I waited some more, giving Erica more time, until I sensed Sledge nearing once again.

I added a third fake vomit. A nice long one. "Bleeeeeeeeeeeaaaaaarrrrrgggghhhhhhhhh!" And then I steadied myself against the planter, trembling like I was ill.

"Are you okay?" Sledge asked, finally sounding worried about me.

"I could really use some water," I gasped.

"Right. Okay. I'll go get you some." Sledge seemed thrilled to have a reason to get away from me and the pile of theoretical vomit I was creating. "I'll be back in a bit!" He raced off toward the public bathroom.

The moment he had disappeared around the corner, I ducked back inside Epic Heli-Skiing. Erica was bent over the computer, quickly dragging files to a flash drive.

"Sledge went to get me some water," I told her. "It ought to take him a minute or two."

"Don't need it. I'm done." Erica plucked the flash drive out of the computer, stuck it in her pocket, and blew past me, heading for the door. "They didn't have any security at all on this computer. Not even a password. It was so easy to crack, even *you* could have done it."

I let this dig slide and dropped in behind her as we emerged back outside. "What'd you get?"

"The logs for the past few days of helicopter skiing. So I could see exactly where Leo Shang went." Erica sniffed the air, then looked at me curiously. "I don't smell any vomit," she said. "Didn't you vomit?"

"Nope. I faked it."

"You did a heck of a job. I could hear you all the way inside. It sounded like you were puking up your own intestines."

"Thanks." Erica didn't compliment me much. I was willing to take whatever I could get.

She led me across the public square, in the opposite

direction Sledge had gone, and we slipped into yet another ski equipment store, where we hunkered down between some racks of winter jackets. Erica pulled a small computer from her pocket. I'd seen her father use a similar one once before; it looked like an amped-up mobile phone. Erica jacked the flash drive into it and brought up the data she'd swiped. It appeared as several long columns of numbers, each with a time next to it.

I smiled. I wasn't particularly good with most spy things, like fighting or shooting. But I was great with numbers. "Those are coordinates?"

"Exactly." Erica unzipped her parka, revealing that she was now wearing one of the high-tech black vests from Epic Heli-Skiing. "This is a backcountry skiing vest. It has built-in GPS tracking."

"You stole that!" I said, a little too loudly.

"I commandeered it," Erica corrected. "It's evidence. When heli-skiers go into the backcountry, there's serious avalanche danger. This vest has some built-in protection against those, but should all that fail and someone end up buried, the GPS will lead rescuers to them. When Epic Heli-Skiing is out there, their clients wear these at all times—and they always have the GPS on." She pointed to the columns of coordinates. The numbers changed slightly every few seconds, though only by a fraction of a decimal point. "As you can see, the GPS is incredibly accurate, pinpointing the location of each skier down to the inch throughout the entire day."

Out the window, I saw Sledge returning with a cup of water for me. He paused in the public square where he'd left me and looked around. He seemed quite relieved I was no longer there for him to deal with. Then he drank the water himself and headed back into the office.

Erica pointed to the last column of coordinates. "Now, the helicopter also has a GPS unit, so if it crashes, rescuers can find it. This is the data from a heli-skiing trip five days ago, and you can see that the coordinates from the helicopter match those of the skiers when the skiers are in the helicopter, but differ when the skiers are actually skiing."

"Yes," I agreed. "When did you learn all this about helicopter skiing?"

"The other night, after I learned that Leo Shang was doing it, I spent a few hours familiarizing myself with the sport. Research is very important in our line of work." Erica brought up another screen full of coordinates. "Now, these are from yesterday: the day you saw Leo Shang wearing that button-down shirt. Notice anything interesting about them?"

I stared at the screen as Erica scrolled through the numbers. It didn't take long to notice what she meant. "The coordinates for the skiers and the helicopter are exactly the same."

"Exactly. You were right. Leo Shang *didn't* go heli-skiing

that day. He never got out of the helicopter. Instead, he used that chopper for something else. Some kind of reconnaissance, most likely."

"Even though there was a pilot from Epic flying it?"

"Why not? Shang could have bribed the pilot to do what he wanted. Or maybe the pilot didn't even know what was going on. He might have figured he'd lucked into an easy day, giving some rich guy a sightseeing tour instead of chasing skiers around."

"So what do we do now?" I asked. "Tell your grandfather?"

"For starters." Erica flipped the computer off and stuffed it into her pocket. "Plus, it looks like I'm gonna be flirting with you heavily tomorrow. There's only two days left until Operation Golden Fist goes down. You need to get closer to Jessica Shang, and you need to do it fast."

FLIRTATION

Northwoods Basin

Vail Mountain

December 29

1300 hours

"That's what I want to see, Ben!" Woodchuck exclaimed enthusiastically. "Those are excellent turns!"

I slid to a textbook stop next to my fellow classmates, who had been waiting for me halfway down the run. They all cheered for me.

Jawa proudly fist-bumped me. "You've gotten ten times better since yesterday! How'd you do that?"

"I just practiced yesterday afternoon," I replied, doing my best to sound humble. It was hard, though. Because I had finally found something athletic that I was actually good at.

Ever since I'd arrived at spy school, everyone else had constantly bested me at tests of skill and feats of physical prowess. Erica was capable of anything, from climbing a sheer rock face to beating up ninjas—often at the same time. Chip, Jawa, and Zoe were all impressive as well. Warren wasn't, but he was so good at camouflaging himself that our instructors tended to overlook his other flaws. (They often overlooked him, period, because they couldn't find him.) Meanwhile, I had been constantly humiliated: flattened by kung fu masters, winded from long runs, flunked off the artillery range for nearly wounding people. Sports had never been my thing.

But something had clicked with skiing. My ordeal coming down Simba the day before had pushed me to the next level. Vail had received more than two feet of snow overnight—and more was falling—and I had skied through it far better than any of the other beginner students. I had even managed to get down some advanced runs without wiping out.

Meanwhile, Erica was still struggling. She wasn't bad, really. She simply wasn't fantastic at it. But this was incredibly frustrating to her. Erica had the opposite issue with skiing that I did: It was the first physical activity she'd ever come across that she *hadn't* mastered with ease. That morning, while I'd been getting cheers and kudos, she'd been getting sympathetic pats on the back and the occasional "Nice try."

She hid all her frustration from Jessica Shang, though. Instead, for Jessica's benefit, she remained in character, upbeat and harebrained, shrugging off each wipeout with a ditzy giggle.

She was also in full-on flirtation mode with me. Now, in front of the entire class, she came up beside me and blatantly fluttered her eyelashes. "You are soooo good at this!" she cooed. "Maybe *you* ought to be the one giving me lessons."

Even though I knew Erica was acting, my face still flushed. I felt like it was a hundred degrees outside instead of snowing. "Sure. Maybe today after class."

Over Erica's shoulder, I caught a glimpse of Jessica frowning. I also got glimpses of everyone else in class, staring at Erica in shock. Seeing Erica flirt—even when they knew it was fake—was like seeing a flying cow. It simply didn't seem possible.

"That's very sweet," Woodchuck teased, "but for right now, *I'm* still the instructor here. We're going to all head down this run one at a time to the lift, and I want to see each of you make your parallel turns as well as Ben just did. Sasha, you first."

"Okay. Here goes nothing!" Erica cried gamely. She pushed off with her poles and wobbled down the hill. She struggled through a few turns, making them without any of her normal grace, crying "Oopsie!" with each one.

The rest of us lined up to watch her. To my surprise, Jessica pulled up next to me. "Hey," she said, nice and friendly, as though she hadn't been giving me the cold shoulder for the past day and a half. "What is up with that girl? I thought she was all into your friend."

"It didn't work out," I lied. "Mike met someone else."

"Really?" Jessica seemed pleased that Erica had failed to land Mike. "So now she turns around and throws herself at you?"

"She's not throwing herself at me. She only asked me for some help skiing."

"Yeah, right." Jessica laughed and shook her head. "She's so sad."

I turned to her, trying to hide my surprise. Mike had been right. Jessica wasn't exactly fluttering her eyelashes at me the way Erica had done, but she was definitely being friendly again—and it all seemed to be in response to Erica's interest in me.

Erica was now well down the run from us, so far we could barely hear her "oopsies" anymore.

"Okay, Warren," Woodchuck announced. "Your turn. Rip it!"

"Check this out," Warren told the rest of us proudly. He

jammed his ski poles into the ground, intending to launch himself onto the slope. Instead, as he slid forward, he caught his ski tips on both poles. The skis stopped short, Warren's boots popped out of his bindings, and he flopped forward into the snow.

Chip, Jawa, and Zoe all broke into laughter.

"Very impressive," Chip teased. "Most people wait until they've actually skied a bit before wiping out. But you did it right out of the gate."

Warren staggered to his feet, spluttering. He had a face full of fresh snow. Somehow, it had gotten into his goggles, blinding him. "It's not funny," he told Chip, although, since he couldn't see, he said it to a tree instead.

"That's right," Woodchuck agreed, although it was obvious that he actually thought it was *very* funny. "Zoe, why don't you head on down while I get Warren back on his skis?"

"Sure thing." Zoe started down the slope. She was getting the hang of skiing herself and performed quite well.

Down at the bottom of the run, Erica snowplowed to a stop, then cheered for herself as though she'd just won the World Cup downhill. "I did it!" she yelled up to us. "No falls! Woo-hoo!"

Jessica sighed dismissively, then asked me, "You're not really going to give that dingbat a lesson this afternoon, are you?"

"She's not that dumb," I said, acting like I was really into Erica—which wasn't really acting at all. "She's nice. And I don't have anything else to do."

"You could come by the hotel again," Jessica said coyly. "I never did get to show you our suite."

I turned to her, surprised. I didn't like the games she was playing, but I faked enthusiasm anyhow. Like I'd forgotten all about Erica. "Sure!" I told her. "I'd love to!"

INFILTRATION

The Arabelle Hotel

Presidential Suite

Vail, Colorado

December 29

1600 hours

Jessica stayed close to me the rest of the day.
Close enough that Erica and I didn't have much time to discuss what I should do once I was in the Shangs' suite. So, at the end of our lesson, in the bustle of storing our ski equipment, Erica deftly slipped what looked like a pack of gum into the pocket of my parka and jammed a radio transmitter in my ear. "I'll be in touch," she informed me, and then melted into the crowd.

Jessica took care of getting me into the suite. Dane Brammage and the other guards obviously didn't want me there, but Jessica faced them all down in the lobby of the Arabelle. "I'm only taking Ben up to show him our place," she said crossly. "That's all. What's the point of my father renting an entire hotel if I can't bring guests into it?"

Dane gave me a wary look, and then, to my surprise, spoke to Jessica in fluent Chinese. Obviously, it was done so I couldn't understand him—and it would have served its purpose well had Erica not been able to overhear the entire conversation through my radio. Erica couldn't translate everything to me as it happened—if she spoke to me, that overrode her ability to hear what the others were saying—so she told me, "Keep quiet so I can hear this," and then eavesdropped as Jessica and Dane bickered back and forth. Through it all, Jessica grew angrier and angrier, until she finally stamped her foot and launched into a furious tirade, yelling at Dane for more than a minute. Even though I didn't know what she was saying, it was still kind of scary. In fact, even Dane himself seemed frightened of her—and he was a professional criminal. "All right," he conceded, speaking English once again—and looking a bit shaken. "You can go up. But only for a little while."

He didn't let us go up alone, though. And he frisked me first.

"For crying out loud," Jessica snapped. "He's a kid from my ski school, not an assassin."

Dane kept patting me down anyhow. "It's your father's orders," he told Jessica. "Anyone who comes into the suite gets searched." Luckily, he was only looking for weapons and the pack of gum Erica had given me was small enough to escape his attention. Once he had confirmed I wasn't packing heat, he crowded into the elevator with us and rode up to the top floor.

"Sorry about that," Jessica told me, rolling her eyes. "My father can be *way* too overprotective sometimes."

"Yeah," I agreed. "Parents are the worst." I didn't really believe this, but I was doing anything I could to forge a connection.

"You're lucky," Jessica said. "You got to come out here without your family. I've got Daddy and all his apes tagging along with me."

"Hey!" Dane said, sounding genuinely hurt. "I'm just doing my job."

Jessica ignored him. "This is supposed to be a vacation and Daddy's acting like it's yet another business trip."

The elevator reached the top floor and opened directly into the Presidential Suite. We stepped off into a beautiful entry hall lined with white marble.

"Maybe it *is* another business trip," I said, as innocently as I could.

Jessica looked at me curiously. "What's that supposed to mean?"

I shrugged. "My dad never just goes on vacation. Instead, he drags us all along to these stupid conventions and works the whole time."

Jessica frowned, like I'd struck a nerve. For a second, I was afraid she was angry at *me*, but then she started ranting about her father. "You're probably right. My father never takes any time off either. He probably *is* here for some business thing. . . ."

While she talked, I quickly cased the suite. It took up the entire top floor of the building, and it was even more decadent than I'd expected. It had a wide-open floor plan with an enormous living room, a dining room with a table for twenty, and a gourmet kitchen. A hallway led off to my right, toward what appeared to be at least six bedrooms. It all seemed a bit excessive given that only two people were staying there. There were big windows with incredible views of the ski mountain, a wide wraparound balcony with a Jacuzzi that probably would have been great if it weren't only fifteen degrees outside, two fireplaces—both with fires roaring in them—Tiffany chandeliers, and a grand piano. There were also two other guards posted there, one by the balcony door and one by the piano. Both wore suits and stood ramrod-straight, looking like they'd been at attention all day, even though no one but them had been in the suite.

Dane ushered us through the entry hall and into the living room. The other guards both glanced at me warily, obviously wondering what I was doing there. Dane subtly pointed to Jessica.

If Jessica noticed any of this, she didn't let on. Instead, she was rambling on about her father. "Daddy promised me he wasn't going to work on this trip," she was saying, "but he's doing it anyhow. He was on the phone doing business all last night. He didn't even stop for dinner with me. I wonder if he's really even been skiing during the day. For all I know, he's been sneaking off to deals. . . ."

"Would you like anything to drink, Ben?" Dane asked. His tone was surprisingly kind, given how standoffish he'd been around me so far. I got the impression he was trying to divert us from talking about Leo Shang's business.

It worked. At least where Jessica was concerned. "Hot chocolate?" she suggested, before I could answer.

"Sure," I agreed. "If you have it."

"We have anything we could possibly want," Jessica told me. "We just have to call the restaurant and they'll bring it up."

"Then what's the kitchen for?"

"People who like to cook, I guess." Jessica picked up the room phone and dialed the restaurant. "Hey, this is Jessica. Can you send up two hot chocolates? Oh, and some graham crackers and chocolate and marshmallows too." Jessica looked to me excitedly. "We can make s'mores in the fireplace!"

"Cool," I said supportively, wondering what it was about the mountains that made people want to make s'mores.

"I hate to interrupt this awesome date you're having," Erica said, inside my ear, "but you need to can the small talk and get some work done. Ask if you can go to the bathroom."

As usual with the earpiece, the conversation was one-way. I couldn't argue to Erica that I was *trying* to get work done. I had to suck up the criticism, turn to Jessica, and ask, "Is there a bathroom here?"

Jessica laughed. "Only seven of them. There's one in the hall."

She pointed. So did Dane. He was standing right next to it.

"Thanks," I said, and slipped inside.

The bathroom was more nicely decorated than my entire house. Every fixture was gold-plated. The toilet was fully automated. The lid rose automatically for me as I entered, which I found kind of disturbing.

"Sit down," Erica told me. "Let them think you're gonna be in there for a bit. We have a lot to discuss."

I wasn't exactly sure how to convey that I was going to be a while through the bathroom door, but I did my best. I dropped my pants to my ankles as loud as I could and sat down on the toilet with a loud sitting-on-the-toilet sort of sigh.

To my surprise, the toilet began to play music. It was probably supposed to be comforting, some sort of melody to soothe you while you pooped, but the whole idea of a musical toilet just weirded me out.

"Okay," Erica said. "You don't have much time in that suite. Here's the basic gist of that showdown in the lobby: Dane didn't want to let you up there, but Jessica told him that if he didn't, she'd go outside the hotel and make a scene. It might seem like Dane gave in to her, but the whole goon squad definitely has their guard up. The moment you got in the elevator, the guys in the lobby called Leo Shang. I'm watching them right now, and from the way they're behaving, I'll bet Shang is on his way back—and he's not going to be happy when he gets there. So . . . take out the gum I gave you."

I did. The reason it had looked like a pack of gum was that it *was* a pack of gum. Or at least, it was the pack the gum came in. I opened it to find five small black objects. Each was a disc the size of an M&M.

"Those are bugs," Erica explained. "There's adhesive coating on them, so they'll stick to anything. Each has a range of only about twenty feet, so you'll need to spread them out through the suite. Place them as centrally as you can. They'll cover more area that way. Understand?"

"Mmm-hmm," I agreed, trying to make it sound like a toilet-related noise in case Dane was listening through the door.

"Good. And get Jessica back to talking about her father. Fast. Whatever you can find out is crucial. Once Leo catches you up there, he's probably going to flip and block you from ever getting close to his daughter again. So stop sitting around and get to it."

I wanted to point out that I was only sitting in the first place because Erica had told me to. Instead, I kept quiet and hopped back off the toilet. It flushed automatically, the music stopped, and the lid closed again. I plucked the five bugs out of the gum pack and stuck them to my wrist inside the sleeve of my undershirt. Then I yanked up my ski pants, made a show of washing my hands—again, in case Dane was listening through the door—and exited the bathroom.

Jessica was now seated on a couch by one of the fireplaces. She had removed her parka and was leafing through a glossy magazine. "Hey," she said. "You can take your jacket off if you want."

"Thanks." The heat seemed to be cranked up to the eighties in the room, and with two fires going, I was already starting to sweat under my ski clothes. Although it was very possible that I was sweating due to fear as well. It was incredibly nerve-racking to be in enemy territory with armed goons scrutinizing my every move. I shrugged off my jacket and looked for a place to hang it.

"Dane, can you take that?" Jessica asked.

Dane dutifully stepped forward and accepted my jacket, though it was clear he didn't appreciate being made into a butler.

"Thanks," I said again. Luckily, the sleeves of my undershirt were just long enough to keep the bugs hidden.

"So?" Jessica asked, waving around the suite. "What do you think?"

"It's amazing," I said. "Can I see the rest of it?"

"Sure!" Jessica hopped off the couch and led me back down the hall. Alarmed, Dane instantly moved after us. Jessica didn't appear bothered that he was upset. If anything, she seemed pleased that she was rattling him.

There was a small table in the hallway by the elevator. It served no purpose except to hold an extremely large vase of flowers that had probably been flown in from halfway across the world at tremendous expense. As I passed it, I quickly stuck one of the bugs under the table, where it clung like a piece of gum on the base of a school desk. It was a move I'd practiced plenty of times in my Intro to Enemy Surveillance class, and I did it so fluidly, Dane didn't even notice. Or at least, he didn't *appear* to. I figured the bug would cover any conversation spoken around the elevator.

One down, four to go.

Jessica blew past the first few doors off the hallway. "These are all extra bedrooms. I think this place holds, like, sixteen people. Or maybe it was twenty. Anyhow, there's a lot of rooms we don't need."

"Not counting the whole rest of the hotel," I pointed out.

"Well, Dane and the other guards are staying here too."

"Still, you're renting out *an entire hotel*." I tried to think of a tactful way to get back to the subject of Leo Shang, then decided I didn't have enough time for subtlety. Instead, I did my best to sound concerned, rather than suspicious. "Why do you need all this space? And all the guards? Is your family in danger?"

Jessica laughed. "No, Daddy just likes his privacy. Here's my room." She led me into a bedroom that was larger than my entire house. There was a whole other sitting area, a flatscreen TV, and another piano—just in case the one in the living area wasn't enough.

"My father likes privacy too," I told her, "but he doesn't rent out entire hotels."

"No offense," Jessica replied, "but I'll bet your father can't afford entire hotels."

"*No one* can afford entire hotels. Except your father and maybe a couple sheiks."

"I guess. Wait until you see *his* room." Jessica led me back into the hall.

I quickly stuck the second bug underneath the keyboard of the piano and followed Jessica. It wasn't a great location, but I didn't have time to find a better one. Two down, three to go.

Jessica opened the door to her father's room. Given the rest of the suite, I'd prepared for it to be impressive, but even so, the sheer size of it took my breath away. It was bigger than the Ski Haüs motel. For the life of me, I couldn't imagine why anyone would need a bedroom so large—especially when they had the whole rest of the suite.

I plucked another bug off my wrist as I started through the door.

Only, Dane stepped in front of us, blocking our way. "Sorry, Jessica, but your father doesn't want anyone else in here."

"Oh, lighten up," Jessica taunted. "I'm just gonna show him the room real fast."

Dane stepped aside, waved an arm to the master suite, then stepped right back into our path again. "There. Now he's seen it real fast. Please return to the living area."

Jessica growled in frustration. "This is ridiculous. This is my suite too. What does Daddy think we're gonna do? Steal his shoes?"

Dane's bulk filled the door so well, I could barely see any of the room behind him. Only a sliver of it. I caught a glimpse of an unmade king-size bed with dirty clothes strewn on it. A silver case the size of a steamer trunk poked out from behind the bed.

The case didn't seem like normal luggage, but it didn't appear I was going to get a closer look. Dane wasn't about to let us in the room. So I quickly stuck a bug on the side of the doorjamb. Since the bedroom was much bigger than the bug's twenty-foot range, I'd just have to hope that, if Shang did discuss anything important, he would do it near the door. Three bugs down, two to go.

Dane spoke to Jessica in Chinese again. He sounded very annoyed.

Jessica heaved an angry sigh, spun on her heel, and stormed back toward the living area. "Looks like the tour's over, Ben. I'm not even allowed to show you my whole suite."

I followed her. "What'd he say?"

"Nothing," Jessica muttered.

"Actually," Erica said in my ear, "he said, 'You have already tempted fate by bringing this boy up here. If you push it any further, don't be surprised when your father cancels the rest of this vacation.'"

It occurred to me that even though Jessica's father had given her far more than most people could ever dream of, she was still annoyed by the boundaries he'd set for her. So

I decided to see what I could do with that. "Is your father always like this with your friends?"

"Always," Jessica echoed. "He's the world's biggest control freak. If you think this place is big, you should see our house. We have our own movie theater, an Olympic-size swimming pool, a trampoline room . . . But does he ever let me even bring anyone over there? No. I've never been allowed to have a movie night, or a slumber party, or anything. And half the time when I make friends, I swear, he scares them off. I don't know how, but he does it. One day they're nice to me—and the next they act like I've got the plague."

We arrived back in the living room. Dane resumed his place by the entry hall, staring at me ominously. The other two guards hadn't moved, but they now fixed me with equally intimidating stares. I glanced toward them. "I can see how that'd happen."

"It makes me angrier than a wet panda," Jessica seethed.

I didn't have the slightest idea what she was trying to say in English this time, so I didn't even bother trying to correct her. Instead, I did my best to be supportive. "I don't blame you."

"Ben," Erica said in my ear. "I just heard from my grandfather. Leo Shang's caravan is en route to the hotel and moving fast. You have five minutes left, max."

All three guards' hands went to their ears at the same time. Each of them probably had an earpiece as well. And they were all getting similar information. Only, they were getting it from Shang.

Jessica flopped on the couch, exasperated. "I know it must seem insanely cool to be as rich as I am, but it *sucks*. I mean, I like having a huge house and a private jet and our own island and all the ponies I want, but . . . it'd be nice to be normal for once. To go somewhere without all these jerks . . ." She waved a hand toward the guards.

"Now, that's just mean," Dane said, sounding hurt once again.

". . . or to have a friend who likes me for just being *me*," Jessica continued. "And not the fact that I'm rich."

"I didn't know you were rich when I met you," I said supportively. "And I liked you for being you."

Jessica gave me a shy smile. "Really?"

"Really," I said, and I meant it. I was actually starting to feel kind of sorry for her. I sat on the couch next to her, shifting another bug to my free hand. "I don't care that you're rich."

"You'd be the first." Jessica's eyes suddenly narrowed suspiciously. "And you've been asking an awful lot of questions about what my father does."

This caught me completely by surprise. "Er, yeah," I stammered, scrambling to come up with an answer. "Because I, um . . . I thought he, uh . . . might be a criminal."

Which was probably a mistake.

Jessica gaped at me in shock. Dane and the other guards in the room tensed.

"Tell me you didn't just say that," Erica said in my ear.

But I had. And there was no way to undo it. I held my breath while Jessica and her guards stared at me. The most uncomfortable silence I had ever experienced filled the room.

And then Jessica burst into laughter. "Daddy? A criminal? That's ridiculous!"

Dane and the guards laughed too, like this was the funniest thing they'd ever heard.

I did my best to hide my relief, then soldiered on, acting like I'd been joking all along. "Well, he *is* kind of suspicious. He's got, like, a billion dollars. And all these security guys. And when I met him in the lobby the other day, he was, well . . . pretty scary."

"I know." Jessica sighed. "He can be a huge pill sometimes. But I swear, he's not a criminal."

"So he's really going helicopter skiing every day?" I teased. "Not plotting some sort of world domination?"

Jessica giggled. "Well, he did spend yesterday in a secret underground lair with a bunch of evil world leaders."

I laughed along with her, definitely getting the vibe that her jokes were merely jokes. Either she truly believed her father was an honest businessman—or she was one heck of an actress.

Dane and his fellow goons didn't seem to think any of

this was funny at all, though. They were growing more and more on edge by the second.

"Okay, Romeo," Erica said over the radio. "Shang's caravan is pulling up right now. T minus three minutes until he's up there."

I wanted to stick the fourth bug under the coffee table, but Jessica and all three guards were staring right at me. So for the moment, I held back and gave my best acting a shot. I asked, nice and innocent, as though it had just occurred to me, "Who *is* your father skiing with?"

Jessica stopped laughing. "What do you mean?"

"You guys didn't come here with any friends, right? Because they'd be staying in the hotel. So who's your father skiing with every day?"

Jessica pursed her lips thoughtfully. "You know, I'm not sure."

"Is he just going by himself?"

Jessica considered this some more. "No. He must have some friends here. The other day, right before he left, I heard him say he was going to see someone named Molly."

The moment she said this, the three guards in the room grew even more alert than they already were.

I pretended not to notice.

"Molly who?" Erica pressed.

"Molly who?" I repeated.

Jessica looked at me suspiciously, as though I had just asked one question too many. So did the three guards.

"I have an aunt named Molly who lives near here," I said quickly, trying to cover. "It'd be really weird if your dad knew her."

Jessica's suspicions seemed to fade. "You're right, that would," she agreed. "I think he said her name was Molly Denham. Or something like that. Is that your aunt?"

"No," I said.

Dane was suddenly at our side, doing his best to look like he was being a gracious host, rather than a guard trying to divert us from what we'd been discussing again. "Hey, kids, I just got word that your hot chocolate is on the way up, along with your s'more fixings. Maybe we should get the fireplace ready."

"Okay!" Jessica agreed enthusiastically, completely diverted. She leapt to her feet and went to move the grating from in front of the fireplace.

"Obviously, you struck a nerve there," Erica told me. "The big guy's doing damage control. And Shang's coming in hot. Making a beeline from the car to the elevators. Not looking happy."

I got to my feet as well, acting like I was trying to help Jessica, though I really took the opportunity to finally stick the fourth bug underneath the coffee table. One to go.

"I *love* s'mores," Jessica said to me. "Don't you love s'mores?"

"I do," I said, even though I didn't like them all that much. I was doing my best to be agreeable, trying to figure out how to get her back onto the subject of her father's business before he showed up again. "S'mores are awesome."

Jessica picked up an enormous fireplace poker. "Think we could roast the marshmallows on *this*?"

"If the marshmallows were each ten pounds," I said.

Jessica laughed once more, and then a thought struck her. "Hey, remember when I told you my father would take me heli-skiing at the end of the week if I got good enough?"

"Yeah?"

"Well, maybe you could come with us too!"

"Really?" I asked, genuinely surprised. "Are you sure your dad would be okay with that?"

"Sure. He's not *always* a jerk. I know he seems scary at first, but he's a big old teddy bear when you get to know him." Jessica's eyes were alive with excitement now, the firelight dancing in them. "So what do you say? It'd be soooo much fun."

"Sure," I said. "I'd love to go with you."

"All right!" Jessica exclaimed happily. "This is gonna be great!" And then, to my surprise, she gave me a hug.

It wasn't a big, meaningful, "I've fallen in love with you"

hug. It was a more of a quick, friendly, "hooray, we're going to go heli-skiing" hug. But Jessica was still a beautiful girl, and she smelled like rose petals, and it would have been really nice . . .

If her father hadn't walked in at that very moment.

The elevator doors pinged open and Leo Shang stormed out. He was probably already angry that I was there in the suite, but now, having seen his daughter hugging me by the fireplace, his face contorted in rage. "What is going on here?" he demanded.

Jessica sprang away from me, startled. "Oh, hi, Daddy!" she said. "Ben and I were just about to make s'mores!"

"That didn't look like making s'mores," Leo growled. "I want him out of here. Now."

The guards quickly sprang into action, swarming toward me.

"Daddy!" Jessica protested. "It was only a hug!"

Leo shifted into Chinese to speak to his daughter. Although I couldn't understand it, I definitely got the gist. It seemed to be along the lines of "First you brought this boy up here when you knew you weren't supposed to, and now *this*." Jessica tried to plead her case, but it only made Leo angrier, which made Jessica angry right back at him.

Meanwhile, the two Chinese guards took me by the arms, lifted me off the ground, and carried me to the door.

Like I was a piece of furniture, rather than a human being. With my arms constrained, I didn't have a chance to place the fifth bug.

Jessica's argument with her father was growing even more heated. She was screaming at him now, livid at the way he was dealing with me. And he was just as livid at her.

Dane met me at the elevator with my ski parka. The other two guards allowed me to use my arms just long enough to put it on, then picked me up again.

The elevator pinged open again. The waiter stepped off with the hot cocoa and s'more fixings, saw the two guards holding me while Leo and Jessica argued volcanically, and stepped right back into the elevator, figuring this probably wasn't the best time to intrude.

The guards threw me inside the elevator as well.

Jessica stormed away from Leo Shang, heading for her room. She yelled one last thing to him as she went, shifting into English, probably for my benefit. "I just spent half an hour trying to convince Ben that you were actually a nice person! And then you show up and act like the worst father in the whole world! I hate you!"

The elevator doors slid shut.

As they did, I caught a final glimpse of Leo Shang. He no longer looked angry at Jessica or me. Instead, he looked devastated by what Jessica had said to him.

"Whoa," said the room service waiter as we descended to the lobby. "What was that about?"

"I don't know," I lied.

"Looked like he wanted *you* out of there in a big way," the waiter said, then held up the tray. "Want a s'more?"

I took a single graham cracker. I was so shaken from the stress of my visit to the Shangs', I didn't think my stomach could handle anything more. "Thanks."

The elevator opened at the lobby. Two more menacing guards were waiting for me there.

The waiter immediately pointed at me. "That's the guy you want. I had nothing to do with any of this."

The guards brusquely escorted me out of the hotel, though at least this pair let me walk under my own power, rather than carrying me. They shoved me out the front door, then formed a human blockade there.

I set off down the street.

"Well," Erica said in my ear, "that was intense."

I waited until I was well out of earshot from any other people, then asked, "What set her off so much at the end there?"

"Leo told her she was grounded. No ski school for her tomorrow. Or the rest of the week. Looks like you just lost your contact." Erica didn't sound upset with me about it, like this was a failure on my part. She simply said it like it was a fact.

I still felt like I'd failed, though. "Are they leaving town?"

"Doesn't sound that way. Whatever Leo's plotting, it's still in the works."

"I only placed four bugs. I didn't have time to get the fifth down."

"Four's better than none. And you didn't have much time. I knew Shang wasn't going to be pleased to see you, but he ran you out of there a lot faster than I expected. What got him so angry at you?"

"Jessica hugged me."

Erica didn't say anything in response. I looked around for her, figuring she had to be somewhere close, where she could keep an eye on the hotel—and me. But I couldn't see her anywhere.

"Erica . . . ," I began.

"Grandpa wants you to return to base, ASAP. Going to radio silence now." With that, my earpiece went dead.

I was caught off guard by how abruptly this happened. It wasn't unusual for Erica to be blunt, but she'd been even more blunt than usual. As though she was angry at me.

I suddenly got the sense that someone was watching me. I turned back toward the Arabelle.

Leo Shang stood at a window on the top floor, looking down at me. Even though he was quite far away, I could still make out his gaze. There was total and complete hatred in it, all focused directly on me. I had no idea if he was so angry simply because his daughter had hugged me—or if he suspected I was up to something more—but it was terrifying either way. I shivered, then hurried toward the Ski Haüs, fearing what Leo Shang had in store for me.

EAVESDROPPING

The Ski Haüs

Vail, Colorado

December 29

1830 hours

That night, my motel room became mission con-trol. Everyone crowded into it, grabbed what space they could, and hunched over their computers. There was no time to go out for food. We ordered pizza and everyone scarfed it down while they worked.

Hank, Jawa, Zoe, and Warren, who were all learning Chinese, were put on bug duty. They sat on the beds, each eavesdropping on a different one of the bugs I'd placed, transcribing everything they heard to English on their laptops, alerting us if anything of interest came up. Erica had commandeered the tiny bureau, where she was using her computer to try to figure out who Molly Denham was. Alexander was pacing about, on the phone with various people at the CIA, updating them on our progress and discussing how to proceed. And Cyrus was debriefing me by the bathroom, going over everything that had happened in the Shangs' suite.

Only Chip wasn't there. He'd been dispatched to the Arabelle to keep watch over it, just in case Leo Shang made a move. (Chip had been selected for this assignment because he was the only member of the team who didn't realize it wasn't as glamorous as it sounded. He'd been thrilled to get out of eavesdropping duty—only to discover that keeping tabs on the enemy at night in a ski town in winter was extremely dull and exceptionally cold.)

"I want you to really *think* about everything you saw in Leo Shang's room," Cyrus told me, taking a bite of pepperoni, meatball, ham, and sausage pizza. "Then tell me all about it."

I sighed. Cyrus had already been grilling me for an hour and he kept coming back to the master suite. "Like I said, I barely got a glimpse of it. I've already told you everything I saw. . . ."

"No," Cyrus corrected. "You've only told me everything

you *remember* seeing. Which isn't much. After all that memory training we gave you, that's the best you can do?"

"I'm doing my best."

"Well, do better. Remember *more*."

I started to protest that this was ridiculous: How could I possibly force myself to remember something that I obviously couldn't remember? But I was sure that would only annoy Cyrus, and he seemed annoyed enough with me as it was. He had already described the results of my foray into the Shangs' suite as "borderline pathetic."

So I tried to recall the tiny bit of the room I'd seen. But I could still think of only one thing. "The silver case—" I began.

"You've already mentioned that," Cyrus interrupted.

"Because it's important, isn't it? It looked a lot like the cases SPYDER used to move nuclear missiles around in, only a bit smaller."

"So your theory is, what? That Leo Shang has a small nuclear missile in his bedroom?"

"Er . . . maybe."

Alexander walked past, on the phone. "We have credible intelligence that Shang has been doing some sort of aerial reconnaissance," he was saying. "No, I don't know what he was reconnaissancing. But we believe his activities are suspicious." He listened a bit, then cupped his hand over the phone and looked to his father. "They say we need more evidence than that to authorize further action."

"I'm working on it," Cyrus muttered, then yelled to the eavesdroppers. "Bug team! What's going on?" He pointed to each of them in sequence.

"The guards in the living room are currently discussing their fantasy football teams," Zoe reported.

"Leo Shang is making calls to China in his room," Jawa said. "But as of right now, they've all been about legitimate business dealings."

"Dane Brammage has seriously bad gas," Hank said. When everyone groaned, he added, "Hey, it's not *my* fault Ben put the bug so close to the hall bathroom."

"Jessica Shang is on the phone with her mother in her room, complaining about her father," Warren said. "She's still very upset. She just called him an onion waffle." Warren reconsidered that for a moment. "Sorry. She called him a bully. I misheard. You see, Chinese is a very complex language and the slightest difference in inflection can lead to very different—"

"Erica!" Cyrus called out, before Warren could prattle on any longer. "Any luck?"

"None." Erica sighed. "Given that 'Molly' can be a nickname for either 'Mary' or 'Margaret' in addition to just being plain old 'Molly,' there is a very large number of potential

Molly Denhams in the world. However, there's only one person with any of those names in the CIA's criminal database, and it's unlikely she saw Shang this week."

"Why not?" Alexander asked.

"Because she's dead," Erica replied. "And she has been for forty years. So she probably doesn't do much helicopter skiing."

"Unless she's a zombie," Warren suggested. "Maybe Shang's evil plan is to bring the dead back to life."

Hank smacked him on the back of the head. "The only thing that's dead around here is your brain."

"Anyhow," Erica went on. "I'm trying to narrow down potential suspects by looking at those Molly Denhams who live in Colorado or those who might be in Colorado at the moment, but it's going to take a while. I've found two possibilities so far, but both washed out. One's pretty much the squeakiest clean person I've ever come across—teaches kindergarten, runs a Brownie troop, makes sandwiches for the poor—and she hasn't left Denver all week. The other one is only four years old."

"Well, keep at it," Cyrus said, then returned his attention to me. "If you'd like to remember anything else about that silver case, now would be a good time. The clock's ticking, and as of right now, that's our only lead."

"What about the information Erica got about the

helicopter?" I asked. "That was proof Leo Shang wasn't actually skiing."

"But it's not proof that he was doing anything illegal, either," Cyrus retorted.

"How about the helicopter pilot?" Jawa suggested. "He must know something about what Shang was doing up there. Why hasn't anyone talked to him yet?"

"Because he's gone missing," Cyrus replied.

Everyone paused in what they were doing and stared at him. Except Erica, who already seemed aware of this information.

"Like, dead?" Warren asked, paling.

"I don't know," Cyrus admitted. "The guy didn't show up to work today, and no one's heard from him since he flew Shang around yesterday. So, yeah, dead's a possibility. But it's not confirmed."

"Well, isn't *that* evidence Shang is up to no good?" Zoe asked.

"No," Cyrus corrected. "In fact, a missing person is the *opposite* of evidence that Shang is up to no good. Because said evidence is missing. Which brings us back to our mysterious silver case." He returned his attention to me, his eyes boring into mine. "You honestly can't remember *anything* else about it?"

"No," I said, feeling like this was a major failure. Also,

I was pretty freaked out by the fact that the helicopter pilot had vanished. If Shang had gotten rid of someone who'd simply flown him around, what would he do to someone he was *really* angry at—like me?

"Did it have any telltale markings on it?" Cyrus pressed. "Nuclear symbols, a skull and crossbones, anything that would indicate it wasn't just a big old piece of everyday luggage?"

"It wasn't everyday luggage," I told him. "It was built to hold something besides clothing."

"You can prove that?"

I grimaced. "No. It's just a hunch."

"Then for all we know, this case is just a busted goose."

"What's that?" I asked.

Cyrus frowned, like he was annoyed I didn't know this piece of CIA lingo. "A busted goose is a distraction. In the wild, when a mother goose wants to protect her ducklings from a predator, she pretends to have a broken wing to lure them away. Sometimes, our enemies do the same thing. They put something out in the open to pull our attention away from what we should really be focused on. For example, the CIA once had an agent stationed in Damascus, on the lookout for a big-time arms dealer. Well, this agent spots a suspicious-looking fellow with sunglasses and a shifty demeanor and a metal case handcuffed to his wrists, and he tails him. Turns out, the guy's a busted goose. The idiot agent gets distracted by him and the arms dealer ends up moving an entire tank right through the city without being noticed."

Alexander set down his phone, looking hurt. "Dad, for the last time, I *really* thought I had the right guy. It was an honest mistake! Anyone could have made it."

"Not anyone competent," Cyrus muttered. "The guy you followed was the most obvious decoy I've ever heard of."

"No, he wasn't," Alexander argued. "I've fallen for way more obvious decoys than that." He suddenly realized what he'd said. "Wait. That didn't come out right."

While he and Cyrus bickered, I sagged in my chair, wondering if the silver case was important or not. It had certainly seemed suspicious, but then, I had no proof that it wasn't merely designed to *look* suspicious.

"Can't we just send someone to infiltrate the suite and see what's in the case?" I suggested.

"Such a move would be exceptionally dangerous," Cyrus told me. "I'd be willing to authorize it if we had credible evidence that the case is the real deal. But without that, it's too big a risk. I can't put this mission on the line for a busted goose."

I nodded understanding and returned to racking my brain, trying to come up with the evidence Cyrus needed.

Unfortunately, I kept drawing a blank—and being penned up in the tiny room with so many other people wasn't helping. It felt as though everyone else was waiting for me to come up with something, increasing my feelings of failure and frustration.

Warren was so fixated on me, he wasn't even watching what he was doing and dropped a piece of pizza on the bed.

"Warren!" Jawa snapped. "You got tomato sauce all over my pillow!"

"It's no big deal," Warren told him. "Just call housekeeping for a new one."

"Housekeeping?" Jawa shot back. "At this place? They all went home hours ago. That's now *your* pillow."

"Fine," Warren said petulantly. "I like the smell of pepperoni."

I sat up suddenly. Cyrus was right: I *hadn't* remembered everything. "Housekeeping!" I exclaimed.

"What about it?" Cyrus asked.

"The bed wasn't made in Leo Shang's room," I explained. "And there were dirty clothes on it. But Leo had been gone all day. Now, if you were renting out an entire hotel for yourself, don't you think the housekeeping staff would clean your room? I mean, this place is a dump and they still make our beds every day."

Erica looked up from her computer, intrigued. "Ben's

right. The Shangs have the hotel's entire cleaning staff at their disposal. The only reason the room would be a mess is if Leo Shang didn't want them in his room. And that man is fastidious. He's the only person in this entire town who wears button-down shirts. So it follows that he's hiding something in there."

"We've been thinking all along that he rented the entire hotel for his own privacy," I said. "But how much privacy does anyone need? They have a suite the size of a mansion for only two people. You'd think that would be enough. But suppose it isn't just about privacy? Suppose Leo Shang is *hiding* something inside the hotel. If he's renting the whole place out, he controls the entire staff, the restaurants, and all the common areas. No one goes anywhere without his permission. . . ."

"Except his daughter," Zoe pointed out.

I swung back toward Cyrus, who didn't look nearly as frustrated with me as he had before. Now he looked pensive. "I realize that's only circumstantial evidence," I said, "but it's still evidence, right?"

"I think Ben's got something," Erica said. "It seems pretty obvious that Shang's trying to keep something secret in his room."

Cyrus didn't say anything. Instead, he grabbed his phone and called Chip.

He had the volume up loud enough that I could hear when Chip answered. "Hello?"

"Has anyone left that hotel with a large silver case?" Cyrus demanded.

"Not that I've seen. Of course, I'm only watching the main entrance. . . ."

"That's the only one that matters. They'd need a vehicle to move this thing."

"Oh. Hey, it's really cold out here, and I'm freezing." I could hear Chip's teeth chattering over the phone. "Any chance I can come back there and warm up?"

"No," Cyrus said, and hung up. Then he grabbed his jacket, heading for the door.

Alexander looked to him expectantly. "Where are you going?"

"To break into Leo Shang's room. I'm gonna find out what's in that case."

"While Shang and all his men are there?" Warren asked.

"There's no time to waste," Cyrus replied. "It isn't gonna be easy, but I've handled plenty worse in my time."

"Can I come?" Alexander asked excitedly. Like he was ten and his father was off to see a baseball game.

"Forget it," Cyrus told him. "This is a delicate operation. I can't have you screwing it up."

Alexander slunk off to pout.

Meanwhile, Erica sprang to her feet and intercepted Cyrus. "I'm the best break-and-enter person on this team."

"You're only the *second* best," Cyrus corrected. "I taught you everything you know, and I've still got gas in the tank. Besides, I need you working this Molly Denham thing."

"This Molly Denham thing is boring," Erica told him. "Make Zoe do it."

"I'm eavesdropping," Zoe pointed out.

"On two guards talking about fantasy football," Erica reminded her.

"Actually, now they're talking about who'd win in a fight: Superman or Iron Man," Zoe admitted.

"Leo Shang is still talking business," Jawa reported.

"Dane Brammage is still on the toilet," Hank said. "Man, what did that guy eat?"

"Jessica just asked her mother if she could stuff a chicken up her nose," Warren said, then reconsidered. "Oh, wait. Maybe she said she needed a tissue."

"On second thought," Cyrus told Erica, "take over for Warren. We should probably have someone who actually understands Chinese listening to the Shangs. Warren, you handle the Molly Denham thing."

"Grandpa . . . ," Erica started to protest.

"Right now, I'm not Grandpa. I'm the mission commander," Cyrus said. "And I just gave you an order."

Erica stormed over to the bed where Warren was sitting and told him, "Move."

Warren did exactly as she'd asked, handing over the headset and withdrawing to where Erica had been researching Molly Denhams.

Cyrus headed for the door again. This time I was the one who stopped him. "Agent Hale, before you go . . ."

"For criminy's sake, what now?" Cyrus groused.

"I'm sorry, sir," I told him. "But I'm a little worried Leo Shang is onto me."

Cyrus shook his head. "We've been eavesdropping on his suite ever since you bugged it and we haven't heard anything to that effect. His anger toward you appears to be solely based on his disapproval of you personally, not on any suspicion that you're a spy."

"You didn't see the look on his face when I was leaving today. He was *really* angry. It looked like a lot more than mere disapproval."

"Well, he'd just caught his daughter hugging you. And our intel suggests he is an extremely overprotective father."

"I understand that, but . . ." I paused, hesitant about adding the next part for fear that Cyrus would be dismissive of it.

He glanced at his watch impatiently. "Benjamin, for all we know, the safety of the free world may be at stake here. I don't have time for dramatic pauses."

So I said what I was worried about. "Yesterday afternoon, when I was out on the mountain after my lessons, I got the idea that someone was spying on me. I never got a good look at him, but it could have been one of Shang's men."

"It wasn't," Cyrus said definitively.

"Why don't you think so?"

"Because it was me."

I took a step back, surprised. "You? I thought you were tailing Leo Shang yesterday."

"Leo Shang was in a helicopter all day. And as you may recall, we don't have a helicopter ourselves. So that left us waiting by the helipad for him to return. As that task wasn't particularly challenging, I left my son in charge of it. I felt there was another threat that needed assessment."

It took me a moment to realize who he meant. "Mike?" I asked.

"Yes."

"You think my best friend is a threat to the CIA?"

"Oh, I don't *think* he's a threat. I *know* he's a threat. And he has been for some time. To begin with, last winter he infiltrated our campus as part of a SPYDER plot. . . ."

"He was duped into that."

"And yet he still did it. Despite numerous signs around the campus perimeter indicating that trespassing on that property is against the law. His actions then mandated a major disinformation campaign to dissuade him of the truth about our facility. Given your conversation with him on the slopes yesterday, however, I think we can assume that campaign was a failure."

"You heard that?" I asked, concerned.

Cyrus tapped the hearing aid in his ear. "I don't wear this because I'm deaf. I wear it because it's actually a unidirectional long-range listening device."

Everyone in the room had stopped eavesdropping on the Shangs and was now eavesdropping on us.

"What's this all about?" Zoe asked. "Is Mike onto us?"

"He's had some suspicions," I told her. "But I think I've put them to rest."

"You have done no such thing," Cyrus informed me. "If anything, you're directly responsible for his suspicions. After all, you have repeatedly failed to hide your spy skills and maintain a proper non-espionage persona in front of him."

"I've done my best," I argued.

"Then your best leaves a great deal to be desired. As I'm sure you're aware, academy policy is that friendships with civilians are discouraged, and your egregious handling of this one is a prime example of why that policy exists. And then, as if Mr. Brezinski weren't already enough of a threat, you allowed him to come here and jeopardize an active mission."

"I didn't have anything to do with him coming here. It was a coincidence."

"Poppycock!" Cyrus exclaimed. "There is no such thing as coincidence! Every action is the result of another action—and in this case, your actions, such as your ill-thought-out discussion at the zoo with him the other day, led to this debacle."

"Wait," I said. "How'd you know I went to the zoo with Mike the other day?"

"I'm a spy. It's my job to know things."

"Were you spying on me then?"

"I don't have to detail my personal schedule to a second-year student," Cyrus huffed. "Your friend is a significant threat to the CIA and the Academy of Espionage. We do not take threats lightly at the CIA. Instead, we assess them and determine the appropriate action to take."

"What kind of action are we talking about here?" I asked warily.

"That's classified."

"You can't do anything bad to him!" I exclaimed. "He's only a kid!"

Cyrus glared at me, fire in his eyes. "I'm fully aware how old he is! I'm not an idiot! And frankly, there are plenty of other things I would much rather be spending my time on than this fiasco. But I'm stuck with it, because I have taken responsibility for you and you have repaid me by bollixing this up. You may have performed adequately on the missions you have served on so far, Ben, but where your life outside the academy is concerned, you have been cavalier, foolhardy, and feckless. I've been forced to work overtime to ensure this doesn't all blow up in our faces, which I do not appreciate one bit. So now, if you'll excuse me, I have some actual spy work to do for once, and I'd like to take care of it."

He yanked on his jacket and stormed out of the room.

Everyone averted their eyes from me, pretending like they'd been too busy eavesdropping on the Shangs to witness my dressing down. Everyone, that is, but Warren. He sang gleefully under his breath, "Oooh. Looks like golden boy's in trouble."

"Shut up, Warren," Zoe said. "Ben's ten times the spy you are."

"Not according to Cyrus," I said, slumping into a chair. "He said I've 'performed adequately.' That's it."

"That's it?" Alexander Hale echoed. "That's the nicest thing I've ever heard my father say about anyone who wasn't Erica. My whole life, he never told me I performed adequately at anything. Even when I did. I know I've had my share of mishaps, but there have been plenty of things that I was perfectly adequate at. And did I ever hear one bit of praise? No. The nicest thing he ever said about anything *I* did was 'at least you didn't kill anybody.' And that was about a math test in fourth grade."

I turned to Erica. She seemed unusually on edge, as though she was concerned about Mike herself. "Do you know what he's planning for Mike?" I asked.

"I don't have any idea what my grandfather's thinking," she told me coldly. "As you can see, I'm not a particularly crucial part of his plan."

"Yeah, you're just a cog in the machine," Jawa said curtly. "Like the rest of us, for once."

"Cram it," Erica muttered.

"It's not so fun when someone treats you the way you always treat us, is it?" Jawa pressed.

"Lay off her, will you?" Zoe asked. "We're supposed to be working as a team here."

"A team?" Hank laughed. "We're not a team. We're a bunch of lackeys doing busywork for Cyrus Hale while he goes and gets all the glory."

"My father isn't going to steal all the glory," Alexander said defensively.

"Oh, right, that's your move," Hank told him.

With that, everyone started bickering back and forth at once, their frustrations bubbling to the surface: frustrations with their place on the mission, with how they'd been treated over the years, with everyone else in general.

I walked outside. It was rude, but I needed to get out of there. The room was too hot, too stuffy, too full of people with grudges and issues and competing agendas. Plus, it smelled like wet ski socks. I needed a breath of fresh air.

I stepped into the parking lot, took a deep breath, then exhaled a cloud of frozen vapor and watched it float away. When I'd first been told about Operation Snow Bunny, it had sounded like great fun: an adventure with my friends in an exotic location. But nothing had gone the way I'd hoped. Our accommodations were crummy, our team was constantly squabbling, Cyrus was never pleased, and my best friend was now considered a threat to the CIA. There was only one day left until Operation Golden Fist and we still hadn't achieved our objective: figuring out what Operation Golden Fist actually was. All I'd done was earn the wrath of Leo Shang.

I looked toward the pedestrian bridge over the highway, expecting to see Cyrus making his way across it toward the Arabelle, but he had already vanished from sight. Although I was annoyed at Cyrus for the way he'd treated me—and everyone else, for that matter—I hoped he would be successful in infiltrating the Shangs' suite and finding out what was in the mysterious case. I actually found myself wishing it would be something incredibly dangerous, like a nuclear bomb or a few hundred vials of some infectious disease, because then it would be concrete proof that Leo Shang was up to something evil and he could be immediately arrested. Then the case would be closed, I'd be safe again, and the whole mission would be wrapped up so we could all go home and get back to our normal lives. Well, our abnormal lives, at least.

Only, Cyrus's breaking and entering didn't work out the way anyone hoped.

DISCOVERY

Blue Sky Basin

Vail Mountain

December 30

1000 hours

Breaking into the bedroom of a target in a heavily guarded hotel wasn't easy. It took Cyrus four hours of surveillance and plotting, followed by ninety minutes of grueling physical exertion in subzero temperatures, pinpoint timing, and nerve-racking stealth. Ultimately, he managed to infiltrate Leo Shang's room as Shang slept and access the mysterious silver case—only to discover it was full of dirty underwear.

He wasn't pleased about this.

I was relieved of mission duties the next day. I probably wouldn't have had anything to do as it was, since Jessica, my target, had been grounded at her hotel and banned from ever seeing me again, but Cyrus made it *feel* like I was being punished. I was sent off to ski school, as usual, but he made it clear this was to get me out of the way. "As long as the CIA sank all the money for this snipe hunt, we might as well have you learn something," Cyrus groused, then booted me out of the motel room.

Zoe, Warren, and Erica were sent with me, as they all needed to work on their skiing more than I did. Meanwhile, Hank, Chip, and Jawa were kept back, assigned to surveillance of the Shangs. Erica protested, of course, insisting that she would be of far more use on the investigation than she would on the slopes, but Cyrus wouldn't be persuaded.

"It's December thirtieth!" Erica argued. "D-day for Operation Golden Fist! You need every person you have on this and you're sending me out to take some stupid ski lesson!"

"You need another ski lesson," Cyrus told her. "You ski like a wounded cow."

"So why not let me do something I'm good at? Like everything besides skiing? I'm the best agent you have on this mission!"

"*I'm* the best agent I have on this mission," Cyrus

corrected. "And I'm in charge of it, not you. You're learning to ski today and that's final."

Erica backed down, though she made no secret she was unhappy about it. She joined the ski lesson with Zoe, Warren, and me, but she remained sullen and peevish the entire time, making her perhaps the first person ever to view going skiing as a punishment, rather than a reward.

Meanwhile, Woodchuck was as upbeat as ever. If he knew things weren't going well, he didn't let on. Instead, he was determined to have us enjoy our day.

Woodchuck felt we were now good enough to head to one of his favorite places at Vail, an area called Blue Sky Basin. It was the most distant section of the resort, butting up against the wilderness of the White River National Forest, so far from town that you had to take multiple lifts and ski runs to get out there. Because of the trek, though, Blue Sky tended to be much less crowded than other areas of the resort.

Under most other circumstances, we probably would have considered it a fantastic ski day. The snow had finally stopped falling, but two feet of fresh powder lay on the ground, creating what Woodchuck referred to as "radical conditions." The sun was out, we were surrounded by gorgeous mountain views, and the snow sparkled like fields of diamonds. All around us, we could hear whoops of joy as skiers encountered virgin swaths of powder.

I wasn't feeling particularly joyful, though. I was still upset about how everything had fallen apart on our mission. And to make matters worse, Warren kept needling me about it. My failure was like a Christmas present for him.

"You sent Cyrus Hale to uncover a suitcase full of dirty underwear!" he exclaimed, laughing hysterically. We were riding up the main lift at Blue Sky, which took eight minutes. Zoe and Erica were on the chair in front of us, so I was stuck with Warren and Woodchuck, riding thirty feet above the ground.

"It wasn't a suitcase," I muttered.

"Sounds like a suitcase to me. I mean, it had clothes in it. Dirty clothes. Not a nuclear bomb, like *you* thought."

"I never said it had a nuclear bomb in it. I said it *looked* like the kind of case that a nuclear bomb might be in."

"Well, you were wrong." Warren laughed again. Even Warren's laugh was annoying. It was very high-pitched, making him sound like a hyena on helium.

"Just because Cyrus didn't find something in that case last night doesn't mean there wasn't something important in it earlier," I pointed out. "Think about it. Dane Brammage *knew* I'd seen into that room. Leo Shang was freaked out that I was in the hotel at all. So they easily could have moved whatever was in the case. They have an entire hotel to hide it in."

"Then why'd they put dirty laundry in the case?"

"To throw us off. If the whole case vanished, that'd be suspicious. But dirty clothes made it look like it was just a suitcase."

"Yeah, but why would they go through all that trouble? As far as they know, you're only a kid. They don't have any idea you're CIA."

I swallowed, not liking the only good answer to that question. "Well, maybe they *do* know I'm CIA."

Warren snickered again. "If that's true, then you've screwed up even worse than I thought."

The sound of an explosion suddenly echoed through the air. It was muffled, meaning it wasn't too close, but it was still near enough to startle all of us. Most kids our age probably wouldn't recognize the sound of heavy artillery exploding, but we were quite familiar with it from school. On the lift chair ahead of us, I saw Erica stiffen alertly, ready for an attack.

"Relax!" Woodchuck called to her. "It's just the ski patrol."

"The ski patrol uses a howitzer?" Erica yelled back suspiciously.

"Yes. To trigger avalanches!" Woodchuck explained. "There's been a ton of snow over the past few days. That creates perfect avalanche conditions. So the ski patrol goes out and triggers them *before* unsuspecting skiers do. See?" He pointed to our right, where a large basin known as Earl's Bowl was roped off to keep people out. In the distance, along a steep ridge, we could see a white cloud rising from where the howitzer shell had hit. As we watched, a large patch of snow sheared off at the top of a cliff and poured down into the woods at the bottom. "If it weren't for the ski patrol, that might have taken out some innocent people," Woodchuck said solemnly.

The discovery that I was heading into an area with the potential for death by avalanche didn't do much to lift my spirits. Or, unfortunately, to dampen Warren's.

"So, if Shang is onto you," he teased, "you think he might try to kill you?"

"I'm kind of hoping that's not the case," I replied. "But if he *was* planning anything, we'd know about it, right? We listened to the room all night and didn't hear anything."

"Well," Woodchuck pointed out, "if Leo Shang was really onto you, then wouldn't he suspect you bugged the room?"

"Oh," I said, suddenly feeling queasy. "I guess."

Warren snickered again, as though the idea of my being a target was the funniest thing in the world.

I found myself imagining that laugh turning into a scream as Warren suddenly fell off the chair and plummeted to the ground far below us.

Then I shoved that thought aside and tried to think of what to do. If Leo Shang really did want me dead, would his men already be tailing me? If so, I couldn't have been heading to a worse place than a remote mountain peak on the edge of the wilderness. And up on the chairlift, I was helpless. I swung around to look at the chairs behind us. I could see only the next six, but there didn't seem to be any of Shang's goons back there. There weren't many people there at all and they were all normal-size humans, as opposed to Shang's beefed-up mountains of muscle. We had reached Blue Sky before most of the other skiers. Despite this, I remained extremely worried about my safety. Maybe I was being paranoid, but then again, Shang's helicopter pilot had already mysteriously disappeared. I didn't want to be next.

I needed to discuss my potential danger with Erica, right away. However, it wasn't really the kind of conversation I was supposed to shout at the top of my lungs from one chairlift to the other.

Then it occurred to me that I might not have to. I was wearing the exact same ski outfit I'd worn the day before; after all, I had only one. The radio transmitter Erica had given me to infiltrate the Shangs' suite was still in the pocket. I stuck it in my ear, wondering if Erica had her radio on.

She did. Her radio didn't seem to be in her ear, as I could

only hear her faintly. I figured it was still in her pocket as well, probably in her parka, as it was picking up everything she and Zoe said.

I was about to try to get their attention when I heard Zoe ask, "So, what do you think about Mike?"

Rather than interrupt, I kept silent. I wanted to know what Erica thought I should do about Shang—but I really wanted to know the answer to Zoe's question, too.

"I don't think he's as big a threat as my grandfather does," Erica replied.

"I don't mean do you think he's a threat," Zoe corrected. "I mean, what do you think of him as a boy?"

"What are you doing?" Erica asked, sounding extremely confused.

"Trying to have girl talk," Zoe replied.

"What's girl talk?"

"Um, pretty much exactly what it sounds like. We're girls, and we talk about interesting stuff."

"Like possible threats to national security?"

"Er, no. Like boys."

"Why would I want to do that?"

"Because it's fun."

"It doesn't sound fun," Erica countered. "It sounds like an interrogation."

"I guess it is," Zoe admitted. "But I promise, it's way

better than that. And it goes both ways. We get to ask each other questions about boys. If you want, you can go first."

"Is this a covert conversation?"

"Absolutely. We're both sworn to secrecy."

There was a pause as Erica mulled this over. Then she said, "Do you like Warren?"

"Warren?" Zoe shrieked, loud enough so we could hear her back on our lift. Then she lowered her voice so only Erica and I could hear it and said, "Ew, gross! No way."

"Did you hear that?" Warren asked me excitedly. "Zoe's talking about me! I think she's into me."

I almost felt bad about letting Warren cling to this. But then he said, "See, girls like me because I *don't* screw up my missions."

I ignored him and went back to eavesdropping.

"Okay, your turn," Zoe said. "Do you like Mike?"

"Kind of," Erica said.

To my surprise, this made me feel almost as bad as learning that my life might be in danger.

Zoe wasn't satisfied, though. "You can't say 'kind of.' You have to say 'yes' or 'no.'"

"Why not?"

"Because 'kind of' is evasive. If you were interrogating a bad guy and you asked him if he was planning a terrorist attack, would you let him off with saying 'kind of'?"

"That's different. There's no room for nuance where public safety is concerned."

"The same goes for boys. You don't 'kind of' like a boy. You 'kind of' like asparagus. With boys, you either like them or you don't."

"Not necessarily. I could like them as a friend."

"First of all, you don't have friends. Second, we're not talking about liking someone as a friend. We're talking about *like* like. Like, would you want to date the guy?"

"I don't want to date *anybody*. Personal relationships get in the way of effective espionage."

"Not necessarily."

"They certainly did this week. Ben got all turned around with this Jessica business when Mike came along. And he was definitely upset when I started paying attention to Mike. . . ."

"Well, Ben really likes you."

"I'm well aware of that. And so, when the time came to win Jessica back over, he overdid it. He rebounded toward her much too hard, leading her on romantically instead of just trying to be friends with her."

"I read the transcripts of everything you and Ben said yesterday," Zoe said. "It didn't seem like he was leading Jessica on to me."

"The transcripts don't convey emotion. I *heard* Ben and I can assure you, he was leading Jessica on. I mean, he got her to hug him. That's not appropriate friend behavior."

"Actually, it kind of is."

"I don't think so. And she did it in front of a roaring fire, no less. And Ben made no attempt to stop her. Or to set any kind of boundaries at all. Trust me, Ben wasn't merely trying to befriend Jessica. He was trying to romance her—and it all blew up in his face."

I almost took the earpiece from my ear, feeling even worse than I had before. I hadn't thought I was doing any of what Erica said, but maybe I was wrong. Maybe I *had* overplayed my hand, leading Jessica on, getting her to hug me, and then ruining everything.

But then, to my surprise, Zoe started laughing. Hard. "Oh my gosh," she gasped. "Erica, you're hilarious."

"What's so funny?" Erica demanded.

"You know so much about everything in the entire world," Zoe explained, "except yourself."

"What are you talking about?"

"You're jealous of Jessica Shang! Because she hugged Ben."

"That's the dumbest thing I've ever heard in my life," Erica snapped. Only, while this was exactly the sort of thing I'd heard Erica say plenty of times, the way she said it didn't sound like Erica at all. Instead, she sounded strangely ill at ease. As though Zoe had struck a nerve.

Zoe seemed to sense this too. "I don't think it's so dumb," she said. "And just so you know, you don't have anything to worry about. Ben has no interest in Jessica Shang."

"He has a crush on her," Erica said flatly.

"He only thinks she's pretty," Zoe emphasized. "But he *likes* you. A lot. And if you're jealous of Jessica, I'm betting you like him, too."

"This conversation is over," Erica said.

"Oh, come on!" Zoe protested. "You need to deal with your feelings, not avoid them."

"I'm not avoiding my feelings," Erica replied. "We need to stop talking! Listen!"

Zoe stopped talking and listened. I ceased eavesdropping and focused on my surroundings too.

We were almost at the top of the mountain. The end of the lift was only a few chairs ahead of us. Beyond it, I could see a flat, wide-open plain of snow, which ended abruptly in what must have been a sharp drop.

The lift machinery was quite loud, whirring and clanking as each new chair arrived. I could barely hear anything over it.

But there was something. A thrumming noise. Distant, but getting louder.

"All I hear is a helicopter," Zoe said.

"It's coming toward us," Erica explained.

Zoe didn't question this. Neither did I. Erica might not have understood her own emotions—or anyone else's for that matter—but if anyone knew how to tell the direction a helicopter was traveling merely from the sound, it was her.

I swiveled around in my seat, scanning the surrounding mountains. Despite the clear day, it was hard to pick out the helicopter, but I eventually found it: a black blur on the western horizon, quickly growing bigger as it approached.

"Is something wrong?" Woodchuck asked, sensing my unease.

"Erica thinks so," I told him, pointing. "There's a helicopter coming this way fast."

"So?" Warren asked. "It's probably just search and rescue."

"Those are red." Woodchuck's face was creased with concern. "That one's not. It looks like it's for heli-skiing, but those are supposed to stay well clear of the resort."

My phone suddenly started ringing. So did Warren's. And Woodchuck's. And Erica's and Zoe's. At exactly the same moment. And they rang with the very specific ringtone we used to specify an emergency alert.

Before any of us could answer, though, the helicopter started shooting.

SNEAK ATTACK

Blue Sky Basin

Vail Mountain

December 30

1015 hours

Luckily for us, there was a small control room at the top of the ski lift. Our chairs moved behind it just in time. The bullets ricocheted off it and shattered the windows, but they didn't reach us.

Still, the control room wasn't much protection. Especially since it shielded us from only one direction. Unfortunately, there wasn't much other cover on the mountaintop. Only a small stand of trees fifty feet away.

Ahead of us, Erica and Zoe's chair arrived at the end of

the lift. The two of them leapt off it and raced for the trees.

The helicopter roared over our heads, so low that the wind from its rotors pushed down on us like an open hand.

My chair reached the end of the lift and Woodchuck, Warren, and I sprang off it, poling as hard as we could after the girls.

Thankfully, there weren't any other skiers on the mountaintop at the moment. What few were around had already started down the slopes and were well clear of the gunfire. Which left only us to serve as targets.

And as targets went, we were awfully good ones. We were now right out in the open. If the stand of trees had been downhill from us, we could have at least skied to it quickly; instead, we had to cross flat ground. That wasn't easy on skis. Especially with two feet of new snow piled up. We all had to go with a combination of pushing with our poles and galloping along with our skis on, which was like trying to sprint with two-by-fours nailed to our shoes. In addition, we were at one of the highest points at the ski resort, nearly two miles above sea level, so the altitude was taking a toll on Warren, Zoe, and me. I felt like I could barely breathe in the thin air. Our progress was agonizingly slow.

To the east, the helicopter banked, coming around for another attack.

"We are screwed!" Warren cried. "We're sitting ptarmigans out here!"

"Ptarmigans?" Woodchuck asked.

"Don't get him started," I gasped.

I pushed on my poles as hard as I could, straining with every ounce of strength, racing for the safety of the trees. Zoe and Warren did the same. Even though both were beginners, in the heat of the moment, they were handling themselves well. Woodchuck was right beside us.

However, Erica suddenly veered off, away from the trees and out into the open.

"What are you doing?" I yelled.

"Saving your butts!" she yelled back. "Get yourselves to cover!"

The helicopter was coming back, moving quickly toward us again.

I now saw what Erica was heading for: A Sno-Cat was parked at the edge of the snowfield. It was a large vehicle with treads instead of tires, used to groom snow and do other maintenance around the resort. This one had a trailer hitched to the back, also with treads instead of wheels, and atop that sat one of the ski patrol's avalanche howitzers.

Erica didn't have enough time to get there, though. The only shelter between her and it was a lone outhouse, set atop the mountain since it was several miles to the closest real bathroom. Erica popped off her skis and dove behind it as the helicopter opened fire again. Bullets shredded the tiny building, then raced across the snowy plain toward us, leaving a trail of tiny geysers. We reached the safety of the trees just in time. The bullets ricocheted off the trunks, snapping branches and annihilating pinecones.

The helicopter roared overhead once again.

"Ben!" someone yelled.

I peered out from the trees and saw Mike Brezinski getting off the ski lift. The helicopter hadn't been aiming for him, but he'd seen the attack. His face was now whiter than the snow around us and his eyes were wide with something I had never seen him show before: fear.

"Mike!" I yelled back to him. "Get away from us! Before they come back!"

But Mike was too frightened to listen to me. After all, heading out to the slopes would mean staying in the open, while the trees looked like safety. He kept pushing toward us.

Meanwhile, Warren wasn't looking too good. He'd turned green with nausea. "They almost got me," he gasped. Then he bent over and threw up.

"Wow," Zoe said, unimpressed. "Way to handle yourself in the heat of battle."

"It's my first time!" Warren whined. "I've never been shot at before! Not with real bullets!"

"Neither have I," Zoe told him. "And you don't see me upchucking my breakfast."

The helicopter banked again, preparing for a third attack.

Erica was back on the move, racing for the howitzer.

Mike reached the cover of the trees in record time. He was panting heavily, completely shell-shocked with fear.

"You need to get out of here," I told him. "Away from me."

"No way," he argued. "I'm not going out in the open! There's a maniac shooting from a helicopter out there!"

"That maniac is shooting at *us*," I told him. "As long as you're with us, you're in danger."

"At *you*?" Mike asked, incredulous. "Why would someone be shooting at you?"

There didn't seem to be any point in lying to him anymore. "Well, it's like you guessed: I'm a spy."

Warren threw up again.

The helicopter swooped back toward us. We tried to maneuver around in the trees, putting the trunks between us and it.

"You're a spy?" Mike gasped.

"Why do you sound so surprised?" I asked. "You accused me of being one the other day."

"I know, but I didn't think you were a *real* spy!" Mike exclaimed. "I thought you were just doing training and stuff! This is insane!" He pointed at the incoming helicopter. "Those people are trying to kill you!"

"Yeah, that happens a lot," I said.

The helicopter had changed its style of attack. Now, rather than racing over our heads, it approached slowly, then hovered right outside our stand of trees, searching for a gap to shoot through.

It was close enough that I could see one of Leo Shang's thugs was at the controls. Meanwhile, Dane Brammage sat in the open doorway, brandishing a machine gun. He found the gap between us, lifted the gun to his shoulder, and took aim at me. I saw him smile, as thought he was going to enjoy killing me.

And then Erica fired the howitzer.

The charge slammed into the rear of the helicopter, blowing the tail right off it. The rear rotor careened through the air, slicing through a nearby tree like it was a celery stalk. Mike, Zoe, Warren, Woodchuck, and I were all thrown to the ground by the blast. A hail of pinecones, knocked loose by the concussion, rained down upon us—along with a few startled squirrels.

Without its tail, the helicopter spun wildly out of control. Dane was flung from it like a rag doll, landing in the deep snow in the distance. The pilot desperately tried to get away from the trees. He managed to pull a short distance away, but then wobbled back in.

"Evasive action!" Woodchuck ordered.

We were already on the move. Even Mike, without any training at all, grasped that staying put was dangerous. We all raced out one side of the stand of trees just as the helicopter slammed into the other. The big rotors shaved the tops off a few pines, then thwacked into the thicker trunks, snapped off the helicopter, and cartwheeled through the air toward the Sno-Cat.

Erica leapt from the vehicle, stepped into her skis, and raced away just as the rotors came flying in. With a resounding *thunk*, they embedded in the Sno-Cat's roof like a lawn dart.

The rest of the helicopter crashed to the ground. The pilot leapt out and scrambled away.

Erica met up with us just as the copter exploded. We were pelted by more dislodged pinecones and squirrels. The woods promptly caught fire, blocking our way back to the ski slopes.

The Sno-Cat caught fire too. The helicopter rotors had punctured its gas tank. It started to burn quickly, the fire licking at the pile of howitzer ammunition that sat on the trailer.

Ahead of us, a flimsy rope fence lined the edge of the snowfield, right before the slope dropped away steeply. There was a small gate in it, but it had a bright red sign marked with a skull and crossbones, informing us that going beyond the gate was leaving the Vail resort area and heading into the White River National Forest wilderness area, which would normally be a very bad idea because there was no easy way out, there were no rescue services, there was extreme avalanche danger, and there was a decent chance we could die.

Normally, I might have paid attention to a sign like this. But there were extenuating circumstances.

Dane Brammage was still alive. In fact, despite being flung from a moving helicopter, he didn't appear to have so much as skinned a knee. Apparently, the snowdrift he'd landed in had not only cushioned his fall, but it had also protected his machine gun. Dane snatched it up out of the snow and came after us.

We charged through the gate. The slope beyond it went downhill fast. It was exceptionally steep, wide open, and treeless, far tougher than anything I'd attempted before, but we had no other options. We dropped onto the slope as Dane opened fire again. His bullets whistled over our heads.

Mike and Woodchuck hit the slope with the most grace, zipping downhill quickly. Warren hit the slope without any grace at all. Instead, he hit the slope with his face—and then his backside—and then his face again as he somersaulted down the hill. Zoe and Erica didn't do much better. I managed to stay upright a good way down, but then I rushed a turn and wiped out myself.

Thankfully, the snow on the slope was extremely deep, covering anything that would have been painful to land on—like sharp rocks—with several feet of pillowy softness. I tumbled through it all like a sock in the dryer, losing my skis and poles, until I settled into more of a controlled skid down the mountain. To each side of me, Zoe and Erica were doing the same thing, having lost their skis as well. We were basically sledding without sleds, rocketing downhill on our backs with our feet in front of us, carving gouges through the snow.

Behind us, Warren was still tumbling, giving a yelp every time he thwacked into the ground: "Ouch! Oof! Oh, my nose! Ow!" He was gathering snow as he rolled, turning into a giant snowball with arms and legs sticking out of it.

Eventually, the slope bottomed out, flattening enough to slow our descent. Mike and Woodchuck each skidded to a stop, panting with exhaustion. Erica, Zoe, and I tumbled into a pile beside them, tangled in a jumble of arms and legs but unharmed.

Warren crashed into a tree. The giant snowball he'd become burst on impact. His helmet slammed into the trunk so hard, it cracked in half. Thankfully, Warren's skull was protected, but he was knocked loopy from the impact. "I want a pony," he murmured, and then collapsed backward into the snow.

I'd ended up underneath both Zoe and Erica. They pried themselves off me and we all stared back up at the slope we'd come down. It appeared to be at least a thousand feet tall. We were at the bottom of a narrow gully, with an equally tall slope boxing us in on the other side. Climbing out again was going to be extremely difficult, if not impossible.

And then Dane Brammage appeared at the top of the slope. I saw the sunlight glint off his gun as he took aim at us again.

Before he could fire, however, the howitzer and all its munitions exploded. A massive fireball erupted at the top of the hill, blowing Dane over the edge of the cliff. He sailed through the air high above us, his eyes so wide with fear that I could see them even from where I stood. I didn't notice where he landed, though.

I was too distracted by the avalanche.

SNOW SAFETY

White River National Forest

South of Vail, Colorado

December 30

1030 hours

The explosion of the howitzer had been deafen-ing, and the noise echoed all over the walls of the canyon. The great sheet of snow that clung to the wall directly above us fractured and groaned.

"Uh-oh," Woodchuck gasped. "That's not good."

The snow began to slide. It hurtled down the mountainside toward us, roaring like a freight train.

Erica, who had just disentangled herself from Zoe and me, leapt back on top of us again. Beside me, I saw

Woodchuck doing the same thing to Mike and Warren.

"Hang on to me!" Erica screamed. Even though she was right next to me, I could barely hear her over the oncoming snow. Erica yanked a cord under her jacket, and a large yellow air bag suddenly inflated from her back.

The snow reached us a split second later. Without Erica's air bag, we might have been crushed beneath it. Instead, we were buoyed to the top, like a cork floating on water. The snow still threatened to rip Zoe and me away and drag us under, but we clung to Erica with all our might and let the avalanche carry us down the valley. I caught a glimpse of another yellow air bag close by—Woodchuck clutching Mike and Warren—but mostly all I saw was a jumble of white snow and blue sky as I was tossed about.

It was like riding a tidal wave made of snow. We were traveling at frightening speed; the sides of the valley were merely a blur as we raced past them. At the front of the wave, just ahead of us, massive trees snapped like toothpicks and vanished into the sea of white.

The avalanche lasted only seventy-three seconds, but it seemed much longer. And then, almost as suddenly as it had started, it was over. The avalanche petered out and we found ourselves well down the canyon from where we'd begun, lying atop a pile of snow so thick that the tops of the trees were barely poking through it.

We all lay where we were for a few seconds, spent from the ordeal—and thrilled that, after a helicopter attack, a tumble down a steep slope, and an avalanche, we were still alive. Everyone, that is, except for Erica. She quickly hopped to her feet, dusted herself off, and said, "Well, let's get going." As though this sort of thing happened to her every day.

"Going where?" Zoe asked.

"Down the canyon," Erica said, like it was obvious. "We certainly can't go back the way we came. It would have been tough enough to get back up that slope *before* the avalanche. And for all we know, Dane Brammage is still back there. That guy is ridiculously hard to kill. But I've studied the satellite maps of this area and I know there's a highway and a small town at the end of this canyon. Maybe five miles away. If we hurry, it shouldn't take more than a few hours."

"Erica's right," Woodchuck said. "If everyone's okay, we really shouldn't dawdle."

I stood up, checking my various body parts to make sure they were all still attached and working. I had what felt like several tons of snow down my jacket and pants, which had chilled my nether regions, but other than that, I seemed to be fine.

Zoe seemed to be fine as well, although Warren remained pretty loopy. "Guys!" he exclaimed, still lying on his back. "These are the perfect conditions for making snow angels!"

He waggled his arms and legs in the snow to prove it.

"We might need to get him to a doctor," Zoe suggested.

Mike also looked to be all right, physically at least. Mentally, he was in shock. He gaped at all of us, trying to make sense of everything. "So, all of you are spies too?"

"In training," Zoe said helpfully.

"In training?" Mike echoed, then shifted his gaze to Erica. "You took out an enemy helicopter with a howitzer!"

Erica shrugged. "I'm at the top of my class." She unzipped her ski parka to get the snow out of it, revealing the source of the yellow air bag she'd inflated. She was wearing the black vest she'd swiped from Epic Heli-Skiing. When she noticed me staring at it, she said, "I told you this had avalanche safety precautions built into it."

"And you wore it today just in case something like this happened?" I asked.

"You know me. I always like to be prepared." Erica pulled her phone out of her pocket and sighed, annoyed. "Ugh. There's no coverage in this stupid canyon."

"We *are* in the wilderness," Woodchuck pointed out, deflating his air bag. His had come from an avalanche vest as well; I assumed that, being a survivalist, he probably wore his all the time.

I checked my own phone. I didn't have any reception either.

Erica told Woodchuck, "I need to get in touch with my grandfather. Fast. He needs to know the Shangs are onto us."

"I'll bet he's already aware." Woodchuck helped Warren to his feet. "That emergency alert we got right before the helicopter attack was probably from him. But even so, we need to reestablish contact. There'll be cell reception in town. So let's move out." He led the way down the valley.

Warren wobbled after him. "Are we going for a hike?" he asked dazedly. "Cool! I've got some granola bars if anyone wants one!" He dug one out of his pocket, only to find it had been crushed in the avalanche. "Shoot. Looks like my granola is no longer in bar form."

The rest of us dropped in behind Woodchuck, and we worked our way down the canyon. The avalanche zone ended shortly, the huge pack of snow sloping back down to earth, and we entered a thickly wooded area. Less snow lay on the ground there because it was all caught up in the tops of the trees above, but it was still deep enough to have to trudge through. There was also a semi-frozen creek meandering along the canyon floor. This made for slow progress, and being in ski boots didn't help. They were painful enough to walk a short distance in; a prolonged march was torture. Plus, now that we were in the shade, the temperature had dropped like a rock.

"Everyone, be extremely alert for hypothermia and

frostbite," Woodchuck warned. "Ball your fists inside your gloves or put them in your pockets to keep them warm. And if you have any chills or shivering, let me know immediately so we can stop and warm you up."

We all nodded obediently.

It surprised me to see Erica following anyone, rather than assuming the lead, but she seemed far more concerned about her inability to contact her grandfather than about who was in charge. It occurred to me that she was worried about him. And possibly her father, too.

"I'm sure Cyrus and Alexander are all right," I told her. "If anyone can handle himself against the Shangs, it's your grandfather."

"Well, he couldn't have handled them *worse* than I did," Erica muttered.

"What are you talking about?" I asked. "You blew up their helicopter! If it hadn't been for you, we'd be dead!"

"They should never have gotten as close as they did. My mission today was to protect you."

"It was? I thought you were just supposed to be learning to ski. . . ."

A cold look from Erica stopped me in midsentence.

"That was all just a cover?" I asked.

Erica nodded. "Grandpa thought there was a chance they were onto you."

"Why didn't you just tell me?"

"He thought you might freak out if you knew your life was in danger."

I considered that, then nodded agreement. "He was probably right."

"Only, I screwed up," Erica said, livid at herself. "I should have been aware that helicopter was incoming much earlier. But I allowed myself to get distracted."

I noticed Zoe grimace at this, feeling bad for being the one who'd distracted Erica.

"There wasn't anything you could have done differently," I said. I was directing my words to Erica, but I was really speaking to both of them. "We were on the lift. We couldn't have gotten off any faster than we did."

"I should never have allowed us to come this far toward the wilderness," Erica said. "That was a grave mistake. I was thinking I could keep a better eye on our surroundings if there were fewer people around. It didn't occur to me there might be an aerial attack. . . ." She trailed off, staring at me thoughtfully. Then she said, "Take off your jacket."

"Now?" I asked. "It's freezing."

"Take it off."

I did and handed it over to her. Erica quickly examined it, working her hands over every seam and rifling through the pockets. "Aha," she said, and with a flourish, she removed a small black square with a curl of wire sticking out of it.

"What's that?" Mike asked.

"A GPS transmitter," Zoe replied.

"They must have planted it on you last night," Erica told me. "While you were bugging *them*."

I groaned, feeling like an idiot. "Which means they were onto me the entire time."

"Not necessarily," Erica corrected. "But you were definitely getting Dane worked up while you were with Jessica. And that was probably my fault too. I was making you push the boundaries. So I'm guessing he tagged you just to be on the safe side." She smashed the transmitter on a rock, then threw my jacket back to me.

I quickly zipped it back on.

"There's one other possibility," Zoe suggested to me. "Maybe Shang doesn't suspect you of being a spy at all. Maybe he just wants to kill you because you hugged his daughter and he's a really overprotective father."

As ridiculous as that seemed, I couldn't quite discount it. To my surprise, Erica didn't either.

"Maybe," she agreed. "If there was anyone evil enough to want to sentence someone to death for hugging, it's Leo Shang."

We reached a section where the canyon walls closed in until it was almost claustrophobic. There was little room left on the bank alongside the stream, occasionally forcing us onto rocks that poked through the water. My heels were starting to blister in my ski boots. And to make matters worse, Warren insisted on singing "Ninety-Nine Bottles of Beer on the Wall."

"So . . . ," Mike said. "Can someone tell me exactly what's going on here?"

"No," Erica said. "It's classified."

"Aw, c'mon," Mike pleaded. "I nearly got killed because of you guys!"

Erica gave him a suspicious glance. "Come to think of it, how'd you end up exactly where we were today?"

Mike looked away, his usual confidence wavering. "I . . . uh . . . followed you guys."

"Why?" Erica asked.

"Because of *you*," Mike told her. "I've been calling you. But you never called me back."

"You gave him your phone number?" Zoe asked Erica.

"Of course not," Erica said tartly. "I don't give anyone my real number. For security reasons. I gave him a fake. It calls a CIA dumping box for incoming messages."

"Ah," Mike said. "Well, that explains why I didn't hear back from you. But I wanted to see you again, so . . . I sort of tailed you guys today."

"Why didn't you just call *me*?" I asked.

"Well, we left things in a weird place," Mike explained. "I thought you were being a dink for lying to me about being a spy. Although, given the helicopter attack and all, I'm guessing you were trying to protect me."

"Yes," I said.

"I had no idea you were on a real mission," Mike replied. "With real bad guys and everything. I thought, when you were asking for my help with Jessica, you were just trying to date her, not infiltrate some terrorist group." Mike looked away sheepishly. "I guess I really screwed things up when I surprised you on the gondola the other day."

"You did," Erica told him, before I could figure out a nicer way to say it.

Mike picked his way across some rocks in the stream, then suddenly looked back at Erica, his mouth agape. "Oh my God."

"What now?" Erica asked.

"You're not Sasha Rotko," Mike said. "You're *Erica*."

"I know that," Erica replied.

"I mean, you're *the* Erica," Mike tried to explain. "Ben's Erica. From school. The one he dated."

Erica gave me a pointed look.

Zoe burst into laughter. "What are you talking about? Ben and Erica never dated!"

"That's not what Ben told me," Mike said. And then he

suddenly understood. "Wait. Was that some sort of cover story?"

"No." Zoe giggled. "Just wishful thinking on Ben's part."

"Oh." A sly smile crept across Mike's face. "Wow, Ben. I guess *everything* you told me about school was a lie."

"It wasn't a lie, exactly," I explained. "You misinterpreted something, and it was easier to let you believe it."

"Yeah, right," Mike said.

Thankfully, before he could tease me any more, a pair of helicopters roared overhead. They were painted red and heading up the canyon, toward the avalanche site. Zoe started waving her arms to flag them down, but Erica stopped her. "What are you doing?" she demanded.

"Signaling for help," Zoe said. "That's the ski patrol. They could rescue us!"

"For all we know, those are Shang's men," Erica warned.

"Those are ski patrol choppers," Mike said helpfully. "They're red."

"Shang's men already stole a helicopter from the heli-skiing company today," Erica pointed out. "What's to say they didn't steal the ones from the ski patrol too? And even if they didn't, they're certainly listening in on the patrol's radio. If we get in those copters, the moment we get back to town, we'll be ambushed again. For now it's better to let everyone think we were buried in that avalanche. At least that gives us the element of surprise, and right now we need every advantage we can get."

"Now, now," Warren said dreamily. "No need to be such a Gloomy Gus."

"I'd say there is," Erica replied. "Operation Golden Fist is going down today, but we still have no idea when or where—or what the plot even is in the first place. So far, all our mission has done is get us in trouble. We've learned nothing from the Shangs, while we just got caught with our pants down in a surprise attack. We're cut off from our team, we're cold, we're wet, and we're a long way from civilization."

"We still have some granola, though!" Warren added enthusiastically. He whipped out the smashed bar to show us, but lost his grip on it. It plunked into the stream and was quickly swept away. "Oh, crud," Warren whined. "*Now* we're screwed."

"Then we'd better pick up the pace," Woodchuck advised. "The sooner we get out of this canyon, the better."

I was already exhausted from the day's adventure and trudging through the wilderness in ski boots. I could tell Zoe and Warren were struggling too. Even Mike, who was normally a fountain of energy, looked sapped. But we pressed on down the canyon anyhow, going as fast as we could, hoping we could get to civilization again before it was too late to stop the Shangs.

INSPIRATION

Minturn, Colorado
December 30
1300 hours

Like Erica had said, there was a town at the mouth
of the canyon, several miles downstream. It wasn't much of
a town—a few run-down buildings lined along a narrow
road—but as we were exhausted, starving, and chilled to the
bone, it looked like paradise to us.

There was only one restaurant, but thankfully, it was
open. It looked straight out of the Old West, a wooden struc-
ture with a wide front porch that you could imagine outlaws
ambushing the sheriff from. The parking lot behind it was
still so thick with snow that most of the clientele had come

by snowmobile. There were dozens parked there, along with some cross-country skis and snowshoes in a rack by the door, as well as one honest-to-God horse. It was tied to the ancient hitching post, drinking from a trough filled with icy water.

"It feels like we're in some sort of time warp," Zoe commented.

"I have coverage!" Erica announced triumphantly, looking at her phone. "I'll call Grandpa and give him the update. The rest of you head inside, get warm, and grab some food."

We didn't need to be told twice. We quickly funneled into the restaurant, shed our damp jackets, and unbuckled our ski boots. I felt an incredible sense of euphoria as the pressure was finally relieved on my blistered feet.

The restaurant was decorated with the standard array of stuffed dead animals—there seemed to be a law in the Rockies mandating at least one jackalope per bar—as well as a hundred years of historical detritus nailed to the walls: yellowed photos of the town from the time of its founding, thousands of license plates, NO HUNTING signs with bullet holes blown in them, and random items like wagon wheels, busted skis, and ancient bicycle parts. The patrons were equally random: They wore everything from cowboy gear to Day-Glo snowmobiling suits. Everyone stopped talking briefly to check us out as we entered, then resumed their conversations.

Suddenly I got the strange feeling that there was

something important in the restaurant. I cased it again, wondering if there were any spies for the Shangs there. Then I wondered if I was just being paranoid. Getting ambushed has that effect on you.

Woodchuck pointed all of us to a table and went directly to the waitress. "What's the fastest thing you can make for us to eat?"

"Eggs, I guess," said the waitress.

"Right. We'll have six dozen eggs, please. Scrambled will be fine."

"And bacon!" Zoe added.

"And sausage!" Mike put in.

"And pickles!" Warren suggested.

"Bacon and sausage," Woodchuck told the waitress, then said, under his breath, "Forget the pickles."

My phone buzzed in my pocket. I pulled it out. Now that we had reception, all my text messages had arrived at once. To my surprise, most of them were from Jessica Shang. I scrolled through them quickly, hoping one might say something important, like "Heard my dad tried to have you killed. Sorry. I'm so angry at him, I'm going to tell you what his evil plans are. . . ." Instead, they were all a bit more normal:

Furious at my father for grounding me today. What a massive jerk!

And:

Looks awesome out there. Can't believe I'm stuck inside.

As I got further along, they got a bit testier, as Jessica grew upset that I wasn't texting back.

Where R U?
Thought we were friends.
R U still freaked out because of my father?

It seemed that I really ought to write back to her, though I wasn't exactly sure what the proper response should be. Plus, I was having trouble focusing on it. I continued to have the nagging sense that I was missing something in the restaurant. It felt as though my observational skills were kicking in, only not quite well enough. Like I'd seen the important object—whatever it was—but hadn't fully grasped it at the time. I looked around again, more slowly this time, doing my best to take everything in, to not let a single item escape my grasp.

"So," Mike said. "What happens now?"

"Well," Zoe said, "I guess Cyrus and Alexander will come get us. That's Erica's grandfather and father. They're both CIA too. And then, um . . . I'm not sure. Figuring out what the bad guys are up to is usually Ben's job."

"Really?" Mike turned to me, intrigued. "You're that good?"

"I'm okay," I said.

"He's way better than okay!" Zoe corrected. "Ben's the best! Every time he's faced the bad guys, he's figured out their plans."

Mike's eyes widened. "Every time?" he repeated. "How many missions have you gone on?"

"Not that many," I said humbly, still trying to focus on the room.

"This is his *fourth*," Zoe told Mike. "Which is huge, given that he's only been at spy school a year. A lot of kids never get to go on a single mission the whole time they're there. But Ben has uncovered moles and saved the president. . . ."

"The president of the United States?" Mike asked, amazed.

"Aw, that's nothing," Zoe told him proudly. "Last fall Ben saved all of New York City from getting blown up!"

Mike stared at me, stunned.

"Zoe's exaggerating," I told him. "I didn't save the *whole* city."

"Well, he saved a lot of it," Zoe stressed. "He's exceptionally good at thwarting the plans of bad guys. So now I guess we just need to give him some time to think things over so he can figure out what the Shangs are up to and then we can go thwart *their* plans too."

"Wow," Mike said. "And this whole time, everyone thought you were just going to a nerd academy."

"That's the problem with being a spy." I sighed. "Everything's supposed to be a secret. Even when you save the world, everyone back home still thinks you're a dork."

I had imagined this event plenty of times: the moment when Mike finally learned my big secret and realized I was much cooler than he thought. But now that it was here, it wasn't quite as wonderful as I'd hoped. Because at the moment, the past didn't matter at all. What mattered was the present, and despite Zoe's belief in me, I had no idea what Leo Shang was up to. Even after three days on the case, I was drawing a giant blank—and time was running out. If I didn't figure out what Operation Golden Fist was soon, I'd have failed. And failure in spy school was far more than just a bad grade on your permanent record. It meant chaos, destruction, and a lot of other terrible things. . . .

Across the room, one of the snowmobilers shifted in her seat, revealing a metal sign nailed to the wall behind her. It was old and rusted, dented a hundred times over. PROPERTY OF CLIMAX MOLYBDENUM MINING, it read. GUARDS ON PREMISES. NO TRESPASSING.

I sat up, suddenly forgetting all about food or anything else.

The waitress stopped at our table, bearing glasses of water for all of us.

"Is the Climax Mine somewhere near here?" I asked.

"Sure is!" she said. "It's just a few miles up the road. Half the town works there." She plunked the glasses down and headed back to the kitchen.

"What's all this about the Climax Mine?" Zoe asked.

"Look," I said, pointing across the room.

"Oh!" Warren cooed. "Another jackalope! How do you think those things get in their burrows with those big horns?"

"Not the jackalope," I said. "The sign! Jessica Shang misheard her father. He wasn't saying he was going to see 'Molly Denham.' He was going to see '*molybdenum*.'"

"I'll be danged," Woodchuck said. "I can't believe the Climax Mine is *here*."

"You've heard of it?" I asked.

"Sure. I wrote a paper on it back when I was in spy school, for my history of espionage class. I knew the mine was in the Rockies, I just didn't realize we were practically on top of it."

"Whoa," Mike said. "Slow down. What is this molly-whatever stuff?"

"Molybdenum," I corrected. "It's one of the elements."

"Its primary industrial use is to make steel much stronger," Woodchuck explained. "It's extremely important for making weapons, especially large-scale ones. The Germans first figured that out back during World War One. They were building these massive cannons that could fire one-ton shells for more than ten miles, but the cannons were tearing apart from their own explosions. Then the German scientists realized adding molybdenum to the steel would prevent that from happening—but there was only one place on earth known to have large deposits of it: the Climax Mine. So the Germans sent a covert team out here and essentially stole it from the owner. Then they starting mining molybdenum and shipped all of it to Germany."

"The Germans captured an entire mine *inside* Colorado?" Mike asked. "And then used it to make weapons they fought us with? And we let them do it?"

"Yes," Woodchuck replied. "In fact, the United States didn't even notice the mine was in German hands for three years. It was a major intelligence failure. Of course, there wasn't a CIA back then—or much of any organized spy network, really. Climax was one of the reasons the government realized they *needed* an intelligence agency. Once we found out what was going on, we took the mine back from the Germans, and it's stayed in American hands ever since. To this day, there's been only one other major deposit of molybdenum found in the entire world."

"Where?" I asked, although I was pretty sure I could guess the answer.

"China," Woodchuck replied.

"I'm betting there's a good chance Leo Shang controls it," I said. "Anyone have a working phone?"

"Already on it." Mike had his phone out and was Googling the answer. "I don't see anything about the owner, but it's called Huangshan. . . ."

"Huangshan!" Zoe exclaimed. "I saw Jawa type that name, like, ten dozen times while he was eavesdropping on Shang's business calls last night!"

"Do you know what Shang was saying about it?" I asked.

"No. That was Jawa's bug to deal with," Zoe explained. "But Shang was certainly talking about Huangshan a lot."

The waitress came over with a plate piled high with bacon and sausage. "Eggs are coming, kids. But I figured you wanted this fast."

She set it on the table, and we all dove in, spearing meat on our forks and wolfing it down. Everyone except Warren, who groused, "Where's the pickles?"

It was pretty much the best thing I'd ever tasted.

"One thing," Mike said, through a mouth stuffed with sausage. "So Shang owns another molybdenum mine. What's the big deal with him looking at this one? That isn't a crime, is it?"

"No," I admitted. "But Erica heard him say he was plotting something for today. And he's definitely been secretive, acting like he's going heli-skiing when he's not, renting the entire hotel and hiding something in his room. . . ." I trailed off, a horrible thought occurring to me.

"What's wrong?" Zoe asked.

"I think I know what Operation Golden Fist is." I snapped to my feet and pulled my jacket back on.

"Where are you going?" Woodchuck asked me. "We've still got eggs coming!"

"I need to talk to Erica right away." I grabbed a handful of bacon, rebuckled my ski boots—doing my best to ignore the resurgence of pain—and headed through the restaurant. "Cyrus needs to hear about this!" I raced out the door into the parking lot and found Erica nearby.

Unfortunately, she was unconscious. She was sprawled on her side in the snow not too far from the horse.

I ran to her side to check on her. To my relief, she was still breathing.

It occurred to me a little too late that I'd just dropped my guard in a very big way.

"Get your hands up, Ben," someone said from behind me. "And don't try anything funny. I've got a gun."

I knew the voice. I did exactly as ordered, turning around to face my nemesis:

Murray Hill.

SHOWDOWN

Minturn, Colorado
December 30
1330 hours

Murray wasn't much older than me, but he had been a dangerous covert agent for SPYDER. The last time I'd seen him, he was running for his life as a missile was about to blow up a good bit of New Jersey. Despite there being hundreds of CIA agents around, he'd escaped and disappeared without a trace. He hadn't changed much since then; he was still as slovenly as ever. His hair was unkempt, his posture was terrible, and the thick parka he wore was splotchy with food stains. He was flashing the same cocky smile he always did when he had me at the business end of a gun and spoke with his same lackadaisical attitude, like he was having a great time. "Hey, Ben. It's good to see you."

Since he'd caught me by surprise, it took me a few moments to manage to say anything. I had a thousand questions all vying to be asked at once. "Where did . . . ? How . . . ? When . . . ? What are you doing here?"

"I'm competing in the halfpipe at the X Games," Murray said sarcastically. "What do you *think* I'm doing here? I'm working for the bad guy."

"You mean SPYDER is working with Shang?"

"SPYDER?" Murray laughed. "Those jerks don't know anything about this. That whole organization is a mess since you blew their headquarters up."

"So you're not working for them anymore?"

"Those dirt bags left me at the scene of the crime to be their patsy while they all fled the country! That was completely uncool. I'm not about to work for people who don't respect me. I'm a freelance evil agent now."

"There are freelance evil agents?" I asked, unable to hide my surprise.

"Oh, yeah. Tons of them. SPYDER was unusual. There's not a whole lot of organizations out there dedicated to causing chaos and mayhem full-time. A guy like Leo Shang pulls off maybe one or two evil schemes a year, if that. In fact, sometimes he's gone years without doing *anything* evil. So there's no point in him having a bunch of guys like me on the payroll twenty-four seven. Instead, he hires us all for a scheme, we come in, we get the job done, and then we move on."

"Like Dane Brammage?"

"Yeah, that slab of meat is a freelance too. It's way better than working for SPYDER. The pay's higher, the accommodations have been top-notch, and I don't have to worry about anyone setting me up as a patsy and blowing me up. The only problem with this plan has been the weather. I am freaking freezing!" Murray shivered and rubbed himself with the arm he wasn't using to hold a gun on me. "Ski people are crazy, coming someplace this cold on vacation. What do they have against the beach?"

I glanced toward the restaurant door, hoping someone else from the gang would be heading outside soon. Murray's major weakness was that he loved to talk. I figured if I could keep him on his favorite subject—himself—I could stall long enough for someone to come to my rescue. "So, have you been here with Shang this whole time?"

"In Vail? No. Believe me, if I'd been here, there's no way you would have gotten anywhere as close to Jessica as you did. I was in China, handling some really important stuff this morning. I got in on the ground floor on this one. In fact, a lot of this whole thing was my idea. So I fly in to help put the final pieces of this plan into action and hear Leo's having a cow because some kid's charmed his way in with Jessica. Well, the alarm bells go off for me. I ask if there's a picture of the kid, and he shows me, and I'm like, 'Holy guacamole, that's no normal kid. That's Ben Ripley!'"

"So then you're the reason I was almost killed today."

"No, no, no. The reason you were almost killed today is that you can't stop poking your nose into other people's business. You know the risks with the spy game. I'd try to convince you that it's much safer to be a bad guy, but frankly, I've given up trying to recruit you. You've burned that bridge. Or, more to the point, you prevented us from burning some bridges. And totally ruined our plans to cause chaos in Manhattan."

I glanced toward the restaurant door again.

This time Murray noticed. "Looking for your friends?" He grinned knowingly. "They should be along any moment. Ah! Here they are!"

Now the door swung open and my friends emerged. Only, they weren't coming to my aid by attacking Murray. Instead, they filed out with their hands up: Zoe, Warren, and Woodchuck. To my relief, Mike wasn't with them. The others were all followed by a girl about Murray's age. She had long brown hair tied in a ponytail, giant lavender earmuffs, a nose ring, and a gun, which was trained on my friends.

"You don't think I'd come here without backup, do you?" Murray asked me slyly. "Ben, this is Jenny Lake, my cohort in crime . . . and my girlfriend." He waggled his eyebrows as he said this. "Jenny, this is Ben Ripley."

"Oh, hey!" Jenny said, seeming genuinely friendly and excited. "It's nice to meet you! Murray's told me so much about you."

"Nice to meet you too," I said. Not because it really was nice to meet her, but because it was kind of a reflex.

Zoe shot me an annoyed look. "Ben, she's a bad guy."

"Sorry," I apologized. "It just seemed polite."

Murray grinned at the others, basking in the moment. "Now, now, Zoe. Just because we're enemies doesn't mean we can't have manners. I'm pleased to see you've been activated. You've worked hard for this. And, Woodchuck, once I heard the CIA was in town, I figured you might be here, since you're Mr. Outdoorsy and all. Though, Warren, you're a bit of a surprise. I really thought you'd have washed out of spy school by now."

"Do you have any pickles on you?" Warren asked. "I am really jonesing for a pickle."

Murray leaned in to me and whispered, "Is it just me, or has Warren gotten weirder?"

"He banged his head on a tree pretty hard earlier," I replied. "Knocked himself silly."

"Ah," Murray said. "That'd explain it."

It occurred to me why Mike wasn't with the others. Murray had no idea who Mike was. And thus Jenny wouldn't have known to look for him either. I wasn't sure exactly how Mike had slipped away, but there was no way to ask anyone what had happened. At the very least, though, I was relieved to know he was safe. Maybe he was even calling the police.

Of course, I couldn't guarantee that. For all I knew, Mike was in the restaurant bathroom, completely unaware that the rest of us had been captured. Or maybe he'd been knocked unconscious himself. If he *hadn't* called the police, the only other way I could think of to get out of this jam was to hope Erica would regain consciousness and kick Murray's butt. Either way, I needed to keep stalling.

I turned to Jenny Lake and asked, nice and friendly, "So, how long have you and Murray been dating?"

"Only a few weeks," she replied. She seemed surprisingly sweet for a villain. "Shang recruited both of us to work this job and we met the first day. The moment we saw each other, we just connected, you know? It was amazing. And ever since then, I've been his little pookie-wookie and he's been my fuzzy-wuzzy bear."

"Awww." Warren sighed. "That's adorable."

Meanwhile, Zoe mimed throwing up.

"Jenny," Murray said. "Now that the gang's all here, we

really ought to take care of these guys. Woodchuck, could you be a pal and carry Erica for me? I'd do it myself, but I tweaked my back doing push-ups the other day." This was obviously a lie to impress Jenny; Murray had always avoided physical exertion like the plague.

Woodchuck obediently picked Erica up and slung her over his shoulder. I'd been hoping that Erica was only faking being unconscious so she could get the jump on Murray. But now she flopped about limply. I was pretty sure this was actual limp flopping and not an incredible act by Erica, meaning she wasn't going to be any help.

"Where are you taking us?" Zoe demanded.

"Oh, not too far." Murray motioned for us to start walking across the snowy parking lot, toward the base of the closest mountain. "Over there should do. I just want to get you away from the restaurant and any witnesses before we take care of you." He looked to Jenny. "The problem with Ben is, you have to get rid of him quickly. If we let him hang around too long, he'll figure our plans out."

"Oh, I've already figured them out," I said.

Murray shot me a skeptical glance. "No, you haven't."

"You're going to set off a nuclear bomb to irradiate the Climax Mine so Shang can corner the world market in molybdenum."

Murray gaped at me in genuine surprise. "You have got

to be kidding me! You did it again! Man, you're good! Pookie, didn't I tell you he was good?"

"You did," Jenny agreed.

"I thought we really had you this time," Murray told me. "How'd you figure it out?"

"It wasn't that hard." I stopped walking, hoping Murray and Jenny would be too distracted to notice. "I know Dane Brammage used to work for this scumbag arms dealer named Paul Lee who hooked SPYDER up with some nukes before. Then I saw the case for something like a nuke in Leo Shang's hotel room. And I know Shang has been doing some sort of reconnaissance in these mountains all week instead of heli-skiing. So when I realized the Climax Mine was close and that he owns the only other major supply of molybdenum in the world, it all just kind of made sense."

"Really?" Murray asked. "Because it seems like a pretty big jump to assume Shang's going to nuke the molybdenum to corner the market."

"Well, there was one more thing," I admitted. "The name of the operation is 'Golden Fist.' And what you're doing is basically the same scheme as in *Goldfinger*."

Murray suddenly looked as rattled as I'd ever seen him. "I don't know what you're talking about," he said.

"*Goldfinger*, the greatest James Bond movie of all time," I explained. "Auric Goldfinger plans to corner the world's gold market by nuking Fort Knox. You're doing the same thing with molybdenum."

Jenny gaped at Murray in astonishment. "Murray! You told me—and Shang—this was your original idea! Did you steal it from a movie?"

Murray turned bright red. "No," he said defensively. "I've never even heard of this *Goldfinger*."

"Yes, you have," Warren told him. "You used to watch it all the time at spy school. Back before you were evil."

"I can't believe you!" Jenny exclaimed. "Shang paid you to come up with a way to take out the competition and you just stole the plot of a movie?"

"I didn't *steal* it," Murray said defensively. "I *modified* it."

"Sounds like stealing to me," Jenny huffed, looking annoyed.

"So what's the big deal?" Murray sighed. "We're bad guys."

"We're only supposed to commit crimes," Jenny pointed out. "Not lie to each other."

"We're about to set off a nuclear bomb!" Murray exclaimed. "And you're upset at me for a little plagiarism?"

"This is about trust," Jenny said curtly.

The two of them were quite distracted now. They seemed to have completely forgotten about marching us across the parking lot to our deaths. I glanced toward Erica, hoping to see her awake. If there was ever a good time to catch the enemy by surprise, this was it.

Only, Erica still lay limply across Woodchuck's shoulder.

"Trust is important to me," Jenny told Murray. "I need to know that when you say something, you mean it."

"Of course you can trust me," Murray said. "I never lie."

"You lied to us all the time!" Zoe pointed out. "When you were a mole at school, you did *nothing* but lie to us."

"That was different," Murray argued. "That was business." He turned to Jenny. "You deceive people all the time for business!"

"Don't try to make this about me," Jenny said.

Murray groaned. "Do we have to have this conversation right now? In front of the hostages?"

"Why don't we talk about the fact that you're setting off a nuclear device just to make money?" Zoe said angrily. "Innocent people are going to *die* in this scheme!"

"Well, we are *evil*," Murray told her. "That's how these things work. You don't corner the world market in molybdenum by giving everyone a free puppy. And speaking of killing people . . ." He glanced at his watch. "Where the heck are those guys?"

"What guys?" Warren asked.

"The guys who are going to kill you," Murray replied.

This caught me off guard. I did a bad job hiding it, and Murray noticed. Normally, he might have taken some joy in this, but he had grown quite testy during his argument with Jenny. "I'm not as dumb as you think," he told me. "I know what you've been up to this whole time, trying to distract me so that I don't kill you right away, giving Erica a chance to wake up and rescue you. Well, it just so happens that *I'm* the one who's been distracting *you*. I've been waiting for the real thugs to get here so they can take care of you once and for all."

I grimaced, feeling like an idiot now. "So, you were never going to kill us yourself?"

Murray looked hurt. "I may be evil, but I'm not a psychopath. I don't like shooting people. My psychiatrist says I have moral issues. Unlike *him*." He pointed across the parking lot.

Dane Brammage had arrived. Not only was he still alive, but he looked as if getting blown off a cliff and caught in an avalanche had only made him angrier.

"Crud muffins," Zoe cursed. "What does it take to kill that guy?"

Thankfully, Dane was a good distance away, and it appeared that he had lost his gun in the avalanche. But it still wasn't going to be too long before he reached us, borrowed Murray's gun, and took us out.

I gave Erica one final, hopeful glance, praying her condition had changed—but she remained stubbornly lifeless over Woodchuck's shoulder.

Murray clucked his tongue as though he was disappointed in me. "She's not going to save you this time," he taunted. "Sorry, Ben. Looks like your luck has finally run out."

The roar of an engine suddenly cut through the winter air. A snowmobile rocketed out from behind a truck and slammed into Murray. With a yelp, Murray went flying and plopped into a snowdrift. His gun skidded across the parking lot.

"Fuzzy Bear!" Jenny gasped, forgetting to keep her own gun trained on us.

Zoe decked her with one punch. Jenny rocked on her heels and landed flat on her back, unconscious.

The snowmobile driver flipped up the visor of his helmet, revealing his identity: Mike Brezinski. "That guy was bad, right?" he asked. "Tell me I didn't flatten an innocent person."

"He was bad," I confirmed. "Thanks."

In the distance, Dane Brammage had seen what had happened. He roared angrily and started running toward us.

"Looks like we better split," Mike said. He tossed two sets of keys to Woodchuck and Zoe, then pointed to two other snowmobiles parked nearby. "Take those! They each hold two people!"

Zoe and Warren scrambled for one while Woodchuck lugged Erica to the other. I raced across the parking lot to grab Murray's gun.

As I did, Murray lunged for it. Luckily for me, Murray had the speed and reflexes of a koala bear. He didn't come anywhere close to the gun. I snatched it up and aimed it at him.

He raised his hands in fear. "You wouldn't shoot a friend, would you?"

"You're not my friend," I told him. Luckily for Murray, though, I wasn't much for shooting people myself. I was more of a handcuff-the-bad-guys type of person. Only, I didn't have any handcuffs—or anything else to restrain Murray and Jenny—and I didn't have any time, either. Dane was barreling toward me now.

And then the rest of Shang's men showed up.

One of the car-tanks spun into the parking lot, coming our way.

The other two snowmobiles revved to life. Zoe and Warren zoomed out of the parking lot on one while Woodchuck followed with Erica.

I ran back to Mike's snowmobile and hopped on behind him. "Let's go!" I shouted.

Mike hit the gas.

As we raced out of the parking lot, I could hear Murray yelling behind us. "This isn't over, Ben! You haven't seen the last of Murray Hill!"

I didn't even look back.

EVASIVE ACTION

Minturn, Colorado

December 30

1350 hours

The car-tank sped across the parking lot after us.
Whoever was driving didn't even bother swerving around the parked cars. He plowed straight into them, sending them skidding wildly across the icy lot.

Luckily for us, however, the town was built more for snowmobiles than for cars. At the edge of the parking lot, the asphalt ended, but a track across the snow continued on toward the mountains. Ahead of us, my friends veered onto it, though Mike and I still had a few yards to go.

The car-tank sped up behind us. More cars were crumpled

as it bore down, aiming to turn us into roadkill.

Mike gunned the engine and we hit the snowy track, leaving the parking lot behind.

The car-tank tried to follow us. It lunged a dozen yards into the snow, almost catching our snowmobile before sinking helplessly up to its headlights.

"Ha!" Mike yelled as we raced away. "Sucks to be you!"

Mike hadn't ever gone to spy school, so he didn't know Twomey's Rule of Premature Gloating: Never taunt the bad guy until you're sure the chase is over. Because it probably isn't.

Dane Brammage shot around the car-tank on a snowmobile. One of the other goons had given him a submachine gun.

"Uh-oh," Mike said. "What now?"

"Let's lose him," I suggested.

"I'm doing my best." Mike gave the snowmobile everything he could. We churned along the snowy track. I had never been on a snowmobile before. In addition to being incredibly loud and vibrating like a blender set to high, it had no seat belts. All I could do was wrap my arms as tightly as possible around Mike's chest and hope that we didn't fall off.

This made it hard for me to see what was going on ahead of us, though my friends seemed to be faring all right. Zoe and Warren were in the lead. Next came Woodchuck, who had to drive with Erica in his lap, propping her up between his arms. Somehow, despite being on a noisy, rattling snow-mobile, she was still unconscious.

"How'd you get away back at the restaurant?" I asked Mike. I had to yell at the top of my lungs so he could hear me over the snowmobile's engine, even though we were only inches apart.

"I went to call my uncle!" he yelled back. "I wanted to tell him I was okay. When I came back, everyone was gone! I thought they'd ditched me until I saw all of you out in the parking lot. Who was that kid with the gun?"

"Murray Hill. He's my nemesis."

"You're only thirteen and you already have a nemesis? That's kind of awesome."

"How'd you get the keys to the snowmobiles? Did you steal them?"

"No!" Mike sounded offended. "I'm not a thief! I asked the other diners for them!"

"And they just gave their keys to you?"

"I told them it was an emergency. They were all super-nice. Of course, I didn't realize we'd be getting chased like this!"

Shots rang out. Bullets plugged the snow around us.

"Or shot at!" Mike added.

Dane Brammage was gaining ground on us. And behind *him*, Shang's men had commandeered some other snowmobiles. I presumed they had simply stolen theirs, rather than asking for them nicely.

We reached the edge of town. The track we were following veered into a forest of aspen trees and we all followed it.

"I heard everything you said back there!" Mike yelled to me. "About the nuclear bomb and all. What's your plan for dealing with that?"

"Er . . . ," I said. "I haven't really worked things out much past 'get away from the bad guys.'"

"You haven't?"

"I was really hoping Erica would have come around by now! She's much better at this stuff than I am!"

A creek came up so suddenly that we didn't even see it until we were soaring over it. We barely made it to the far bank, landing so hard that I was nearly bounced off the snowmobile.

"So . . . ," Mike said, a little awkwardly. "Are you still really into Erica—or is it okay if I ask her out?"

"You want to talk about this now?"

"I was just wondering! Because I definitely got a good vibe from her the other day. And she seems pretty amazing. But if you're still into her, then I'll back off."

Normally, I would never have admitted to having a crush on a girl in front of Mike. It was way too embarrassing. But at the moment, denying it seemed pointless. "I'm still into her."

There was a moment's hesitation before Mike asked, "Really?"

"Yes!"

"Okay. Just making sure. Are there a lot of other girls at this spy school like her?"

"Well, there's plenty of other girls . . . but there's no one like Erica."

We shot out of the aspen trees onto a wide-open plain of snow. It seemed surprisingly flat to me—and then, to my dismay, I realized why. I glanced down at the snow beneath us and saw something bluish glimmering beneath it. "Mike! We're not on land anymore!"

"What?"

"We're on a lake!"

Mike glanced down, then said, "Oh, nuts."

A loud crack rang out. For a second I feared it was a gunshot. But it turned out to be something even worse.

The ice was breaking apart.

Ahead of us, Zoe and Warren's snowmobile suddenly pitched forward as a large section of ice sank beneath it. Both of them were thrown off. They slid across the frozen lake like hockey pucks while their snowmobile toppled onto its side, cracking the ice even more.

Woodchuck was too close behind to avoid it. Instead, he bailed out, taking Erica with him. His snowmobile slammed into Zoe's so hard it flipped into the air, then smashed down, embedding itself nose-first in the ice.

A web of cracks quickly spread from the wreckage, fracturing the lake's surface like a window beaned by a baseball. Bits of the ice broke free and sank, revealing the frigid black water beneath.

Mike veered away, avoiding the worst of this, but the ice was disintegrating beneath our treads as we went. We raced across the lake, hoping it would stay solid long enough for us to reach the far side.

Zoe and Warren had slid to the far side of the lake. They were far enough from the break that the ice was still sturdy enough to hold them, and now they scurried across it to the shore. Woodchuck wasn't so lucky. He was much bigger than them and he was carrying Erica's weight as well. He was doing his best to run with her, but the ice was coming apart under his feet.

"They're not going to make it!" I yelled.

Mike instantly angled toward them, even though this put our own safety at risk.

Woodchuck saw us coming and sprinted our way.

The ice groaned and shifted beneath the upended snowmobiles. They began to sink, gasoline forming a slick in the dark water around them. The cracks in the ice widened and lengthened.

We were only a few feet away from Woodchuck when the surface beneath him heaved. With what seemed to be the last of his strength, he flung Erica toward us.

Mike slowed down so I could catch her.

It's not easy to catch a teenage girl from a moving snowmobile on top of a disintegrating sheet of ice. At spy school, they tried to prepare us for all sorts of dangerous scenarios, and yet I don't think anyone had ever even thought of this one. It was probably a blessing that I only had about half a second to prepare for it; otherwise I might have started obsessing about the thousands of things that could go wrong. But in the few moments we had, I simply reacted, making some quick mental calculations about her trajectory, reaching out as we skidded across the ice, and doing my best to snag the flying unconscious girl. I probably didn't look very suave or debonair while I did it, but I got my arms around her torso and managed not to have her sudden weight knock me off the snowmobile. Then I clung to her as tightly as I could, although her legs still dangled limply off the side.

"Go!" Woodchuck yelled. "Now!" Then the ice beneath his feet gave way and he plunged into the freezing water.

Mike gunned the engine—but we didn't go anywhere.

We'd gained weight and lost momentum. The treads of our snowmobile simply spun uselessly on the breaking ice.

And if that wasn't bad enough, Dane Brammage arrived.

He roared onto the ice, saw the wreckage in the middle, and skidded to a stop. Then he whipped out his gun and took aim at us.

For a horrifying moment, we were right in his sights.

At the last moment, our treads caught. Our snowmobile leapt forward and rocketed across the lake.

Dane's bullets pinged off the ice right where we'd just been.

"Can't you do something about him?" Mike screamed at me. "Shoot him before he shoots us!"

"I'm not very good with guns!" I pointed out.

"Well, try anyhow! He's a big target!"

I pulled out the gun I'd taken from Murray. Even though Dane was about as big as human beings got, I knew there was still relatively little chance I could hit him all the way across the lake.

But then I realized there was a closer target that was a lot bigger.

Zoe and Warren's snowmobile had almost sunk by now, disappearing beneath the water's surface. But Woodchuck's was still sticking upright like a tombstone.

I blasted away at it until I'd emptied the clip.

The last bullet actually found its target. It sparked off a metal runner, igniting the gasoline slicked on the water. The frozen lake instantly caught fire. Flames erupted, creating a haze of smoke that hid us from Dane Brammage.

And then the snowmobile exploded.

A wave of heat rolled over us, briefly making the blustery day feel like summer. Burning pieces of metal flew through the air and clattered across the ice. The frozen surface of the lake shuddered and tore apart. Cracks shot across it like lightning bolts, carving it into pieces.

Zoe and Warren had reached solid ground. Woodchuck, being a master of survival, was swimming through the frigid water. He didn't look *happy* about it—but he seemed to be okay. Mike, Erica, and I made it to a shallower section of the lake just as the ice collapsed under us. Our snowmobile sank, but went only a foot before hitting the bottom. The water lapped at the toes of our ski boots and billowed into clouds of steam around the engine.

Dane Brammage wasn't so lucky. He was a big guy and he'd stopped dead on the ice. He desperately gunned his snowmobile's engine, but before he could get going, the surface split beneath him. He dropped through it, disappearing so fast, it was almost as if the lake had swallowed him.

I kept staring at the water, though, expecting Dane to resurface, stubbornly remaining alive yet again.

"Nice thinking," Erica said.

I looked down at her in my arms and saw her eyes were open. "You're conscious!"

"Wow, your powers of observation are as keen as ever," Erica said.

"Good to see your sarcasm is already fully functional," I replied.

Erica gave me what looked like an extremely fleeting smile, then hopped off the partially sunken snowmobile and started through the ankle-deep water to shore. "What's our situation?"

Mike and I scrambled after her. The icy water seeped into our ski boots, chilling our toes. Normally, this would have been awful, but my feet were already in such pain after hiking so far in ski boots that the numbing cold was actually kind of a relief.

"Dane's underwater," I said, "but I wouldn't count on him being dead yet."

"Me either," Erica agreed. "That guy's tougher to kill than Rasputin. Where are the other bad guys?"

There was a roar of snowmobile engines on the far side of the lake.

"Right there," Mike said.

Shang's remaining men parked their snowmobiles on the opposite shore. The lake between us was no longer frozen, but they could still shoot across it. We scrambled to some large rocks at the shoreline and hunkered down behind them as the bad guys opened fire.

I took in our surroundings. Except for the rocks we were hiding behind, there was little cover on our side of the lake. Our snowmobiles were useless and our only gun had no more bullets. Plus, Woodchuck was still out in the water. He was nearing the shore now, but the cold water was taking its toll. Every stroke he took appeared to be a Herculean effort for him.

"The situation looks pretty dire," I told Erica.

"Maybe not," she replied. "Listen."

It was hard to hear much of anything over the sound of the bullets sparking off the rocks in front of us, but when I focused, I could hear a distinct whirring noise.

"What's that?" Mike asked.

"The cavalry's coming," Erica replied. "I didn't have a whole lot of time to talk to Grandpa before Murray chloroformed me, but I at least told him we needed a rescue." She tapped the avalanche vest she was wearing. "And this is giving him our exact coordinates."

A military helicopter raced around a bend in the river, keeping low to the ground. Cyrus Hale was at the controls. Alexander sat beside him, manning a machine gun mounted in the chopper's nose. He opened fire on Shang's men, who quickly aborted their attack and fled into the cover of the woods. Alexander blasted away at them as they ran, shredding the trees and blowing bushes apart, keeping them in retreat.

Cyrus landed the copter by the side of the lake. The wind from the rotors whipped up a snow tornado and pelted us with bits of ice.

Woodchuck reached the shallow water, but he was in bad shape. His skin was turning blue from the cold and he was shivering uncontrollably. Alexander leapt from the helicopter, ran to him, and helped him to his feet. Mike and I helped drag him toward the copter. Water poured from Woodchuck's clothes onto us.

We boosted him into the helicopter. Zoe and Erica were already inside, armed with emergency blankets and heating pads. They immediately stripped off Woodchuck's wet clothes and swaddled him in warmth.

Warren sat to the side and tore into a box of emergency rations. "I found candy!" he exclaimed. "Ooh! And it's chocolate!"

Mike and I clambered into the helicopter with Alexander. "Looks like you finally got yourselves a chopper," I said.

"Yes!" Alexander agreed, sliding the door shut. "We borrowed it from the Cheyenne Mountain Complex!"

Now that Shang's men were in the cover of the trees, they began taking potshots at us. A few pocked the metal hull of the helicopter.

Cyrus pulled back on the control stick and we rose into the air before the enemy could do any more damage. "Any chance you've figured out what Shang's plan is?" he asked us.

"He's planted a nuclear bomb," I said. "He wants to irradiate the Climax Mine so he can corner the molybdenum market."

"Hey!" Alexander cried. "That's sort of the plot from *Goldfinger*."

"Yeah," I agreed. "Murray Hill stole it."

"It's still dangerous," Erica said solemnly. "A nuke in this area could kill thousands of people and irradiate millions more. Any idea where the bomb is?"

I shook my head. "It's somewhere in the mountains near here, but I don't know the specifics."

"That's a huge amount of land," Zoe said, discouraged. "Finding a single bomb out there would be like looking for a needle in a million haystacks."

We were now several hundred feet above the lake. Cyrus pressed forward on the stick and the helicopter shot forward, racing up the canyon.

"Where are we going?" Mike asked.

"Where else?" Cyrus replied. "To talk to Leo Shang."

NEGOTIATION

Leadville Airport
Leadville, Colorado
December 30
1420 hours

Leadville, Colorado, is the highest town in the United States, perched in the mountains 10,340 feet above sea level. Therefore, it was home to the highest airport in the country—as well as the highest high school, highest ice cream shop, and highest garbage dump. There wasn't much to the airport, only a windswept runway and a few corrugated aluminum hangars. Most visitors used the far nicer Eagle County Airport in the Vail Valley.

Leo Shang wasn't your average visitor, though.

Hank and Jawa had been keeping tabs on him all day, listening to the bugs I'd planted, while Chip stood guard around the hotel. The bugs had ultimately been useless—once Shang had realized I was an agent, he'd suspected the room was miked—but he couldn't keep his sudden departure from the hotel a secret. While Cyrus and Alexander had been rescuing us, Chip had seen Shang and Jessica hurriedly check out, hop into their car-tank caravan, and speed away from town.

The guys had done their best to follow—Hank had a driver's license, a rental car, and high marks in Tailing the Enemy 101—but the caravan had shaken them on Highway 24. There was only one airport in that direction, however, and once Cyrus knew that Leo Shang's goons had planted a nuclear bomb close by, it was easy to guess where Shang was headed. "The guy's about to light up this whole state like a Roman candle," Cyrus explained as we flew toward Leadville. "So he's gonna want to get out of Dodge as fast as he can."

Sure enough, the caravan was racing down the two-lane road toward the airport as we arrived. There were three car-tanks in it. Shang's jet waited on the tarmac. Waves of heat rose from the twin engines, indicating they were primed to fly.

The military helicopter we rode in was much larger than the heli-skiing choppers. It was mostly cargo bay, with a small cockpit and a line of jump seats along the left wall. On the right wall were a sliding door, a winch, and a tether for lowering people down or hauling them back up. Erica, Zoe, Warren, Mike, and I were belted into the jump seats. Cyrus and Alexander were in the cockpit. Woodchuck lay on the floor, wrapped up in so many blankets he looked like a flannel burrito. Thankfully, he'd managed to recover from his hypothermia. He'd stopped shivering and his face was its usual ruddy color, rather than blue.

Several pairs of skis and poles were piled at our feet. It looked as though Cyrus and Alexander had looted them from the ski rental.

Now Cyrus hovered over the runway, pointed toward Shang's jet, and ordered Alexander, "Take that out! Shoot the wings so it can't fly!"

"Er," Alexander said uncomfortably, "I can't."

"Why not?"

"I used all the bullets back at the lake."

"What?" Cyrus roared. "You didn't save any for emergencies?"

"I thought the gunfight at the lake *was* the emergency!" Alexander explained. "I didn't realize there might be two emergencies today."

"If I've told you once, I've told you a thousand times," Cyrus growled, "always keep some spare bullets! But you never learn, do you? You can't do anything right!"

After days of being berated, Alexander finally cracked and stood up to his father. "Oh, that is so like you!" he snapped. "I helped save everyone back at the lake—and do I hear one bit of praise from you? No. But the moment I make one tiny mistake, I hear plenty!"

"This wasn't a tiny mistake!"

"Would it kill you to say something nice to me just once in my life?"

"You know what *will* kill me? That nuclear bomb. Which is going to go off if we don't catch Shang and find out where it is!"

While they bickered, Shang's caravan raced onto the tarmac below us. Erica unbuckled herself, went to the winch by the door, and grabbed the tether that hung from it. It was a large rope with a thick loop at the end, easily big enough to go around her torso.

"Whoa there, young woman!" Alexander warned. "Where do you think you're going?"

"I'm going to rappel down to the tarmac and stop Shang," Erica said matter-of-factly.

"Oh, no, you're not," Alexander told her. "It's way too dangerous."

"Well, we have to do *something*," Erica shot back.

"Not that," Cyrus joined in. "You've been rendered

unconscious once already today. And that was the second time this week. I'm worried about your brain."

"*You* were the one who knocked me unconscious the first time!" Erica pointed out. "And *now* you're worried about me? Shang's going to get away!" She reached for the door handle.

"Do not touch that door," Alexander warned. "If you rappel out of this helicopter, you're grounded."

"I'm not sneaking out after curfew," Erica protested. "I'm trying to prevent nuclear annihilation. If I don't stop the Shangs, who will?"

"Me," Alexander said.

"Oh, please." Erica sighed. "You couldn't stop a car if your foot was on the brake."

Shang's men opened fire on us. Erica hit the deck as bullets tore through the door of the helicopter. Others webbed the cockpit window, forcing Cyrus to take evasive action.

Warren dropped to the floor of the helicopter and curled into a ball. "They're shooting at us!" he cried. He seemed to have recovered from his knock on the head; rather than being loopy, he was back to his normal, weaselly self. "Make them stop! I'm too young to die!"

The helicopter swiveled wildly as Cyrus tried to avoid the enemy fire. The spare skis and poles skidded around the cargo bay, clanging off the sides.

Mike looked to me, concerned. "Does this sort of stuff happen to you a lot?"

"No, this is my first helicopter gunfight," I admitted. "But we can probably trust Cyrus to handle it."

Below us, the caravan was racing down the tarmac toward the jet. The Shangs' car was obviously the one in the center. It was the only one without people shooting at us from it.

Rappelling out of the helicopter was now impossible, and the Hale family was arguing about what to do next. It was becoming extremely evident why Erica always claimed getting emotionally involved could mess up a mission; the Hale family dynamics were so messed up, it seemed unlikely that they would ever agree on a plan of action.

But then something occurred to me. If emotions could mess up *our* mission, then maybe they could mess up Leo Shang's mission as well. The last time I'd seen Jessica, she'd been furious at her father—and I figured that, since he was ending her vacation abruptly, she probably was now even angrier. Given the number of text messages she'd sent me, it seemed she wanted to talk.

So I dug out my phone and dialed her.

I wasn't sure she'd answer, given that there was a gunfight going on, but she picked up on the third ring, sounding even more excited to talk than I'd expected. "Ben! I've been hoping you'd call!"

"Really?" I asked.

"Yes! You really freaked me out when you didn't answer any of my texts. I thought you were mad at me or something."

"No! I just . . ."

"I mean, I can understand why you'd be upset after the way my father treated you. Sorry he was such a jerk. He's being a total nightmare to me, too. He got some rival businessman angry at us, so we have to leave Colorado right now. . . ."

"The people in that helicopter aren't rival businessmen," I said, trying to get a word in edgewise.

Jessica actually stopped speaking for a second. Then she asked, "How do you know about the helicopter?"

"Because I'm in it!" I told her.

Below us, the caravan parked by the jet. The guards leapt out and formed a gauntlet for the Shangs to pass down. They kept shooting at us, forcing Cyrus to continue our evasive action.

Over the phone, I could hear Leo Shang. "Jessica! This is no time to be on the phone! Hang up and follow me!"

Jessica ignored him and asked me, "Why are you in the helicopter?"

"I'm a junior CIA agent! Your father has been lying to you. He's not really a businessman. He's a criminal."

"That's not funny, Ben."

"I know. It's all incredibly serious. Your father didn't bring you here just to ski. You were right about that. He brought you here to plan a crime. A big one."

"Jessica!" Leo Shang was saying. "Get off the phone, now!"

Only, Jessica didn't get off the phone. And she didn't get out of the car. Because, like Erica, she didn't always listen to her father. Especially when she was angry at him. "What are you talking about?" she asked me.

"If we don't stop your father right now, he's going to set off a nuclear bomb in Colorado. He's doing it to corner the molybdenum market. . . ."

"Molly Denham has a market?"

"No, *molybdenum*. It's an element used in making weapons. And your father is trying to destroy the entire U.S. supply of it—even though it means killing a lot of innocent people."

"No," Jessica said. Her voice sounded strained, like she was struggling with the idea that her father was an international criminal. Which made sense; I would have reacted the same way. "He would never do something like that. He wouldn't kill people."

"He's having his men try to kill us right now! They're shooting at us!"

"Maybe he's just trying to frighten you off. . . ."

"No. He's been trying to kill me all morning. He sent Dane Brammage to do it."

I could see Leo Shang was out on the tarmac now, with the door of the car open. Over the phone, I heard him yelling at Jessica. "If you don't hang up right now, you're in big trouble!"

"Daddy," Jessica said sternly, "did you tell Dane to kill Ben today?"

Leo didn't answer right away. And when he *did* answer, it wasn't very convincing. "What kind of question is that? Of course I didn't tell Dane to do such a thing!"

"Then where's Dane?" Jessica asked suspiciously.

"He's, uh . . . getting some snacks for the plane trip."

Jessica didn't buy this for a second. "Oh my God," she gasped. "You tried to kill my friend! That is so uncool!"

"Jessica," Leo said, "we need to get on the jet right now."

"I'm not going anywhere with you!" Jessica screamed at him. "You're the worst father ever!"

"You don't understand what's going on here!" Leo yelled. "Now, get out of that car this instant!"

"Or what?" Jessica yelled back. "You'll kill me too?"

On the tarmac, the gauntlet of guards now looked a bit confused about what was going on. Leo Shang climbed back into the car to deal with Jessica. "You are my daughter and I demand respect! Now, you are coming with me!"

The sounds of a scuffle followed. I heard Jessica scream, "Let go of me!" and then there was a yelp of pain from Leo Shang. The door on the far side of the car opened and Jessica leapt out and ran across the tarmac, heading away from the jet.

Shang leapt out after her, but he was hobbling, like he'd been kicked hard in the shin. "Jessica!" he yelled. Only, he didn't sound angry anymore. He sounded panicked, like a worried father. He might have been upset at his daughter, but he wasn't about to leave her behind to die. "Get back here!"

Jessica kept going, though. So Shang turned to his guards and pointed after her.

The guards obeyed. They all chased after Jessica. She gave them a good run for their money, scrambling like a wide receiver, forcing the guards to spread out across the tarmac.

Which meant no one was shooting at us anymore. Erica quickly leapt back to her feet and threw the helicopter door open.

"Erica!" Alexander yelled. "I thought I told you that's too dangerous!"

"Yeah, you did," she admitted. "But I'm doing it anyhow."

Before Alexander or Cyrus could say another word, Erica slipped the tether loop around her waist and leapt out the door.

"Teenagers," Cyrus muttered. Then, since he knew he couldn't get Erica back into the copter, he maneuvered over the jet. Erica rappelled to the ground beside it.

I stuck the radio transmitter into my ear, then listened as Erica slipped into the jet and took care of Shang's pilot. There was some shouting in Chinese, followed by the sounds of a brief fight, followed by some more shouting in Chinese; only this time, the shouting was coming from someone in pain.

"The jet is secured," Erica reported calmly. As though she'd just bought a quart of milk, rather than defeating someone in hand-to-hand combat.

"The jet's secure," I relayed to our team.

Across the tarmac, Shang's guards finally caught Jessica. She didn't give up the fight, though, writhing and kicking at them.

Cyrus flipped on the helicopter's loudspeaker system and addressed Leo Shang through it. "It's over, Shang. We have commandeered your jet. You're not going anywhere until that bomb is defused—and the longer you stall us, the less time there is to do that. So tell your men to stand down."

Shang turned back toward his jet in time to see Erica closing the door and locking him out. All his bravado immediately drained out of him as he realized the jig was up. He shouted to his men, who dropped their guns and raised their hands.

Cyrus brought the helicopter down beside them and killed the engine. The roar of the rotors dropped to a soft whine as they slowed to a stop.

"Nice work," Mike told me. "You're pretty good at this spy thing."

"Thanks," I said.

Cyrus hopped out onto the tarmac and signaled for the rest of us to follow him. "Zoe and Warren, go pick up those guns," he ordered.

"Yes, sir!" Zoe saluted and, with Warren's help, collected all the guns from the ground, scurrying around Shang's guards.

Meanwhile, Cyrus approached Leo Shang, who had now become nervous and fidgety. "I need to know exactly where the bomb is," Cyrus demanded.

"It won't help," Shang whined. "It's too hard to get to and there's no way to defuse it."

"Let me be the judge of that," Cyrus told him.

"Hold on," Warren said worriedly. "There's no shutoff switch on it?"

"Why would I put a shutoff switch on a nuclear bomb?" Shang asked.

"So you can shut it off!" Warren yelped. "In case of emergencies! So when something like this happens, we don't all die!"

"We don't have to die," Shang said. "We can save ourselves if we leave now. We can all take the jet and get far enough away in the time we have left."

"How much time *is* left?" Cyrus asked.

"Er . . . I'm not quite sure," Shang admitted.

"You're not sure?" Warren wailed. "You mean it could go off any second?"

"No," Shang told him. "We have more time than that. I'm just not sure exactly how much. Dane Brammage set the timer, but I haven't heard from him in a while."

"You might not hear from him at all," Zoe said. "Ben kind of sank him in a frozen lake."

Shang seemed surprisingly unmoved by this. "Well, I guess that leaves more room on the jet. I told Dane to give us until around three o'clock. . . ."

"That's in less than half an hour!" Mike exclaimed.

"I know!" Shang cried. "So let's all get out of here! We still have time to escape!"

"But the rest of Colorado doesn't," Alexander pointed out. "We're not leaving thousands of innocent people to die."

"And if we're going to risk our lives, you're sure as heck gonna risk yours," Cyrus told Shang. "So let's stop the dilly-dallying and get down to brass tacks. Tell me where the bomb is."

Jessica had stopped fighting the guards by now. The gravity of the situation had sunk in.

Leo Shang gave her an angry glare. "This is all your fault," he said.

"My fault?" Jessica replied tartly. "I'm not the one who put a nuclear bomb in the mountains without an off switch."

Zoe and Warren returned to Cyrus's side, their arms full of guns. Cyrus selected one he liked and casually pointed it at Leo Shang.

Shang gave in. "Dane dropped the bomb on a mountain near the Climax Mine."

"What's the exact location?" Cyrus demanded. "Latitude and longitude would be nice."

Shang grew a little embarrassed. "Uh . . . I don't know that. Dane might, but you killed him." He looked at me accusingly as he said this, like I'd screwed up somehow.

"It was self-defense!" I pointed out. "And for all we know, he still might not be dead."

"So all you know is that the bomb is on a mountain?" Warren asked Shang, wild-eyed with panic. "That's not helpful at all! There's like a million mountains around here!"

Cyrus glared at Warren. "You're not helping things."

"I think I might know how to narrow the search down," I said. "The heli-skiing company's copters have GPS tracking systems in them. They're accurate down to the foot. What time did Dane drop the bomb?"

"Around nine thirty this morning," Leo replied. "He commandeered the helicopter from the company, dropped the bomb, and then went off to take care of some other things."

"Like trying to kill us?" Zoe asked pointedly.

"Er . . . yes," Shang admitted.

Jessica turned to Zoe and said, "I just want you to know I had nothing to do with all this. I didn't even know my father ever had people killed. I am so embarrassed."

"That's the helicopter Erica blew up," I continued. "Epic Heli-Skiing ought to have detailed information about where it was at exactly nine thirty this morning. We can use that to get a better bead on the bomb."

"Good thinking," Cyrus said to me. He pointed to Alexander and told him, "Call them right now."

"Yes, sir!" Alexander replied, thrilled his father had trusted him with something. He stepped aside to make the call.

Cyrus returned his attention to Shang. "What's the make and model of this bomb?"

"It's a Soviet Stalin-class X-43 fusion model."

Cyrus whistled through his teeth.

"Is that bad?" Mike asked.

"The X-43 is an old-fashioned model," Cyrus replied. "A leftover from the Cold War. Probably pilfered from a stolen nuclear missile. It's not very easy to defuse."

"Then let's forget about it and just get out of here!" Shang cried.

"That's not such a bad idea," Warren pointed out.

Zoe fixed him with a harsh stare. "Tell me you're not actually siding with the bad guy."

"I'm not siding with him," Warren mewled. "I'm just saying he has a valid point."

Cyrus turned his attention to Mike. "I'm going to go out on a limb here and assume that, since Ben says we can trust you, that means we can trust you."

"You can trust me," Mike agreed.

"Good," Cyrus replied. "I want you to stay here with Zoe and Warren to hold these men prisoner and keep an eye on Jessica until the police get here. I'll leave Woodchuck to help. He should be much more useful once he warms up a bit more."

"Sure thing," Mike said. "Although if you need me to help defuse the bomb, I'm happy to do it."

Cyrus gave him a slight smile, like he was impressed. "That won't be necessary. You've done enough service as it is. Ben, Erica, Alexander, and I can handle it, though."

I turned to Cyrus, startled he'd named me. Alexander seemed equally caught by surprise. He nearly dropped his phone in shock. "Really, Dad? You think I can help?"

"Maybe," Cyrus said, and started back toward the helicopter.

That single word lifted Alexander's spirits like nothing I'd ever seen. He was beaming like a kid who'd just received a bicycle for Christmas. "All right! Let's do this!" He raced back to the helicopter and hopped into it.

"This is crazy!" Shang yelled. "It won't work! We're going to die because of your foolishness!" He started after Cyrus, but Zoe stepped into his path, aiming one of his own guns at him.

"Take one more step or say one more word and I'll shoot you," she warned.

"Get out of my way, you little brat!" Shang ordered, then tried to storm past her.

Zoe shot him. But only in the foot.

Shang howled in pain. He hopped around, clutching his foot in his hands and whimpering.

To my surprise, Jessica didn't seem too upset by this. In fact, she seemed kind of pleased by it.

"I only took off the last knuckle of your little toe," Zoe informed him. "You won't miss it. But try anything else and I'll aim higher next time." She then leveled all the guards with a gaze that made her look just as scary as Erica could be. "That goes for all of you. Anybody else want to call my bluff?"

The guards all shook their heads and backed away from her respectfully.

"Good," Zoe told them. "Now sit down."

The guards and Shang all sat like a bunch of well-trained golden retrievers.

Only Jessica remained standing. She raised her hand politely, like a kid in school.

"Do you have a question?" Zoe asked.

"Yes. Can I say something to Ben?"

I stopped on my way to the helicopter and turned back to her.

"I suppose," Zoe replied. "Sorry I shot your father."

"He obviously deserved it," Jessica said, glaring at Leo. Then she turned to me and yelled across the tarmac. "I'm sorry about all of this! I had no idea what Daddy was plotting, I swear."

"It's not your fault," I yelled back to her. "Sorry I had to lie to you."

"I understand why you did it. I hope defusing that bomb is simple as cake."

"You mean 'easy as pie'?" I asked.

"Yes! That's it! Good luck." Jessica blew me a kiss.

Despite the fact that I was pretty much scared out of my wits, this made me feel slightly better. "Thanks," I said. Then I turned back to the helicopter.

Erica was now standing beside it. Since we'd captured Shang's men, she didn't need to hold the jet anymore. She was glaring at Jessica angrily.

Mike dropped in beside me. "Whoa," he whispered. "Looks like someone's jealous."

"No, she's not," I said, still not ready to believe this.

"Trust me," Mike said. "I know that look. She wants Jessica to back off. 'Cause she's into you."

We arrived at the helicopter. Cyrus had already climbed in and taken the controls. Alexander was still on the phone with Epic Heli-Skiing.

"We've got coordinates!" he announced. "This morning, starting at nine twenty-eight, their helicopter hovered at the same point for two minutes and thirty-five seconds, 39.4102 degrees latitude, 106.2256 degrees longitude."

"Sounds like our spot," Cyrus agreed, then fired up the rotors.

Erica looked at me expectantly.

I turned back to Mike. I had the disturbing feeling this might be the last time I saw him—or any of my friends—ever again. "Thanks for everything," I said. "You've been the best friend I could ever ask for."

"Why are you talking all sappy like that?" Mike asked. "This isn't the end of the world."

"It could be," I pointed out.

"Nah. You can handle it." Mike gave me a big, confident grin. I could tell that, beneath it, he was actually really worried—but I appreciated the vote of confidence anyhow. "Now go take care of business."

"Okay," I said, and hopped into the helicopter.

Erica followed me in and shut the door behind us. Cyrus lifted off before we were even strapped into our jump seats.

I looked out the window, watching my friends and enemies drop away beneath us. All of them were looking toward us with a mixture of hope and fear, wondering if we'd be able to save the day.

I wondered that myself.

Cyrus pulled on the stick and we banked toward the mountains, heading straight for a live nuclear bomb.

NUCLEAR DISARMAMENT

White River National Forest, Colorado

39.4102 degrees latitude

106.2256 degrees longitude

December 30

1450 hours

It was easy to spot the Climax Mine from the air. It was a great big scar on the landscape. A massive chunk of wilderness more than a mile wide was simply gone. Where there had once been snow-capped mountains and green trees, there was now only brown dirt, industrial machinery, and tailings ponds, huge pools of water stained disturbing colors by unnatural chemicals. It looked as though a tiny piece of New Jersey had been transplanted to the middle of Colorado.

I could also make out several dozen people at work in the mine, going about their jobs like it was any other day, completely unaware of their impending doom.

Spotting the bomb wasn't quite so easy. Even though we knew the exact location of the helicopter during the drop, right down to the inch, the bomb wasn't sitting out in the open at that very spot. Instead, it had tumbled down the snowy slopes and was now at some other, unknown point on an awfully big mountain.

Alexander, Erica, and I stood at the windows of the helicopter, scanning the ground below with binoculars while Cyrus hovered over the drop zone. Unfortunately, all any of us could see were rocks, trees, and snow.

"Maybe we should have brought some of the other guys," I said to Erica.

"Like Warren?" she asked dismissively. "That kid couldn't find a bomb if it was taped to his butt."

"Zoe could have helped," I replied, and then added, "Mike, too."

Erica gave me a sideways glance, then returned to her binoculars.

"He helped a lot today," I said. "If it hadn't been for him, we'd be dead. He saved us while you were unconscious. Hopefully, your grandfather understands he's not a threat anymore."

"He's even *more* of a threat now," Erica pointed out. "He knows the truth about us. He knows we're spies. And he knows about the academy. That's a huge risk."

"So what's Cyrus going to do, kill him?"

Erica made a noise I'd never heard her make before. It took me a moment to realize what it was. To my amazement, Erica had actually giggled.

"What's so funny?" I asked.

"There are other ways to deal with someone who's a threat besides killing him."

"Like what?"

"Recruiting him."

I lowered my binoculars to stare at Erica in shock. "You mean Cyrus has been thinking about recruiting Mike all along?"

"I have no idea what Grandpa has been thinking," Erica admitted. "But I'm sure recruitment is an option. Like you said, Mike did well today. Of course, that won't mean diddly if we don't find this bomb and defuse it."

Before I could pursue the conversation any further, Alexander gave a triumphant shout. "I see it!"

He pointed below us. On the eastern flank of the mountain, something metallic glinted in the sunlight. Unfortunately, it sat in the worst place imaginable. The only way to get down to it was to descend an exceptionally steep slope of snow through a minefield of jagged rocks. And if that wasn't bad enough, the bomb sat only a few feet from the edge of a cliff, which dropped away into a canyon so deep, it looked like it went straight through the earth.

"They couldn't have dropped it into a nice flat meadow?" I groaned.

"I've got more bad news," Cyrus announced from the cockpit. "There's nowhere for me to land the copter. I'm gonna have to keep it in the air. So you'll have to go down and defuse that thing yourselves."

"Ourselves?" I had already been nervous at the thought of being anywhere near the bomb, but now my stomach started doing backflips.

As usual, though, Erica took it all in stride. She walked back to the pile of skis and poles in the cargo area and said, "Let's go."

I followed her. We were still wearing the same ski boots we'd had on that morning. Cyrus hadn't brought us a change of footwear. My feet were in agony, but now the boots were finally going to come in handy again. I searched for a pair of skis with the right size bindings to clip into.

Alexander didn't grab a pair himself, however. "Um," he said weakly. "I don't think I'll be able to join you. I, er . . . I can't ski."

Even Erica seemed surprised by this. "Not even a little?"

"No," Alexander admitted. "All those bedtime stories I used to tell about leading evil criminal masterminds on wild chases down the slopes of the Karakoram Range . . . I made them all up."

"I knew that," Erica said flatly. "But I thought you at least had some *idea* how to ski."

"No," Alexander said. "I tried once. But on my very first run I skied into a tree and sprained my groin. So I never did it again."

"Well, maybe you could walk down the slope somehow," I suggested. "It'd take longer, but we could still use some help defusing that bomb."

"Oh, I think that'd be even more of a bad idea," Alexander replied. "To be honest, bomb defusion was never really my forte. In fact, I'm quite awful at it. I failed every one of my simulations. Ever. I get a little shaky when I get nervous." He held up a hand to show us. It was trembling like a sapling in a hurricane. His fingers were twitching so badly, I could barely see them.

"If you can't ski and you can't defuse a bomb," Erica said, "then why did you volunteer to come along?"

"Moral support?" Alexander ventured.

Erica sighed and turned to me. "Looks like it's just us, then."

I didn't really want to go either. Heading down to the

bomb merely looked like a couple hundred good ways to die. But if no one went, we were going to die anyhow, and it seemed better to die valiantly rather than chickenhearted in front of Erica.

I finally found a pair of skis with bindings that fit my boots and hoisted them to my shoulder. "Have you ever defused an X-43 before?" I asked Erica.

"No. I've never even seen an X-43. They're pretty rare. But Grandpa knows them—and he'll be on the radio to talk us through it. Then, once we're done, Dad will hoist us back up on the tether." She turned to Alexander. "You *can* work the winch, can't you?"

"I think so," Alexander said. He didn't sound quite as sure of himself as I'd hoped.

"So let's get moving," Erica told me.

We carried our skis to the door of the helicopter and clipped them on. Cyrus lowered us as close to the mountaintop as he could get. Alexander threw open the door.

Even though we weren't too far above the slope, it was still going to be a big leap from a helicopter onto a sheer descent. On skis, no less. It was even more treacherous than the slope we'd attempted before the avalanche that morning.

I gulped in fear.

And then Erica put a hand on my shoulder and whispered

in my ear, "I know you can do this. You're a better skier than I am—and I'm good at everything."

It wasn't exactly the greatest compliment in the world, but it bolstered my confidence enough. "Okay. Let's do it."

Erica leapt out of the helicopter. She didn't even take a second to gather her nerve. She simply jumped, the same way she might have leapt off the bottom step of a staircase.

She stuck the landing on the slope, carved a nice turn around some jagged rocks, and started her way down. Despite her failure on her first run a few days before, she had improved greatly.

Like Woodchuck had said, a great deal of being able to ski something was simply *believing* you could ski it.

So I jumped out of the helicopter too.

The fall was the worst part. It probably took less than a second, but it felt much longer, and every last bit of it was terrifying.

Then I hit the mountain. The snow was so soft and deep, it was like landing in a giant cushion. The next thing I knew, I was skiing. It was awfully frightening, given that the slope was steep and full of sharp, head-splitting rocks and it ended in a precipitous drop to certain doom—but there was something exhilarating about it as well. As I carved my turns and followed Erica down through the virgin powder, it occurred to me that this was the type of thing people shelled out big bucks to go helicopter skiing to do—minus the cliff and the nuclear bomb, of course—and I suddenly understood why. I was experiencing a physical high, and for a few seconds, the entire mission was quite enjoyable.

And then I wiped out.

One moment I was upright and life was good, and the next I was tumbling downhill toward a cliff and life was about to end very quickly. My skis flew off, my poles sailed away, and a few pounds of snow ended up in my pants. The sheer drop at the end of the slope rushed toward me.

I dug my heels into the snow as hard as I could, forcing them down until my boots hit the hard rock beneath the powder. My feet rattled along the ground, finding no purchase, while I sluiced through the snow and the cliff came closer and closer. . . .

Until, suddenly, my boots connected with a big rock, jarring me to a sudden stop.

The cliff edge was only ten feet away. Now that I was so close to it, I could see that the snow jutted over the edge a bit, like the frosting on a cupcake, making me wonder if there was even less solid ground between the cliff and me than I'd suspected.

Just to my right sat the bomb.

It was the size of a microwave oven, housed in a metal shell that was stamped with dozens of words in Russian, all of which appeared to be warnings. For people who couldn't read Russian, there were also several skulls and crossbones, indicating trouble.

Erica slid to a stop beside me. I'd passed her while tumbling down the slope. "You made that a little more exciting than it had to be," she said, then tossed her poles aside, shed her jacket, and removed her avalanche vest. Beneath it all, she wore her standard utility belt. She plugged a radio into her ear and said, "Okay, Grandpa. We're here."

I inserted my own radio just in time to hear Cyrus reply, "Good. Is there a metal casing on the bomb?"

"Yes," Erica replied.

"Take it off. And be careful. One wrong move and Colorado gets a new crater."

"I'm well aware how dangerous this is." Erica removed two Phillips-head screwdrivers from her utility belt and handed one to me.

Six screws held the casing atop the bomb. Erica went to work on them.

Even though we were surrounded by snow, the sun was out and all my exertion and nerves had already made me start sweating. I took off my jacket and gloves as well, freeing my arms and fingers, and started on the screws.

The snow groaned and shifted around us, tilting slightly toward the edge of the cliff.

Erica popped out the first screw. "Grandpa, tell Dad to get that tether ready."

"Is there a problem?"

"There's a decent chance the whole snowpack we're sitting atop is unstable and about to slide over the edge of the cliff. So yes, I'd consider that a problem."

"I'll see what I can do. Try not to get distracted."

That was easy for Cyrus to say. He wasn't *on* the snowpack on the edge of the cliff. But I did my best to focus, pulling out one screw, then another, trying to ignore the groaning snow and the sickening sense that we were slowly drifting with it.

Erica popped out the third screw.

I got another out a few seconds later. "Done."

"Okay," Erica told me. "Grab the casing with both hands and we'll lift it off. Very carefully."

I grabbed the casing. So did Erica. We lifted as gingerly as we could. It came off with surprising ease, revealing the guts of the bomb beneath.

There were two yellow canisters marked with radiation symbols and more skulls and crossbones. They were strapped together with duct tape and surrounded by a nest of red wires, all of which were connected to a digital timer.

The timer indicated there were only two minutes and five seconds left until detonation.

My stomach was well past doing backflips. Now it did a triple axel roundoff with a twist.

Even Erica seemed shaken. "Crap on a cracker," she said under her breath.

"Another problem?" asked Cyrus.

"We have less than two minutes to defuse this thing," Erica reported. "And there's a whole rat's nest of wires."

"Just clip the red one," Cyrus told her.

"They're *all* red," Erica informed him.

"They are?" Cyrus asked. "Curse those Soviets! Everything always had to be red with them."

"So which one should I cut?" Erica asked.

"It's hard to know without looking at it," Cyrus said.

There were now only ninety seconds left on the timer. Erica pulled out her phone. "I'm going to take a picture and send it to you," she said, then glanced at the screen. "Actually, scratch that. I don't have any reception."

"I'm afraid you're going to have to wing it, then, sweetheart," Cyrus said.

"Wing it?" Erica's normally calm voice cracked. "But . . ."

"No 'buts,'" Cyrus said. "You know more about bombs than any girl your age. More than most people, period. You can do this."

Erica nodded, gathering herself, and then looked at me. "One of these wires must connect to the detonator. The rest are triggers. So we need to find the right one and yank it. If we pull the wrong one . . . we all go kablooey."

I inspected the bomb. I couldn't even see the detonator. It was wedged below the yellow canisters beneath the snow. And it looked like every wire was snaking down toward where that might be.

The snow groaned and shifted again. A few chunks by the edge split off and dropped into the canyon.

The sound of the helicopter's rotors grew louder and louder. A wind kicked up around us. I figured Cyrus was lowering the copter toward us, and Alexander was probably playing out the tether, but I couldn't take the time to look up. I needed every bit of focus, every last fraction of a second to scan the tangle of red wires, looking for the one that would shut the bomb off.

There were only sixty seconds left.

I didn't have the slightest idea which wire was the correct one to cut. And neither did Erica.

But then something occurred to me. "Why would all the fake wires be triggers?" I asked.

"Because that's the way bombs are made," Erica said.

"Is it? I mean, building in a whole bunch of triggers seems kind of overzealous, doesn't it? That assumes someone's going to be defusing the bomb, which probably doesn't happen very often. I mean, I know *we've* had to defuse a bomb before, but overall, that's pretty rare, right?"

"I suppose," Erica said.

"Honestly, I've never defused a bomb in all my years in the Agency," Cyrus admitted.

I looked to Erica, who seemed just as surprised as I did. *"Never?"* she asked.

"It's not like this kind of thing happens every day," Cyrus replied.

"Well, maybe all these other wires are just a busted goose," I suggested. "They're only there to distract us. You know, so we waste time trying to figure out which wire's the right one, until it's too late."

Erica considered this. A few more seconds ticked by. We were down to only twenty-five.

The snow groaned and shifted more. A large chunk only three feet from us fractured off and fell away.

"I don't have any better ideas," Erica admitted. "Let's pull all the wires."

"Really?" I asked.

"It's better than doing nothing. If the bomb's gonna blow, it's gonna blow."

"I agree," Cyrus chimed in. "Yank them."

So we did. We ripped every last wire out of the bomb.

It didn't blow up.

But the timer didn't stop, either. It kept on ticking down. Eight seconds. Seven seconds. Six.

I looked to Erica helplessly, out of ideas.

She was looking at me the same way.

And then, to my astonishment, she kissed me.

I had encountered a great number of startling things since coming to spy school, but this rocked my world more than all of them put together. It was very quick—after all, the world was about to end—but it was definitely the greatest few seconds of my entire life. I was terrified of dying, but at the same time, oddly thrilled that I was getting this experience in right under the wire.

The timer ticked to zero.

Nothing happened.

Erica pulled away from me, looked at the bomb curiously, then rolled her eyes. "Oh, man," she muttered. "We disconnected the bomb, but not the timer."

It took me a bit longer to recover. "So . . . we're not going to die?"

"Not from the blast. Plummeting is still a likely option, though." She glanced up toward the helicopter and spoke over the radio. "We need that tether ASAP."

"We're getting it there as fast as we can," Cyrus replied.

"Well, get it here faster," Erica said. She was behaving as though the kiss had never happened, back to her normal, rational, unemotional self.

But then, I needed Erica to be her normal, rational,

unemotional self in that moment. Because I was on the verge of freaking out.

The snow we were on was definitely sliding toward the edge of the cliff. And even though the bomb we were with hadn't exploded, it was still a nuclear bomb. Dropping it from a great height might very well still set it off.

The helicopter hovered fifty feet above us, as close as Cyrus dared get. Any closer and the rotors might have clipped the steep slope. Alexander was lowering the tether as fast as he could. The big reinforced loop at the end dangled just above our heads.

Erica stood to reach for it. The snow shifted ominously with her movement.

She was about to grab the tether when a wind kicked up, jostling the helicopter. The loop swung past her fingertips.

"There's a spool of filament wire on my utility belt," she told me. "Tie one end to the bomb, then get ready to move out. We're going to have to act fast."

I grabbed one end of the filament and did as ordered. It wasn't easy, though. My hands were growing cold without my gloves, and the thin wire was hard to handle with my numb fingers. Plus, the bomb and I were both sliding toward the edge of the cliff. I raced to get the wire looped around one of the yellow canisters, then tie a knot.

More snow dropped away into the chasm, only a foot

away from us. The chasm was now so close I could see down to the bottom of it. It was like standing at the top of a sky-scraper.

The tether swung back over us. Erica lunged and grabbed it. "Ben! Time to go! Now!"

"One more second," I said, struggling to cinch the knot.

"Now," Erica ordered.

I pulled the knot tight, then stood. The snow under us heaved and rushed toward the edge of oblivion.

Erica already had the tether's loop around her torso. She quickly swung it over my head and brought it up beneath my armpits.

A second later, we slid over the edge of the cliff.

Only, we didn't drop. The tether held us in the exact same place, as though we'd stepped onto some invisible plat-form.

The bomb dropped, though. It toppled over the edge of the cliff and plummeted until the filament snapped taut with a twang. Erica grunted in pain from the sudden extra weight. But that was all the discomfort she allowed herself. "We're good," she told Cyrus over the radio. "Get us out of here."

"Roger." The earth dropped away below us as the heli-copter lifted us up.

The tether was pinioning Erica and me together, face-to-face. We were now dangling several thousand feet above the ground, in a freezing wind, with a nuclear bomb tied to us. But we were still alive, and we'd saved a good section of Colorado from nuclear annihilation. So we had that going for us.

Erica plucked the microphone out of her ear and indicated I should do the same.

As we were face-to-face, this seemed like a perfectly good time for another kiss. A much longer one, maybe.

Only, I didn't get it.

"That kiss didn't mean anything," Erica told me. "We were in a tight spot, and you were about to lose it, and I didn't want your last moments on earth to be terrifying."

"Okay." I was disappointed that a second kiss hadn't come, but at the same time, I couldn't help smiling. Because for once in my life, I knew something that Erica was trying to keep secret. I'd overheard her on the lift with Zoe. And Mike, who knew far more about girls than I did, had provided confirmation.

Erica Hale liked me.

Maybe she didn't have a massive crush on me, the way I had a crush on her. And maybe she was way too focused on becoming a spy to even consider having a boyfriend. But she at least liked me enough to be jealous of Jessica Shang, which was something.

Which meant she was lying. She hadn't kissed me merely

to calm me down in my final moments alive. Erica had thought those were her final moments too. She'd *wanted* to kiss me.

"Why are you smiling?" Erica asked.

"I'm just happy to be alive," I said.

Erica gave me a hard stare, like she didn't believe me. "You can never tell *anyone* about what happened here. If you do, I will find you . . ."

". . . and you'll kill me," I finished. "I know the drill."

We were rising slowly as Alexander winched the tether into the helicopter. In a few seconds, we would be back inside, safe and warm again.

But despite the cold and the height and the nuclear bomb and the fact that my feet were in agony after way too much time in ski boots, I found myself savoring those moments, dangling high above the mountains with Erica. Because I knew Erica as well as anyone. Once we got back home, she would do everything she could to avoid a relationship with me—and to be honest, I now understood why. As Operation Snow Bunny had just proved, emotions could severely complicate missions. And Erica and I had many more missions ahead of us.

So that kiss was probably all I was going to get from her for a long, long time.

And yet . . . she'd still kissed me.

It was a start.

January 1

To: █████████████████████
CIA Director of Operations

RE: Operation █████████

As I'm sure you're aware by now, despite your concerns, our junior agents performed exceptionally well on their recent mission. Not only did they uncover ████████████ but they also were of invaluable assistance in ███████████████████████████████ Due to their efforts, Leo Shang has been captured, along with several associates (although once again, that rapscallion Murray Hill appears to have escaped).

Therefore, I recommend commendations—as well as high grades in Undercover Work and Bomb Defusion—for agents ██████████ and ████████████████ on this endeavor. I also recommend passing grades for young agents ████████████████████████████ and ██████████ ██████████ As for agent ██████████ the less said about his performance, the better. We might consider holding him back a year.

One final note. An issue I have expressed concern about before came back to haunt all of us on this mission: ████████████ However, while young ████████████ appearance at first threatened to derail ████ ████████████ he ultimately proved himself surprisingly capable and resilient in the face of danger. To that end, please disregard my previous recommendation that we deal with Mr. ████████ by termination. Instead, I believe we should recruit him to the ████████████████ He would make a welcome addition to our ranks, and given his performance, possibly even rival ██████████████████ as a young agent someday.

Sincerely,

Cyrus Hale

P.S. My sources indicate that ████████ may not only still be in existence, but fully recovered from ████████████████ and plotting ████████████ ████████████████. In the very near future, we may have to activate agents ██████ and ████ for Operation Muskrat.